Y0-AQT-066

THE HARLEQUIN'S SON

THE HARLEQUIN'S SON

ANDRE LAUNAY

St. Martin's Press
New York

Library of Congress Cataloging-in-Publication Data

Launay, André, 1935–
The harlequin's son.

I. Title.
PR6062.A785H3 1987 823'.914 87-87
ISBN 0-312-00605-5

First published in Great Britain by Pan Books Ltd.

First U.S. Edition

10 9 8 7 6 5 4 3 2 1

And when she could no longer hide him, she took for him an ark of bulrushes, and daubed it with slime and with pitch, and put the child therein, and she laid it in the flags by the river's brink.

And his sister stood afar off, to wit what would be done to him.

EXODUS II. 3,4.

chapter one

He wished he had painted his face white.

All white, with surprised eyebrows and the outline of a tear under the left eye.

No one had known who he was when he had been made up like that, wearing a black and green chequered skull cap and a black and green chequered costume with a frilly collar.

Mon ami Pierrot.

Sitting astride the cardboard moon he had recited the nursery rhyme in perfect French and had won applause.

He had liked that. The warmth that had enveloped him from over the footlights.

'I think I want to be an actor,' he'd said to his mother afterwards. 'I like pretending I'm someone else.'

'Don't we all,' she had replied.

He was eight at the time and had drifted on from there into the delightful world of make believe.

Without anyone knowing he could change from Harlequin to Magician, from Sorcerer to Prince of Darkness, and there was only one person in the whole wide world who shared his fantasies: the person who had first dressed him up for the Pangbourne village concert and had taught him the rhyme in French, his aunt, who was not his aunt at all, but a friend of the family, Tante Louise, as she always insisted he call her. Madame Rimbaud to most adults, Ma Rainbow to the locals.

He wished he was made up as a Pierrot now, or hiding behind a theatrical mask. He wished he was anyone but who he was, what he was, a thirteen-year-old schoolboy from Amhurst College, in a blue Sunday suit, white shirt and Amhurst tie, looking for an identity. But then the whole reason for him standing there in front of the impressive glossy black door, with its brightly polished brass bell-pull and brightly polished brass knocker, was to find out who he was.

His friend Hooker's idea.

'You've got to have an identity Saranson,' he'd said, 'and the best way to do that is to get to know your father.'

He pulled the bell, but it made no sound at all, so he lifted the knocker and hammered it twice, loudly.

He had rehearsed his introductory speech enough times not to falter. If the door was opened by a maid, or a butler, he would say, 'I am Alexander Saranson, and I would like to see the General.' If it was opened by the General himself, he would just say, 'I am Alexander Saranson, sir, and would like to have a word with you.'

Hooker had also suggested he should think more maturely; none of this 'little boy play-acting' stuff. 'If you have to have a false personality as a prop then for God's sake think in military terms. Be efficient, smart, fearless.'

There was a noise, an inner door opening, then a bolt being drawn back.

He straightened up, adjusted his tie, placed his hand in his jacket pocket.

The black door opened and an elderly woman with white hair, wearing a flowered apron, looked at him questioningly without a word.

'I am Alexander Saranson,' he said clearly, 'and I would like to see the General, please.'

She opened the door fully to let him in.

From a white lobby into a cream hallway, stairs leading up to a well lit landing, military prints on the walls, Persian rugs on the parquet floor, crossed spears, crossed swords, helmets, a stuffed elk's head. It was exactly as he had imagined it should be.

The woman pointed to an upholstered chair and he sat down on the edge of it as she disappeared down the corridor and turned right under an archway.

The conservatory. The General was probably in the conservatory. Alexander hadn't just walked up the drive to the front steps of the magnificent house, he had gone right round the estate first and had studied the mansion and all its outhouses, and he had seen the glass roof of the conservatory above the garden wall, with its promise of tropical plants.

'He won't eat you,' Hooker had said. 'Some animals eat their children, but one must presume that he is human.'

The woman reappeared round the corner and beckoned to him to follow.

Through the archway to a green baize door and through the green baize door he was shown into the vast conservatory, as expected.

There were small palm trees and bright green plants with massive leaves which he suspected might be carnivorous, there were orchid-like blooms and bulbous fruit growing out of terracotta pots, but his attention was drawn to the man sitting in a white wing-backed cane chair, staring at him over a leather-bound book.

He wasn't an old man, but he wasn't young either. Sandy hair going grey, a sandy-grey moustache, cold, penetrating blue eyes.

His father?

The expected joy did not materialize.

His reaction, rather, was of fear.

This man was another headmaster, another housemaster, not a blundering fool like his grandfather, but someone he would not be able to get round easily. There was no warmth there. He was not the sort of man to whom Alexander would be able to say, like he could say to Tante Louise, 'Today I am a Government Secret Agent or the Commander of a Space Mission.' He would not be receptive to that sort of fantasy. If humans ever ate their children, he was exactly the sort of human who might eat him. He was a seasoned lion in his own jungle.

'Yes?' the General asked of him, not hiding the fact that the unexpected interruption in his reading was offensive.

'I'm Alexander Saranson, sir.'

The General contemplated him.

The blue eyes stared him in the face, then looked straight down at his shoes.

'Polish your shoes,' Hooker had warned, 'Whatever else, polish your shoes.'

'You are Sarah's boy,' the General said.

'Yes sir.'

'Why did she send you?'

'She didn't sir. I came on my own accord.'

The General closed his book and placed it on his knees, sat up a little in his throne.

'What is it you want?'

In at the deep end. Close the eyes. Take the dive.

'Are you General Sir Geoffrey Saranson, sir?'

'Yes, I am.'

'I thought, sir, that perhaps you might be my father. I thought we should meet.'

There was no flicker of the face muscles, no twitching of the fingers, no movement of the feet, just the steady stare of the cold blue eyes that registered a change from the irritated to the surprised.

Abruptly the General placed his book on a small white table beside him and got to his feet.

He was tall, neatly dressed in clothes that were not normally neat: corduroys, a checked shirt, a loose heavy-knit cardigan. His brown shoes were as polished as the large green leaf he was now stroking.

'Interested in tropical plants? This is a Mangosteen, grows mainly in the East Indies. I planted the seeds myself. It's six years old now. About half your age I suppose. How old are you? Twelve is it?'

'Thirteen, sir.'

'And you're at Amhurst College I see.'

'Yes, sir.'

'Like it?'

'Yes, thank you sir.'

The General disappeared behind some foliage for a moment to reappear on the other side of one of the small palm trees.

'Did your mother suggest to you that you were my son?'

'No sir. I presumed it sir.'

'But she didn't tell you?'

'No, sir.'

'Did she tell you that she and I were once married?'

'I found out, sir.'

'Does she know you've come to see me?'

'No, sir.'

The general frowned, briefly, then turned to feel the velvet texture of a greyish shrub and seemed, for quite some time, to be lost in thought.

'I'm sorry about this Alexander,' he said at last, not looking round. 'I would rather you had heard it from someone else, but since you are here and deserve some explanation, I clearly have to tell you myself. You are not my son. I do not know whose son you are, all I know is that you were the reason for the divorce. I was not aware that you had been given my name, but on reflection, as it is your mother's by marriage, I suppose it was inevitable.'

The General then pulled a flat wallet out of his trouser pocket and drew out a ten pound note.

'Your mother was never one to be totally honest with herself, let alone with others, but you must ask her to tell you the truth, which, for some reason, no doubt of her own making, or that of her parents, she has chosen to hide from you.'

The ten pound note was held out.

'This is to cover the expenses you must have incurred in coming here and also to reward you for your bravery which I recognize. I am aware that it cannot have been easy for you to visit me.'

Alexander took the ten pound note gratefully and folded it before slipping it into his pocket.

'I'm sure you can see yourself out,' the General said.

He was dismissed.

He turned and, not looking back, not saying goodbye, blocking any thoughts that might come into his mind, he made his way out of the conservatory, through the green baize door, along the cream passage to the military hallway, to the lobby and out by the polished black door which was opened for him by the white-haired lady.

He wanted to run down the drive, but he checked that impulse. He thought he might cry, but his eyes were perfectly dry, perfectly clear, and there was no feeling of disappointment. It was only when he got to the Lodge gates and turned round to look at the house again, that he saw, to the left, a swing and a slide, and realized that the General had a son, or a daughter, a child of his own. And that hurt.

Was he being watched?

It was impossible to tell, all the square window panes looked black. The General or the white-haired woman might well be observing him.

He walked back up the drive and boldly crossed the lawn to the swing, a simple wooden seat on two long chains hanging from the apex of a triangular frame of royal-blue metal tubing.

He pulled the ten pound note out of his pocket, rolled it up tightly and threaded it through one of the link rings.

It fitted tightly, would not blow away, and one day it would be found and talked about.

He turned and walked back to the Lodge gates and out into the lane.

He was not a General's son.

That belief, which had given him so much confidence in the last few weeks, had all been wishful thinking. His ability to command, his ability to designate, the idea of working towards becoming a House Captain, Head of House, a Prefect or even Head of School, had all been a myth.

In no way could he have inherited a military mind.

And somehow this was an immense relief.

He could sink back now into the comfort of not having such a responsibility, such an image to live up to.

But then, if the General was not his father, who was?

And why were they hiding the truth from him?

Alexander walked for seven miles.

On leaving the General's estate he turned left the way the taxi had come and walked down the lane, not knowing exactly where he was going and not caring.

At the top of a hill he realized he must have gone wrong, but he went on, hands thrust deep in his pockets, ignoring the fact that the sky had clouded over and there was a threat of rain. The lane eventually came to a more important road and he hesitated for a moment looking at the signpost. Upper Beeding, Thakenham, Bramber. Thakenham was only half a mile away, maybe there would be a bus stop and a bus would take him somewhere he knew.

It had never occurred to him that the General might not turn out to be his father. He had expected a hard interview, a protest, a man refusing to acknowledge his existence for some reason, reprimanding him in a military fashion for coming without warning, without an appointment; but he had not expected a denial.

Rather the contrary.

He had thought about a possible welcome, open arms, the love he so much wanted, the admiration, the joy of a father finding a lost son. The fantasy, for obviously that is what it had been, had also included the General driving him back to school in a large army limousine bedecked with military ensigns, an NCO chauffeur in uniform at the wheel. He had even gone into the realms of lunacy being escorted back in convoy with outriders, in a tank, and shooting up the school because the General had just mounted a campaign against private education.

At Thakenham he found nothing but three thatched cottages, one of which was the village store, closed, a letter box in a wall and a small bridge over a stream. No one around, no church, no bus stop. So he walked on to Bramber which was indicated as being a mile further on.

He was going to be late for Evensong, he was in fact going to miss Evensong and possibly Hall, which would mean a beating, a hauling-up in front of Wilcox or The Buzz. He didn't care. He wasn't even sure that he was going back to school at all.

He passed a farm which showed signs of life. Animal life as it turned out, not human. Two morose cows chewing the cud and looking at him over a low fence.

Then it started raining.

Why had they so constantly lied to him?

The General had not been unpleasant. Surprised, shocked even, sad on his behalf, he felt, but not angry. He hadn't done anything appalling by going to see him. The man at least had been aware of his existence. 'Your mother was never one to be honest with herself, let alone others . . .'

It started pelting down now and he stopped under a dripping oak for a few moments, then decided to walk on and get wet. He would arrive at the school soaked and demand to see The Buzz immediately and explain his plight, or perhaps he wouldn't arrive at all. He would, instead, take his own life.

Wouldn't that teach them? His mother, his grandparents? For keeping the truth from him. 'Frightfully sorry Mrs Saranson, but your son was found hanging from an oak tree near Thakenham, his clothes were soaked through. Death by misadventure while of unsound mind.' Hooker would like that.

Hooker would do the autopsy.

It was because of Hooker that he was here. Hooker and his stupid Black Album. That's what had pulled the curtain up on the whole family charade.

'The trouble with Hooker,' Pitts had said, 'is that he's prone to necromancy.'

He had been sitting with Pitts in Travellier's House garden watching Hooker paste another fearful disaster story torn from the morning's paper into his death book.

It was an incredible album, containing the price lists from all the crematoria in the United Kingdom and cuttings from a magazine called *The Funeral Director* with details on embalming.

'They gut you, then stuff you with old copies of the *Sun* and the *News of the World*,' Hooker had informed him with relish.

He also had photocopies of his aunt and uncle's death certificates and details of how they had died. His fascination, he claimed, was inherited from his undertaker grandfather in whose footsteps he intended to follow. He would not be an ordinary undertaker, but the first Cabinet Minister for Undertaking, because Parliament would eventually have to control the disposal of the dead and everyone would be incinerated in a vast crematorium built for the purpose on the Isle of Wight, which would be re-named the Isle of Black. 'In time,' Hooker had gone on, 'the British Isles will become the cemetery of the European Economic Community and make a fortune out of human gas power.'

'You're completely round the twist,' Pitts had said, then Hooker had asked what Pitts' father did and Pitts had replied that he was a boring old solicitor, and Hooker had asked Alexander what his father did and he had replied, 'He's dead,' which had made him the hero of the moment. From then on Hooker had been hell-bent on knowing everything about his father, how he had died, when, how old he was when death had overcome him, his full name, his history, and it had made Alexander realize that he knew nothing about the man. He had never missed his father because he had been brought up by his grandparents and mother who never mentioned him, and so he made up the story that the man had died in the agony of cancer of the bowels, which had satisfied Hooker enormously.

But the subject had not been put to rest. Hooker had asked where his father was living at the time of his demise, whether he had died in hospital or private clinic, and when it had come to supplying his full names, Alexander had shamefully had to admit that he didn't know.

'You don't know your father's own names Saranson? A bit of a creep, aren't you?'

After that he'd avoided Hooker, preferring Pitts' company, but then had been shattered when Pitts had called him an 'innocent' when he'd asked why he spent so much time in the House Captains' room polishing their shoes.

Vexed, he had gone back and complained to Hooker, who had shrugged the matter off with 'What do you expect, Pitts is a tart.' Which Alexander hadn't understood at all.

Hooker had then patiently suggested that Alexander should open his eyes and observe what was going on around him instead of behaving like a prim little turd. Prefects, house captains and even masters liked the company of pretty new boys, and if he didn't know what that meant he'd have to wait till one of them showed him.

Not for the first time the humiliation of being told he was ignorant made him flush with an inner rage. Sex was something he had never understood because it had never been explained to him, and that was because he had never had a father to ask.

Unnerved, he had stuck closer to Hooker, who had then started questioning whether his father had really died. People, Hooker had told him, were never what they seemed, everyone had secrets, had something to hide. Scratch the surface of anyone's past and you'd find a deception underneath. Was he really sure that his father was buried? Where, for instance, was his grave? Or had he been cremated and his ashes scattered over some corner of a foreign field?

Alexander had thought the question ridiculous, but Hooker had explained that he had always believed his own father was dead until he'd found out that his mother had divorced and hadn't the guts to tell him. She had invented his death though his father was in fact in South Africa, remarried with three children!

Adults lied about such things. Women in particular.

He didn't care, but just thought Saranson should know.

Alexander hadn't identified with Hooker's story at all. If his mother was lying, then his grandparents would be lying too, and none of them would ever do that.

But then he'd begun to lose faith in human nature and friendship and honesty, when he'd got home for the Easter holidays. He'd started studying the behaviour of the adults around him, which he had never done before, and that had been unsettling.

He'd soon realized that his mother was rather irritated by his presence in their London house and not a bit interested in what he did all day or how he had got on at school. She'd got nervous too, towards bedtime, and had insisted on closing the door after kissing him goodnight and he'd noticed that the lodger's bed was never slept in.

Then, when they were driving to Hernmead Court, his grandparents' home, he had asked her about his father, how he had died, where he had died, where he was buried, and she'd mentioned a long illness in hospital, then had changed the subject as though it were none of his business.

When he'd settled down at Hernmead, his grandparents accepting his arrival as something that had to be borne rather than enjoyed, he had started asking questions about his father again and had received some very confusing answers.

'Tropical disease,' had been his grandfather's version. 'Serving abroad at the time. Far East. Best not talk about it. Your mother was very upset.'

His grandmother had tried to be more helpful.

'It was a war wound, Alexander, which always gave him trouble. He died in a military hospital. The army took care of his ashes. He was very proud to have a son, so you must do well at school for his sake.'

Their uneasiness about the whole business had intrigued him, so he had probed further.

The family photo albums, he'd discovered, had no pictures of his father, and there were none to be found anywhere else. When he'd asked Hilda Kelly, the housekeeper, about him, she had gone through an elaborate performance with the pots and pans in the kitchen, claiming that she was very busy, in order to avoid answering.

So he'd brought up the subject casually with old Tom Northey, the gardener, and had at last got a positive response.

'He's a General now, isn't he? Surprised they didn't tell you,' he'd muttered, then had added, 'but then again, I don't suppose they would.'

'Why not?'

'Best ask your mother.'

Which he had, when she'd come down for the weekend. She'd had more time for him on this occasion and had obviously been warned that he was prying.

'Your father was a very sick man,' she'd explained. 'He was discharged from the army at a time when his career showed great promise and he invented lots of stories about himself to overcome the setback, which is why Granny and

Grandpa are sometimes confused. He died in a London hospital and was cremated at a place called Golder's Green, where his ashes were strewn in the gardens of remembrance, which was all he wanted. There's no gravestone or plaque or anything like that.'

'Tom Northey told me he was a general and still alive,' Alexander insisted, to which he'd got the too sharp reply, 'You shouldn't listen to servants' chatter darling. And why would Mummy lie to you?'

It was a question that had not gone away.

The sound of an engine made him turn round, a motorcycle roared past, splashing him. He didn't care. He didn't care about anything anymore. Maybe his father was a tramp and he had inherited this sudden desire for walking to nowhere down country lanes with nothing but the clothes he had on his back.

He heard another engine. It was a Renault 4, bright yellow. He thumbed it, hitch-hiking was a beating offence; the car wouldn't stop anyway. But it did, a mad woman at the wheel and two yapping dogs in the back.

'Get in quickly, you're absolutely soaking.'

He got in and she accelerated off before he had time to close the door.

'I'm going to Bramber, where are you going?' she asked. 'Amhurst I expect. You are from Amhurst aren't you? You should be carrying an umbrella. Don't they make umbrellas *de rigueur* at your school? They did at mine. I'll drop you off at the village and you can catch a bus from there, but of course there are no buses on Sundays, so you'll have to walk. Over the hill. I'll point you in the right direction. Maybe you'll get another lift.'

They passed more morose cows and the dogs barked and she told them to shut up and he started shivering.

'I hope you can have a nice hot bath when you get there. And you must take your socks off first thing.'

They reached Bramber and she turned into the car park next to the church, and he got out.

'Thank you very much,' he said.

'Just go on straight up the road and take the first turning on the right – that'll take you up Chanctonbury Hill and from up there you can see the college and Chanctonbury Ring.'

She closed the door on her dogs, got out herself and was gone.

She'd know someone up at the school and probably tell. The Chaplain, no doubt, who'd report it to The Buzz.

He started up the hill. It wasn't that far, well, another three miles, cross country. He was in territory familiar to him because of the beastly runs.

He was now going to miss Hall and would be late for Lights Out. That would worry them.

'Excuse me sir, I have to report Saranson missing.'

'Saranson? Missing? Now remind me Wilcox, which is Saranson?'

'The beautiful one sir. The one with the black hair and large brown eyes sir. Solo choir, sir.'

'Oh that little bugger. Where do you think he's got to then? Any house captains or prefects missing? He's probably gone twinking somewhere with a senior boy and they've got locked up in the changing rooms, or museum, or fives courts, and daren't make their presence known.'

His shoes started squelching, his trousers were soaked through and so was his jacket, but he was stoic and soldiered on.

Soldiered on!

Only this morning, even early this afternoon, he would have believed his stamina was inherited. It wasn't. Not unless his father was a marathon runner, or one of those awful characters who climbed mountains. Perhaps he *was* a mountaineer. He didn't fancy that. Climbing up Everest. He didn't like the cold.

He saw the boilerman's green van before he heard it, coming down the hill towards him. Should he thumb a lift in the opposite direction? The man was obviously going out to the pub for the night.

He decided to ignore it, and put his head down against the drizzle. The ten pound note would be wet through. The van took ages in coming, then drove slowly past and stopped. The man peeped his hooter. 'Oy! You!'

He turned.

'You're from Amhurst, aren't you?'

'Yes sir.' He shouldn't call him sir. He was only a boiler-man, the odd-job man who heated the damned place.

'Where're you goin' then. The school's this way.'

Where had he gone wrong?

'Got lost,' Alexander said, and got in the van.

'What House are you in then?'

'Travellier's.'

'You'll be alright. The Buzz won't hurt you as long as you've got a good story. But you're out of bounds.'

Alexander made polite conversation as they splashed their way up and down the steep, narrow Sussex lanes. He'd seen the boiler man around the cloisters often enough, but had never spoken to him. He learned that he had been at the school for years and shared The Buzz's fanatical interest in bees.

'Both apiarists,' the man said proudly, as they turned in through the school gates. 'Where shall I drop you off, Porter's Lodge?'

'Yes please. Thanks.'

He squelched down the empty cloisters. Dormitory time, but not yet Lights Out. It was just possible he'd get away with it. But at the top of the stairs leading into Travellier's was Goodall, talking to, of all people, Wilcox, the Head of House.

'Hallo Saranson, fall in the river or something?'

'Something, Goodall, yes.'

'I hope you're aware of the concern you've given us all.'

'Sorry, I got lost . . .'

But he wasn't allowed to finish.

'Go dry yourself and put on your little pyjamas and your little dressing gown and report to House Captains in three minutes.'

'Yes Goodall.'

He shouldn't have agreed. He should have gone straight to

The Buzz and told him the whole story. That's what housemasters were for.

There were noises of interest in the dorm which were silenced by Goodall who followed him in and watched him as he took off his soaking clothes in the bathroom, dried himself with the rough towel and put on his pyjamas.

He went to the House Captains' room and was made to stand there in the middle of the carpet while he was examined by all five seniors.

'Well Saranson, you've had us all quite worried,' Wilcox said. 'Another five minutes and the Headmaster would have had to be informed. Where were you?'

'I went to visit someone at Lower Beeding and just couldn't make it back in time.'

'Someone, Saranson? Who?'

'General Sir Geoffrey Saranson. He's a sort of relative.'

'Sort of? Could you clarify?'

'He was married to my mother, but they divorced.'

'Oh, very sort of. Went to chat about a few family problems then, is that it?'

Alexander looked down at his slippers. Brown and beige, checked pattern, rather new. He suddenly felt exhausted and totally helpless. If any of them asked him if the General was his father he realized he wouldn't be able to hold back the tears.

'Domestic traumas aren't acceptable as an excuse for being late Saranson, but you'd best go off to bed now. Come and tell me the details tomorrow, after breakfast, my rooms.'

Alexander was astounded. No beating.

'Thank you Wilcox.'

He went back into the dorm, slipped into his cold bed and whispered to Hooker that he had got away with it.

'You're so naive,' Hooker said.

'About what?'

'About what prefects can do to you.'

'What can they do to me?'

'Serve you up to the Head of School as flavour of the month.'

chapter two

'Little Miss Discontented, that's me,' Sarah Saranson said sticking her tongue out at her reflection in the bedroom mirror. 'I don't like my son, I don't like my father, I don't like my mother and I certainly don't like the colour of my tongue!'

She turned on her naked heels, pressing them deep in the thick white pile of the carpet, and flung herself on the bed, burying her head in the two soft pillows.

'If I weren't so inhibited with all the supposedly right values, I would have slept with dear tall Elliot last night and wouldn't be alone now. But no, not me! I found it necessary to put him off the whole thing and used Alexander as an excuse to be moral.'

She turned over, flung her arms out, her legs out and stared, spread-eagled, at the ceiling.

Poor innocent Alexander. What did he know of her problems? It would be at least another three years before she could talk to him about such things and expect him to understand. All the joy of imagining herself in the future as the single parent of a youthful, handsome son with whom she could share her life, had already been shattered by the dreary, tedious reality of the time and effort it took to bring up a child.

Thirteen-year-old boys were incredibly boring.

And what if, at the end of it all, he turned out to be like his father?

She sat up and reached for a cigarette.

Last night Elliot had lectured her on the evils of smoking.

So she would die of cancer, if she didn't die of boredom before.

Not for the first time, lying comfortably on the pummelled pillows, she contemplated suicide.

It wasn't serious, she wouldn't do it, but she enjoyed

working out the various ways she might kill herself, or her father, her mother, and even Alexander.

Perhaps she was frightened of her son because he was so bright and beautiful.

'You don't cut your wrists across, mother, you run the razor blade down the length of the veins; that way there's no chance of anyone stopping the bleeding.'

It was their only common ground perhaps, morbidity.

He was as fascinated by death as she was.

'You must be proud of Alexander,' Elliot had said. 'He sounds intelligent.'

She had shrugged her shoulders and gone all cold inside.

'He doesn't get it from me,' was all she had replied.

Oh God! Why did she have to deny her pride?

Because she hadn't made him hers.

Her son belonged body and soul to her parents and they made every decision regarding his upbringing, what he should be told, what he should not.

In their view, it seemed, the less he knew about anything the better. So they lied to protect him from the nasty surprises of life and she, like an idiot, lied along with them.

But then the lies had seemed to work. Alexander had accepted their muddled and uncoordinated stories, and hadn't brought up the subject again.

'It's a question of identity Mummy. I sometimes wonder what I'm going to be, and knowing that my father was a soldier helps. I think I may join the Corps next term. What was his rank?'

'Major.'

'Major Saranson. Jolly good. Other boys like to know, you see.'

She'd told her father Alexander's reaction and it hadn't surprised him. 'Needs to have a hero I expect. A dead soldier's ideal. Chap likes to know where he is in society, Sarah. I expect you do too if you think about it.'

She'd thought about it, and she'd had to admit that her dear, dear Papa had been right. His antique values had proved their worth and that was comforting. 'As soon as he starts at Amhurst again any funny ideas he might get will soon be put into persepctive. Besides he'll be too damned busy to think about himself all the time.'

To know exactly what was expected of you, how to behave, how not to behave, she liked that. She liked to know where she was. Oh there had been a time when she had rebelled against her own background, but class had saved her from self destruction over the years.

Was that where she would find peace of mind then? Admitting that she actually agreed with her own parents and enjoyed the same sort of life that they did? She had been pleased to receive Tante Louise's invitation to the annual Pangbourne cocktail party in the Weir House garden. It had almost become the event of the year.

Always during the last week in July, it followed on at the end of the season, after Wimbledon, Ascot and Henley. And she liked all that. Why was she always pretending she didn't? Why didn't she embrace her parents' social scene with open arms and enjoy it, instead of thinking herself what . . . superior? Different? She wasn't different. Sleeping with an unconventional man had not made her different, and it was fourteen years ago that it had happened and time she got over it.

All Tante Louise's fault for making her admit to herself that being married to an ambitious soldier was a life sentence of tedious imprisonment.

They had become friends shortly after Monsieur Rimbaud had died and she had found Tante Louise to be the most exciting person she had ever met.

'I am a lonely widow and I am going to be fifty-six next week, Sahara,' she had said. 'I need the company of young people around me. Come to dinner and help me celebrate.'

It had been the best meal Sarah had ever eaten, and she had not been the only guest. Five couples had come from London. French, Italian, some speaking three languages all at once, and there had been Richard, whom she had known by sight but had never spoken to before.

Richard, a complete outsider as far as she was concerned,

yet ten months later she had given birth to his son.

He had offered her a lift home after the party and had suggested a walk along the river. Masterfully he had taken her hand.

'Your husband's away?' he'd checked.

'Yes.'

'So you're alone.'

'I'm alone.'

'It would be nice if we could do something together.'

Like what?'

He had turned to kiss her on the forehead. 'I'd like us to go to bed together,' and before she could react, he had walked her on accepting her dumbfounded silence.

Her mind had raced then, raced in every direction, towards him, away from him, back to him again, aware only of his large hand holding hers.

'Do you love your husband?' he'd asked.

'Of course.'

'Yet you're holding my hand.'

'I'm trying very hard not to be narrow-minded.'

'Have you ever been unfaithful to him?'

'It's none of your business.'

'But it is my business. I want to sleep with you. I want to know whether its possible or whether I'm wasting my time walking you down this river path.'

His bluntness had annoyed her. It had annoyed her because through it she knew that he was trying to charm her. The all-honest approach. 'I declare that I see you only as a sex object.'

'Are you married yourself?' she'd asked.

'Yes, but my wife is in hospital, with a difficult pregnancy. She has to remain absolutely still or she'll lose the baby, and I can't stand the tension.'

'So while . . .'

'She's imprisoned,' he'd interrupted, 'I want to have sex with you, yes. Down and out sex. No romance. Lust for lust's sake. A physical affair, because it's perfectly obvious that you are as frustrated as I am and we need each other badly.'

That, strangely enough, had not annoyed her because it had

had been true. She knew it, he knew that she knew it and it had jarred her into taking a more realistic view of her situation.

'I think it would be wrong,' she had said, 'and I don't think I could handle it.'

'Wrong for whom?'

'Wrong for your wife and wrong for my husband.'

'I have no intention of telling them.'

'But what about the guilt?'

'Guilt!' he had screamed out into the night, and it had echoed along the surface of the water. 'What is guilt? Explain guilt to me.'

But she hadn't been able to. She had just not found the words.

He had, of course. They had poured out.

'My stronger guilt defeats my strong intent . . . Thank God guilt was never a rational thing . . .' The quotations had been labelled, dated, Shakespeare, Burke, then he had said, very quietly, 'If you don't come to bed with me I'll kill myself, then you'll know what guilt is.'

She had thought that so inane that she had turned on him, incensed, because up till then he had seemed so mature.

'Oh don't be stupid!' she had spat out. 'That is so spoilt!'

And he had looked at her and smiled at her reaction, knowingly, and she had understood that she had allowed herself to be manipulated, for he had led her to reveal that she cared about him. Her annoyance at discovering that he might be silly had prompted her reaction, and that had exposed her disappointment with someone in whom she wanted no disappointments. It was that insight into her character that had won her over.

He played games and had acknowledged that she could play games too.

She had wanted to see him again after that but was not sure that she should, so had talked to Tante Louise trying to convince herself that she was happy with Geoffrey, but

Tante Louise had not allowed that.

'The British army officer is one of the most glamorous personages imaginable,' she'd agreed. 'Most are cultured, well read, poets even, but their background is a disaster for their wives. It is such a male-orientated life, an *Eenglish* male orientated life! And we know what that means.'

'What does it mean?' she'd asked.

'Immaturity, ma chère Sahara, an inability to grow up and dominate a woman as she wants to be dominated. What you need, and you know it, is a lover.'

So she had taken one, Richard, and life had suddenly become wonderful, till the pregnancy test.

Those endless sleepless nights of calculations, of going back over and over again checking the exact dates when Geoffrey had gone to Northern Ireland and when she had been with Richard.

'I'm pregnant Tante Louise, but not by my husband.'

'Are you sure? Are you really sure?'

The expression had not been one of anxiety but one of delight of excitement, of congratulations.

'Now he will divorce you.'

'But I don't know that I want that,' she said meekly.

And Tante Louise had exploded.

'Abort! Abort! If you do not have the courage to be a single parent, then abort. But, ma petite Sahara, remember that denying yourself this child will be denying yourself the only challenge you have ever faced.'

Had Tante Louise been evil? Was she some sort of Machiavelli, a Zvengali who preyed on innocent English girls like herself and encouraged them to misbehave to satisfy some native caprice to prove that the British, with their reserve and sang-froid, were as vulnerable as anyone else to nature's whims?

Without Tante Louise for support she would never have been able to go through with it.

'Visiting that frog again?' her father had reproached her so often.

He could be so incredibly stupid.

'Your father does not think,' Tante Louise had explained. 'You must try and understand him. He inherited a fortune and has never had to work and has never had to think. So he does not.'

'And my mother?'

'Your mother is a very simple woman. If her parents had not been well off and she had not been sent to a good school, which enabled her to meet your father, she would be a *vendeuse* in one of those large stores selling fur coats to luckier women than herself and hating the world just as much as she hates it now. I always play a little game, Sahara, when I first meet people, I always change their background for them. If they are working class I try to imagine what they would be like if they had money. And vice versa. It gives one an insight into their characters. Birthright is fascinating to me and you have a marvellous opportunity to make your life really wonderful, once you are divorced. You will have a little human being to bring up by yourself with no one to tell you how to do it.'

It hadn't worked out that way at all.

'To tell you the truth, Sahara, I have only started enjoying life since my Emile died. Before that I lived his life, not because he imposed it, but because living my life would have been uncomfortable for him, and I did love him. He was a simple but generous man, you see, who liked his work, and his fishing. Not fishing like your father, with a tweed hat and expensive rods and reels bought at the correct shop in St James's, but with a stick, a bent pin for a hook and a worm.'

'Fella's a cook, chef at some frog restaurant,' her father had blurted out on some occasion. 'He doesn't know how to fish. Doesn't know what the word sport means!'

'He's related to a French poet, I understand,' her mother had ventured.

'Serves him right,' had come the riposte.

Oh . . . all the misunderstandings and heartaches that had followed little Alexander's birth. No one had been happy for years.

And now? Was she happy now? Not particularly.

Maybe it was all to do with orgasms.

The lack of them.

She stubbed out her cigarette, then threw herself back on the pillows.

Little Miss Frustrated.

She didn't like Elliot physically; why didn't she admit it? Because she was desperate? Forty-two and Mr Right had never made an appearance. That was all. That was all that had, or rather had not happened. She had not met her match and probably never would.

Alexander's father was the nearest she had ever got, and he had frightened her. That was how she had burnt her fingers.

Once bitten, twice shy.

There was a noise downstairs, letters being pushed through the letter box.

She glanced at the time. A quarter to nine.

She relied on the postman to get her up. She hated the mail but was always curious. One day there would be something nice from someone nicer. Maybe it would be today?

She went down the stairs, thankful that central heating had been installed however costly and however stupid it was to have it on in the summer, but she did like her comfort. She looked at the three envelopes on the floor, one white, the other two buff, and the *Daily Express*. She ignored them all deliberately and went on down to the basement kitchen to make herself her lovely morning cup of coffee. One of her great pleasures in life was drinking coffee and reading the paper in bed. It was one of the wonderful things about privacy and living alone, you could do what you wanted in the morning. When married to Geoffrey she had always felt a trifle guilty reading the *Express*. He considered it a rag. He had his *Times* and his *Financial Times*, so she had taken the *Guardian* but had become irritated by its puns and really was not interested in politics. Now she had the *Express* again with its lovely gossip. The middle-class *Sun*, Geoffrey had called it. So what?

She made her coffee and took it up the stairs and, with

controlled excitement, picked up the three letters not looking how they were addressed which would give away who they were from.

White envelopes usually held the promise of something other than a demand for money.

She drew back the curtains, looked out at the damp drizzly day, was thankful she didn't have to open the shop absolutely on time and snuggled down into bed.

The buff envelopes first.

The dreary water rates and unbelievably the telephone bill again. £122. It was all those calls to her parents and Tante Louise.

Now she studied the white envelope.

Mrs Sarah Saranson,
28 Blake's Garden Mews. SW6.

It was typed clearly, a typeface which was unfamiliar.

She slit it open. The writing paper was expensive and headed THAKENHAM HOUSE, LOWER BEEDING, SUSSEX.

It was from Geoffrey and she immediately felt the blood draining from her cheeks and a knot of nauseous anxiety forming deep inside her.

My Dear Sarah,
I was rather pained over the weekend to receive a visit from your son, Alexander . . .

She closed her eyes, then opened them to read the first line again.

I was rather pained over the weekend to receive a visit from your son Alexander who called on me in the belief that I was his father. I do think that after thirteen years the child should have been told the truth and trust that you will take care of this matter promptly.

My kind regards to your parents,

Geoffrey.

She sank down the length of the bed and deliberately let the letter fall from her limp fingers on to the floor.

Alexander had visited Geoffrey.

She was being reprimanded as she had always been reprimanded. 'I trust that you will . . .' Oh God! It would be with her for ever! 'I trust that you will not burn the toast tomorrow.' Virtually the first words of their marriage. 'I trust that you will not forget to put oil in your new car or it will not remain new for very long . . .'

Alexander had gone to see Geoffrey.

She actually felt quite numb at the thought.

She had this terrible image of him, standing there at the foot of the bed in his pyjamas that night she had been with Harry. 'Mummy, I've just been sick on the stairs,' and Harry pulling out agonizingly in shock. 'For Christ's sake who's that? You didn't tell me anyone else was in the house!'

She had walked in it too, the vomit.

'Go back to your room, I'll be up immediately darling,' searching for her bathrobe in the dark, and for some stupid reason they hadn't put on any lights for fear of revealing their nudity, and the bright circle of Alexander's stupid torch had picked out the decadence of the evening making everything seem worse.

Little Alexander, then ten, had been confused. Sick, feverish, it had been the start of two weeks of scarlet fever and the end of a very brief affair indeed.

Was it from that moment that she had started wishing in her heart of hearts that she wasn't a mother? Started hating her own son?

It wasn't hate. It was fear. Fear of guilt, fear of being accused by him of not being a good mother.

Alexander had gone to see Geoffrey.

'Well of course Daddy,' she would have to explain. 'That is exactly what an intelligent child would do. He knows we're hiding something important from him.'

'Stuff and nonsense.'

The brick wall.

Had she put up a brick wall between herself and

Alexander as well? Obviously. There was no communication between them whatsoever.

She reached for the £122 telephone and placed it on her lap, and picking up the receiver dialled Tante Louise's number.

Comfort, comfort. Advice, advice.

'Louise Rimbaud here,' the French voice answered.

'It's me, Sarah.'

'You are at work so soon?'

'I am in bed paralysed with fear.'

'*Ma chère*, why?'

'I've just had a letter from Geoffrey telling me that Alexander visited him over the weekend.'

'This Alexander, I like him more and more. He will not give up till you tell him the truth you know.'

'Well before I do that I'll have to consult with the powers that be.'

'And those powers, ma petite, will not let you, so you will have to get the child's confidence and tell him something in secret during the summer holidays.'

'The truth?'

'Of course not. The truth would have disastrous effects on him at his age. You will have to tell him an untruth and it will have to be such a good untruth that he will believe it.'

'I'm not very good at deception.'

'Then I will help you, and we will work out something clever between us.'

chapter three

Alexander had a secret room at the very top of his grandfather's house.

The house was old, enormous, with turrets and gables, front stairs and back stairs, corridors and passages, a huge kitchen, a vast cellar, a walled garden, orchards and lawns leading down to the river where there was a boat house with an old fishing punt and his own canoe.

Alexander's secret room was under the only gable that faced south and overlooked the Thames. Through an opening in the brickwork that served him as a window, he could see the white span of Whitchurch Bridge up river, the willow trees of Otter's Island, and Pangbourne Lock beyond, and to the east he could look across Hernmead meadow at Mary Northey's cottage and Hernmead Woods.

The secret room was reached through a low door in Hilda Kelly's lavender bedroom. It was hidden behind a blue damask curtain which protected her hats and dresses, coats and shoes from the dust, the slant of the attic room ceiling forbidding a wardrobe which would have been more practical.

Having parted the curtain and threaded himself between seersucker frock and brown gaberdine raincoat, and stepping cautiously to avoid the sensible low-heeled shoes and rubber galoshes, he would pull back the bolt and enter his kingdom of the long rusty nails sticking out beyond the cobwebbed beams which held the warped roof-tiles in place. He would lie full length on the old straw mattress that had been left there by one of the many skivvies who had once been in the household's employment, and plan his day or stare at the family tree he had painted on a large piece of hardboard.

It was an incomplete family tree with only one branch.

He sat up, swivelled himself round and faced the bright blue opening. Two days ago a pigeon had alighted on the brick ledge blocking out the light. It had scared him and he had taken it as an omen and asked Hilda what the appearance of an unexpected pigeon meant. She'd crossed herself immediately and closed her eyes.

'It's bad news Alexander. A group of pigeons huddled together on a roof means there's going to be a storm, a pigeon flying into the house means a death in the family. Did you see the pigeon in the house?'

'No,' he lied, 'I saw Tibbles dragging a dead one across the courtyard.'

'I'll kill that wretched cat!' she'd said with her Irish fury.

Hilda Kelly was all right. Off her head, but all right. She lied like all adults but only on behalf of others. He could trust her more than most. She was the only servant in the house now, apart from some woman from the village who came in to clean every week-day. Hilda did breakfasts, lunches and suppers, Grandma did the afternoon teas and some of the shopping, otherwise it was poor Hilda who did everything, between Holy Communion on Sunday mornings and Confession on Saturday nights.

So the pigeon had been an omen of death.

Maybe he should threaten suicide.

He fell backwards on the mattress and stretched out, arms alongside his body like a corpse.

The idea appealed to him.

'Really macabre, Saranson,' Hooker would say, 'Really *macabre*.'

Emotional blackmail.

That would really unsettle everyone, especially Grandpa who'd go berserk at the thought of the family name being dishonoured.

'We're ordinary Nottingham people,' his mother had once pointed out, 'Nottingham Lace people. Don't believe a word your grandfather tells you about us having aristocratic blood. The only reason dear Daddy has never had to lift a finger is because *his* Daddy owned a small lace factory and made a fortune out of making mosquito nets for the government during the First World War. That's where all the money comes from. Your Grandpa's grandmother took in washing, and her husband was a bargee on the Norfolk broads.'

Grandpa would be the most vulnerable.

He didn't ride horses but talked quite a bit about belonging to the local hunt. He never really did anything except talk. It hardly mattered whom he talked to as long as there was someone around listening. The one-sided conversations sometimes went on for an hour, more often than not in the morning when Alexander went to his grandfather's room to keep him company while he got dressed.

From the time the old man came out of the bathroom wearing his floppy, wide underpants and cellular vest, till Hilda sounded the breakfast gong, all the important matters of the day would be reviewed, man to man.

In the cupboard-lined dressing room, off the master bedroom, Alexander would stand by the window which overlooked the stables where the two family cars were garaged, and listen to the problems facing a man running a vast estate.

It was in that room one morning that Alexander had first asked about his father. The old man had been rambling on about Tom Northey pruning the apple trees and had mentioned how long the old gardener had been employed by the family, and Alexander had very casually asked whether Tom Northey had known his father, and there had been an exceptionally long silence.

'How did my father die, Grandpa?' he'd asked then, and had got the tropical disease answer that had contradicted his mother's story.

He'd gone down to the kitchen after that where his grandmother was waiting for the kettle to boil to make morning coffee, talking to Hilda who was peeling vegetables.

He had waited patiently till the coffee was made and had offered to carry the tray into the morning room, his grandmother walking nervously behind him fearing he might drop it, not having got used to the idea that he was really quite capable of carrying all sorts of things.

'Do you want some milk dear?' she'd asked, and he had said, 'I'd rather have coffee,' helping himself to a ginger-nut from the biscuit tin. 'Don't spill the crumbs on the floor, Hilda's just vacuumed the room and she'd get angry.'

She'd ignored his request for coffee and given him a glass of milk, so he'd asked her about his father's death which had made her spill the sugar and tell another lie.

He quite liked Grandma despite the smell under her prominent nose. She wore dresses all through the summer and a skirt and twin-set all through the winter. She had no interests except perhaps her daughter about whom she worried constantly, mostly when it wasn't necessary. Sometimes her grey hair looked a bit blue, usually after she'd been to the hairdresser. Grandpa always thought that rather funny.

It was she who had really made it plain that the subject of his father was taboo, something not to be brought up again, something, therefore, that absolutely had to be investigated; and so he had questioned Hilda and Tom Northey who had mentioned the General, and that's where Hooker had come in.

'Ever looked him up in *Who's Who*, or the telephone directory, even?'

It had never occurred to him to do so, but together they had gone to the school library and there it had been in the red box-like book in very clear black and white.

> SARANSON, General Sir Geoffrey Hubert, MC; *b* 1920; *Educ*: Harrow; RMC Sandhurst; Middx Reg 1938; Royal Warwick Reg 1947; C in C Belfast 1972; Ass.sec.Gen., NATO, 1980–82. *Club*: Nav & Milt. *Rec*. Golf.

It had puzzled him, really puzzled him.

'My mother must have realized that I'd find him in here sooner or later.'

'Later rather than sooner Saranson. You didn't think of looking, did you? Besides you're only six years old as far as she's concerned. Parents crystallize us when we're about six because they don't want us to grow up and become brighter than them.'

Hooker hadn't left it at the *Who's Who* entry; he'd gone to the telephone directories, given him London and taken half a dozen provincial ones for himself.

'Look up your name, Saranson, see how many there are, and try and find a General, or a Lieutentant Colonel. Directories aren't always up to date.'

Hooker had found the General in the Sussex book at the address in Lower Beeding.

'Round the corner, he lives round the corner. He's probably paying for your education and is keeping an eye on you.

Go and see him. You've got to. He'll appreciate a son who ferrets around for his antecedents.'

Would he be happier now, not knowing the truth?

He didn't know the truth.

All he knew was what was *not* true.

His mother had met him at Victoria station on the first day of the hols, hardly two weeks ago. The 7.00 train from Brighton arriving at 8.00. Very early for her. But she'd been there, nervous as hell, taken him straight home to Blake's Garden Mews in a taxi and shown him the bribe.

A Sinclair Spectrum Personal Computer which could be plugged into any TV set and tape recorder.

'In return,' she said, 'I want you to leave the delicate subject of your father alone, especially as far as Grandpa and Grandma are concerned. You should never have gone to see Geoffrey.'

'Geoffrey?'

'Geoffrey Saranson, Alexander, my ex-husband whom you visited without anyone's permission three weeks ago. I got a rather angry letter from him. Luckily I've managed to keep Grandpa and Grandma ignorant of what you did, but you should not have gone there without telling me first.'

'You never tell me the truth so I thought I'd find out for myself, that's all. You're always lying!' he'd protested.

'We're not lying darling, it's just that the truth is not very pleasant and we thought we'd save you from it for as long as possible.'

'What is the truth? I want to know.'

It had been rehearsed, the answer, he could tell because it had come out too pat. It had also taken for granted that he knew a lot about adult relationships.

His mother had never spoken to him like that before, taking him into her confidence, and while she had been talking he had sensed, but this was on reflection, he had sensed Tante Louise's influence. 'He is thirteen Sahara. Thirteen-year-olds understand everything these days; girls of that age are on the pill!'

'Before I married Geoffrey,' his mother had said sitting

down next to him on the sofa, 'I fell in love with a friend of his. We had an affair, I became pregnant, but before you were actually born he became very ill and died. Geoffrey took pity on me and we got married so that you could have a name. Unfortunately the marriage didn't work out and we got divorced shortly after. The separation upset everyone dreadfully, specially Grandpa and Grandma, which is why we want to forget the whole thing.'

'What was his name?' he'd asked.

And there had been a pause.

'I'm not going to tell you, not till you're much older because, Alexander, to be absolutely honest, I don't trust you, and you've done enough damage already.'

She'd lit a cigarette and had gazed into the fireplace.

'I will tell you,' she'd then gone on, 'when you're eighteen. Till then I'd like you to forget the whole sorry business. Your father's dead, he's been dead for longer than you've been alive and there's nothing you can do about it. Needless to say I'm sorry but really it doesn't affect you; you've been perfectly happy up till now with me and your grandparents looking after you, and you can go on being so.'

'What about his parents, my other grandparents?'

She clearly hadn't been ready for that one and had answered too quickly. 'They're dead too. They died a long time ago. I never knew them.'

He'd then further bothered her by asking whether he'd be able to change his name by deed poll to his real father's name when he was eighteen and she had mumbled 'probably' and had cleverly switched on a prepared video, *The Return of the Jedi*, which he had missed during the last holidays.

So he had kept quiet after that, but he hadn't kept still.

'I do not know whose son you are,' the General had said. 'I was not aware that you had been given my name . . .'

She was still lying.

Once delivered to Hernmead he'd searched the whole house.

Systematically he had opened every drawer, every wardrobe, every cupboard in every room looking for a clue, for a disclosure of the truth and eventually, finding a set of keys in his grandfather's study which opened the lock of an old leather trunk in the cellar, he had found a number of enlightening documents in a file marked 'Sarah'.

His own birth certificate dated 5 March 1973, with the father's name down as GEOFFREY SARANSON, Army Major; papers relating to the divorce between Sarah neé Midley and Lieutenant Colonel Geoffrey Saranson, dated two years later; there was also a 'Certified Copy' of an 'Entry of Marriage' between his mother and Major Geoffrey Saranson dated 2 April 1971, two years before he was born.

It was the fact that everyone had gone to such lengths to cover up something that he just could not come to terms with, that had made him feel so desperate.

After carefully replacing the file in the trunk and the key back in the study, he had gone down to the boat house to sit in his canoe and stare at the stagnant-smelling water, then had come up here to his secret room where he would now have to remain till tea time, because Hilda had come up for her afternoon break and was listening to the radio.

He would have to do something outstandingly clever to get attention and force his mother and grandparents to be honest with him. The idea of a threatened suicide appealed to him, but it would have to be super-dramatic and embarrass them publicly.

His mother had once suggested that drowning would be the best way of killing himself.

Could he do that?

Could he pretend drowning?

Tante Louise's invitation to cocktails in two weeks' time had excited his grandparents terribly during lunch; could he use the occasion?

The Weir House party would be perfect, if the weather held. The weir pool itself provided an ideal evening setting with its still, deep-green waters as a lacquered stage and the frothing white cascades as a backdrop to the morbid tragedy. Tante Louise's guests would be lined along the terrace and garden frontage, a captive audience, and he would make his entrance in the canoe from behind the weeping willows of Otter's Island, gliding to the centre of the pool and gaining attention by standing up and facing Weir House, a rope round his neck tied to the concrete block his grandfather used for anchoring the fishing punt.

Timing would be of the essence. His grandfather would have to have read a threatening note only a few minutes before he appeared.

Mary Northey could help there. Mary Northey could in fact help him quite a bit, delivering the note into Tante Louise's hand then letting him know by a signal from the river bank that it had been received.

If he wrote on the envelope TO GRANDFATHER from ALEXANDER. URGENT. Tante Louise would be bound to hand it to him, and if by chance she delayed doing so, his unexpected and bizarre presence in the middle of the pool would jar her memory. Besides, Tante Louise could be counted on to dramatize any occasion.

He would appear in some strange garb and her guests, already tiddly on her drinks, would at first think it was some pageant she had organized. Then the awful truth would be revealed.

No one would be able to reach him if he stopped the canoe at the very centre of the pool, not without getting into a boat or swimming, and talking him out of his threat would be impossible without shouting. So his grandparents and mother would be forced to agree to his terms in public, in the presence of hundreds of witnesses.

Pyjamas would look suitably out of place, but probably too ridiculous, a T-shirt and jeans would not be dramatic enough, his blue school suit would be better, but best of all, best of all!, would be a cassock and surplice. A choirboy gliding into the middle of the weir pool on a canoe with a rope around his neck!

Very unsettling, and such a silent spectre-like apparition might symbolize death in everyone's mind.

Excited at the prospect, he decided that as soon as he could, he would go down to his bedroom, get out pen and paper, and make a list of everything that had to be prepared. He had two clear weeks to plan the performance to perfection, Mary Northey would be the only person he would take into his confidence, but only up to a point. He'd invent some story about it all being a joke and would just have to put up with her sniggers as she imagined, wrongly, what the outcome would be.

First thing tomorrow he would go to the local church to see about borrowing a cassock and surplice, but now, until he was released from his temporary imprisonment, he would compose his suicide note, which would have to alarm, threaten and terrify.

chapter four

Dear Grandpa,

You will soon see me in the weir pool in my canoe preparing to drown myself.

I want to die because no one will tell me the truth about my father.

If you want to save my life you must shout out his name loudly and clearly and promise to answer all my questions about him.

I hope you will.

Such an early watery death before so many people would be fearful.

Alexander Saranson (?)

He liked the question mark after his surname best. It was the cleverest part of the note.

But would it work?

When Mary Northey, from behind a tree in Tante Louise's garden, gave the agreed signal, the simple dropping of a white tissue, there were at least sixty guests standing on the Weir House terrace and along the river frontage overlooking the weir pool.

He was on the other side of Otter's Island, hidden by the high grass and a multitude of nettles, and the moment he got the message, he stood up in the canoe and pushed off from the bank with his paddle.

Wearing nothing but his underpants under a purple cassock and white surplice, he was made up, his face powdered white, his eyes darkened under the lower lids for sinister effect, his lips tinged with green. Like a martyr he was bare-footed and from around his neck hung a length of white cord which led to a concrete weight placed on the canoe's bows.

He was a good enough navigator to know just how much impetus to give the slim boat, how to lean slightly to one side or the other to go to the right or left. Before making his entrance into the weir pool itself, he gave one big stroke then stood erect but with his head bowed, both hands clasping the paddle as though it were a penitent's cross.

One of the first people he spotted on the terrace was his grandfather in dark-blue blazer and club tie, reading the note. Next to him, his grandmother in pastel mauve, and next to her his mother with a silly new hat.

Mary Northey had delivered the note without a hitch. He had told her to hand it to Tante Louise and on the envelope he had written 'FOR MY GRANDFATHER from ALEXANDER. URGENT.'

Tante Louise was there, hovering around trying to find out what it was all about; he could also see Doctor Caldicott, balder and taller than most, gin in hand.

Comments reached him pretty quickly across the water, surprised comments at first, 'Oh look!' and 'How super!' and 'A water pageant, how clever!' until someone spotted the rope around his neck and objected, 'Rather dangerous isn't it?'

Agitation in the small crowd, grandfather rushing into the house, Grandma following, Mother, Tante Louise, then all of them coming out again. People shielding their eyes to see more clearly what he was doing.

When the canoe stopped its progress in the centre of the pool, some twenty yards from any bank, Alexander threw the paddle away and watched it plunge upright into the still waters and rise out again like Excalibur.

He was very pleased with the dramatic effect he was creating.

He bent down to pick up a section of the white rope which he had previously severed. No one could see the deception when he held the two ends in his hand. As he straightened up, the canoe rocked precariously causing one highly strung female to scream.

'What are you doing?' his grandfather shouted. 'Alexander what *are* you doing?' He was purple with rage.

Alexander said nothing but remained quite still. He would have to wait for his grandfather to take the initiative, he would have to stand there like an acrobat on a high wire till his demands were met, till his father's name was bellowed out for all the world to hear.

Grandfather consulted Grandmother and Mother, Tante Louise pulled at the doctor's sleeve and all went back into the house.

He waited.

The guests watched, intrigued.

His grandfather came out and leaned heavily over the terrace wall.

'Alexander! Come in now and we'll talk! You're behaving like a very silly boy!'

He shook his head but made no other move.

His grandfather, only just keeping his anger in check, turned to walk back into the house.

Alexander waited.

If he could stick it out, just remain there, a tragic, pathetic figure, a tormented victim begging for understanding, he would get results, or at least some sympathy from the astounded guests.

He turned around and was surprised to see that a number

of people had gathered on the weir's parapet: passengers from the pleasure steamer who had got off at the lock, and customers from the nearby Swan Hotel.

He looked at the guests on the terrace again; there was no sign of mother or grandparents, Tante Louise or the doctor. Feverish discussions were no doubt taking place.

He waited.

The guests waited.

An awesome silence fell on the spectators.

What was the boy going to do?

Grandfather appeared at last with the entourage and they all stood together talking intensely, then to Alexander's surprise a Thames Conservancy launch purred round the tip of Otter's Island, a man in uniform and white cap at the wheel, another in shirt sleeves taking in the scene. The engine was quickly put into reverse and the smooth mahogany boat's progress checked thirty feet or so from him. They were going to be cautious.

Alexander turned round the other way. Two hatless police officers had climbed over the parapet and were coming down the slippery concrete slopes to the water's edge, unbuttoning their jackets.

Would they dive in and attempt a rescue?

He hadn't thought of the police, had never imagined his grandfather would call them.

They had come very quickly, which was impressive, and frightening.

Maybe that's how they thought they would get him to give in. Intimidate him with the sight of uniforms.

He would never back down now.

He shifted his weight from the right to the left foot and the fragile canoe rocked again causing another gasp of alarm to rise from the onlookers.

He had all the attention he wanted.

He moved again, this time stepping back to sit on the stern board so that he could survey the scene more safely.

He dipped his hand in the water and the canoe very slowly swung in a semi-circle.

He was surrounded, there were even people on Otter's Island now, and two skiffs from Hobb's Boat house, low in the water with the curious, were being waved back by the officials in the Conservancy launch.

He'd have to make it worth their while.

He stood up again, deliberately rocking the canoe, aware that the huge concrete weight balanced on the bows was the main focus of attention. That, and the length of white rope.

A sudden move and the block could slip, overturn the canoe and pull him deep, deep down into the depths of the treacherous waters.

Could anyone guess that the rope was cut where he held it tightly against his chest, that he was in fact in no danger at all?

They would hardly take the risk of being wrong.

He crouched down and paddled gently with his free hand to turn the canoe so as to face the house and the guests on the terrace again.

There was activity now by the drawing-room windows, Tante Louise, Mother and Grandmother listening to a police superintendent who was explaining the use of a megaphone to his grandfather.

Family contact was going to be made out loud in public.

The truth would be heard by all.

'Alexander!'

His name crackled out.

There was reproach in the rattled voice, unforgiving resentment, but it did not cover the splutter of the launch's engine as it started up behind him.

He swivelled round to face the attack and was horrified to see the motor boat right on top of him.

'Come on boy, don't be stupid!'

One official kneeling on the deck, arms outstretched ready to grab him, the other with a boat hook aimed at catching the rope.

He threw himself backwards.

He heard screams as he hit the water, heard the splash of the concrete block slipping off the canoe.

He held on tight to the rope.

The hook had missed it, but the block was not dragging him down fast enough. He had to swim down, and his surplice was billowing with air and keeping him up.

He blew bubbles out of his mouth and turned over to see the long dark shadow of the launch directly above him.

How would he explain the cut rope?

He needed to breathe.

God! he suddenly needed to breathe, but he had overdone it and was down too deep.

He kicked out, let go the ends of the rope, pushed with both hands, felt the dreadful weight of his clothes dragging.

He had to blow the painful air out of his lungs, then needed to breathe in. Water filled his mouth. He gulped. He drank, he choked, he could no longer see the surface, there was no way up, all was black, and the pressure round his head and chest became unbearable.

He was drowning.

He was actually drowning and was going to die . . . Then something smacked hard against his chest, pressed down on his ribs, he felt a finger gouging out his tongue and he opened his eyes in sudden broad daylight.

'You'll be all right son, you'll be all right, just take a deep breath and let the air out slowly. Take deep breaths.'

He breathed in hot air, life giving air. The man above him smiled encouragement. 'Breathe in deeply now, more deeply.'

The stagnant, weedy Thames was everywhere inside him, he could feel its slime on his palate, on his tongue, he could smell the staleness in his nostrils.

He coughed, he wretched.

The launch shuddered under him.

He was on the deck and they were speeding towards the bank.

He closed his eyes not wanting to see. He didn't want to see their faces, his mother's, his grandfather's, his grandmother's. He just wanted to disappear, to hide.

Someone lifted him bodily, carried him like a rag doll up

the riverside steps to a soft secluded part of the lawn where he was put down out of sight of the curious.

Tante Louise was there with a cushion, some other woman with a blanket, his mother, with her silly hat, changing expressions every few seconds unable to adjust quickly enough to the situation. Grandpa and Grandma with similar difficulty, staring down at him not wanting to believe what he had done to them.

What would their friends think?

Doctor Caldicott was kneeling over him now, pulling up his eyelids with cold clean finger tips; Mummy, undressing him, removing his surplice, his water-logged cassock but not his underpants. She wouldn't do that to him in public.

'Breathe in and out slowly,' the doctor said.

He breathed in and out slowly.

A stethoscope appeared from nowhere and hopped its way round his chest. He could hear the occasional gurgle, and it hurt in the throat and tasted of mud in his mouth.

'Sit up, there's a good lad.'

He sat up. Tap, tap all over the back, the cold flat disc of the stethoscope again. He breathed deeply without being asked. He cleared his throat, allowed some liquid to dribble out between his lips for effect. It had been a near thing. He had, after all, lost consciousness.

'Physically he's all right,' the doctor declared. 'A few days' rest won't do him any harm, but no going on the river.'

Masterly!

They left him lying on the lawn under the blanket, and then they all went off in a huddle to discuss his future. Grandfather, Grandmother, Mother and the doctor.

Tante Louise raised her eyebrows at him behind their backs and with a quick, sympathetic blowing out of the cheeks, conveyed that she thought he had sailed pretty close to a very dangerous wind.

'Ee can go and lie down on one of the beds upstairs for a while if eet it is a good idea,' she said in her comic French accent.

The doctor thought it a good idea, and so did his caring

family. Get the little bugger out of the way till all the guests and gossips have gone.

Mother and Tante Louise helped him to his feet and, wrapped in the blanket, he followed them along a back path to the tradesman's entrance of the house, away from the terrace.

'You must take off those wet underpants, Alexander,' Tante Louise said as they went through the kitchen, 'Or you will catch cold.'

He stopped to slip them off and handed them to his mother who took them with disdain.

Upstairs he was led down a corridor to a guest room where there were two single beds with patterned covers and matching curtains. Tante Louise opened a cupboard, took out a soft pink towel and handed it to him.

'Dry yourself properly, Alexander, then lie between the lovely clean sheets and have a good rest. I will bring you up a glass of warm milk, or would you like some strawberries, something to fill your stomach?'

He would have loved some strawberries but thought it best not to show signs of well-being. The pretence would have to go on until he had won the battle totally.

'Why did you do such a strange thing, mon petit? Frightening everyone like that?' Tante Louise asked, turning down the bed.

'I have my reasons,' he said simply.

'Oh, I am sure. But it would have been nicer of you not to choose my cocktail party for such a demonstration.'

He whipped off the towel and quickly got into the bed and snuggled down.

'You're such a fine-looking boy, and you have such a fine singing voice, you should not risk your life with such stupid tricks. You could have drowned, you know.'

His mother had disappeared. She couldn't face him, obviously, couldn't risk answering his questions without first consulting dear Grandpa.

'Won't you tell me why you did it?' Tante Louise asked, tucking him in.

He could talk to her, of course. She was so direct, so forthright and honest and interested. And he liked her. Her perfume, her large bosom loosely held up by a pink silk bra that you could see when she bent over, her heavy make-up, her heart-shaped vermilion lips and mauve eyelids.

She was like an actress.

'It has something to do with,' he started, and hesitated, wanting to find the correct words. 'It has something to do with, well, you're here aren't you, talking to me, and my mother isn't. Nor is my grandfather or grandmother. It was something to do with that.'

'Family misuderstandings should not reach such magnitudes at your age,' she said. 'Later, when all my guests have gone you must tell me all about it. For now, rest and try to sleep.'

She left, as she was closing the door, he heard whispers, his mother's voice outside in the corridor, and the doctor's.

They were worried.

They were concerned.

He had dared.

Who dares wins.

But he hadn't won yet.

He wouldn't have won until they had told him the truth, the whole truth and nothing but.

chapter five

Doctor Caldicott came into the Weir House drawing room with the reassuring smile of someone who knows that a major problem they have temporarily become involved with need no longer concern them.

'I've given Alexander a sedative, so he'll probably sleep for some time. I think he's learned his lesson and doubt whether he'll get up to such tricks again, but maybe a good talking to would do no harm.'

He then informed them that he was late for his visit to another patient, and left.

Sarah crossed her legs, leaned her elbow heavily on her knee, pinched her cigarette between two extended fingers and watched the wisp of blue smoke curl upwards in the still air.

Father, mother and herself, all facing the empty fireplace, each waiting for someone else to speak first.

Her own feelings, right then, were of complete and utter weariness with the whole business and a dread that she would be forced to tell her pompous senseless father that Alexander had been to see Geoffrey. Mother would be on her side until that little bit of news had been broken, after which all hell would be let loose.

She had sensed some pride at Alexander's nerve.

She had, for a brief moment, thought of taking the whole matter in hand, whisking him back to London to his true home and telling everyone else to mind their own business. But it wasn't that simple.

She was heavily overdrawn at the bank again and if she made any decisions regarding Alexander without consulting dear Papa first, he would withhold her allowance and generally make things difficult.

So she remained silent, staring with heavy lids into space, awaiting her fate.

Tante Louise came in with a tea tray and plateful of left-overs from the party and set everything down neatly in front of them.

'If any of you want something stronger, help yourselves from the drinks cabinet. I will leave you all alone now.'

'I think the best thing I can do,' Father said when she had gone, 'is write to his housemaster explaining today's outrage and ask him what he thinks we should do.'

'He'll be on holiday dear. Masters have long summer holidays,' Mother pointed out.

'Well, the school will have to do something. The fees are

exorbitant enough. It is their responsibility.'

'I don't think what Alexander did has anything to do with the school dear. Surely it's a family matter. We mustn't put ourselves in the position of having to explain everything to his housemaster. The less the school knows about his real background, the better.'

'The wretched boy has got us drinking tea at eight o'clock on a Saturday evening in this frog woman's house. It's damned impertinent.'

'I don't think that's relevant,' Sarah said.

'What do you think is relevant then, Sarah? He is your son after all, though one would hardly guess it by the amount of interest you take in him!'

'I think we should tell him the truth.'

'Don't be ridiculous.'

'He's very curious about his father and very determined, Daddy,' she tried.

'He's a troublemaker. Good grief woman, he's only thirteen!'

'Boys of thirteen are brighter these days than they were in yours dear,' Mother said. 'They watch television.'

'What's that got to do with it?'

'They learn things they shouldn't.'

'Then he must be stopped watching television. That'll do as one punishment for a start.'

'I don't think punishment is the answer,' Sarah said.

'Well for God's sake Sarah, what is?'

'I think that we should talk to an analyst.'

'You're the one that needs an analyst. What on earth is an analyst going to do except send us outrageous bills to tell us what we already know? The boy's imagination must be curbed. That's all!'

Mother and daughter exchanged glances.

'The first thing we must do is clear the family name. We are, right now, the laughing stock of the whole village, and soon it will be the whole county. Now you may not care about this Sarah, but I do, very much, and young Alexander knows it and must be made to realize that he can't get away with what he did.'

'Are you going to hang him publicly, or put him in the village stocks?' she dared.

'I'm going to have a word with the police inspector to see if we can keep the whole business quiet and maybe pass it all off as a schoolboy practical joke that went wrong. No one but them, after all, saw his note.'

It was going to be all right. A side-stepping operation of the real issue was going to be negotiated, but now was the time to assert herself and get away from them.

'You talk to the police, Daddy, and I'll take Alexander back with me to London and see if I can get some sense into him.'

If, sooner or later, she had to reveal Alexander's visit to Geoffrey, she would at least be able to say she had found out about it after this last incident.

'Do you think you can cope with him?' Father asked, relinquishing his authority over the boy as reluctantly as always.

'He is my responsibility, as you said. Allow me to try.'

'Very well, but make damned sure that he realizes how angry we are.'

Relief on Mother's face. The problem had been resolved. She would be able to take her husband home to Hernmead and calm him down, while Sarah removed her offending son from the rancorous presence.

They all drank their tea in silence then Mother got up to collect the cups.

End of Act One, or was it Act Five? And how many acts were there going to be in this endless disruptive drama?

The dust had been successfully swept under the carpet anyway, again.

She drove back to London alone, happy to leave a sleeping Alexander in Tante Louise's care, happier still to get away from everyone.

It had been a horrific day.

She could have stayed on at Weir House of course, without telling her parents, but that would have meant an evening of going over the awful events, and she had had enough. She didn't want to think of Alexander till she had at least had one good night's sleep, and if possible not to think of him for several days after that.

But she would have to.

She would have to go back and get him in the morning and face the music, and tell him some foolproof story about his father.

What would she tell him?

That he had disappeared into thin air shortly before he was born? That he had gone off to the continent to avoid the responsibility of fatherhood?

What could she do to make it all sound genuine?

Maybe show him the letters he had written to her, care of Tante Louise . . . 'Like Laurie Lee I intend to go walking out one midsummer morning, maybe to Spain or Italy . . .'

She hadn't known who Laurie Lee was until she had asked about him in a bookshop. She'd felt so stupid not having understood. He had written to her again from the south-west of France with another riddle which had once more made her feel ignorant. 'Like Henry Miller I am eating the oranges of Hieronymus Bosch. He is what I wish to be about and what you should be about if you could but shake off the shackles of that dreadful family of yours. You are trapped, you see, by your own fear of insecurity, when the world outside makes no demands. You have to learn to shed the feeling that you must be someone, that you will only be respected if you are a recognizable type. So many of us build shields which do us so little good and a great deal of harm. The majority live the artificial life, that is why the peasant in his raw state is so likeable, and we try to imitate him and fail because we have not learned, as he has through poverty, that none of what we care about is important except to ourselves.'

She had read the letter so many times she knew it by heart and had so often tried to live according to its philosophy, but her yearning for the 'raw state' was not so much a need to live simply, as to re-live those moments when he had freed her of all her inhibitions, that first time he had called unexpectedly at Hernmead Court when her grandparents were out and it was Hilda's day off.

She had been sunbathing down by the old boat house, lying across a rug spread on the grass, feeling slim and delectable, when he had loomed above her, tall, masculine, in his dusty jeans and unbuttoned cheesecloth shirt.

'You shouldn't sunbathe,' he had said, 'You have a beautiful white skin and you shouldn't spoil it.'

He had knelt down and kissed her shoulder and, fearful that old Tom Northey might see them from the gardens, she had got up and nervously put on her bathrobe.

'Would you like a drink?' she'd offered.

And he'd smiled and had taken her arm and had led her into the boat house which, in those days, had been in a terrible state of disrepair, with half the roof timbers rotted and the walls crumbling with damp.

He had taken her to the darkest corner and had pulled the bathrobe off her shoulder to caress her.

'Look at that whiteness. You obviously have no idea how much pleasure pure white shoulders like that can give a man.'

'I always thought men liked dusky maidens with dark skins,' she'd managed.

'They adore dusky maidens with dark skins, but can also get turned on by pure white porcelain.'

He had leaned over her to kiss her neck, then had unexpectedly threaded his hands up under the bathrobe and along the inside of her thigh to press his thumb between her legs.

She had tried to back off, but he had quite brutally pushed her against the wall.

'You're hurting,' she'd protested.

He had opened up her bathrobe, pulled her bikini top off exposing her breasts and had started kissing her, pecking her, biting her, mauling her.

She had become frigid with embarrassment and had looked up and been horrified at the sight of all the cobwebs above and around her. She had shivered.

'I hate it here,' she had said trying to disengage, 'I'm frightened of spiders.'

And he had reached up and drawn his fingers along a beam gathering a length of cobweb and, forcing her down on the dank duckboards, he had drawn it across her throat like a necklace.

'I hate it! I hate it!' she'd cried, but he had grabbed her wrists and stopped her reaching for it.

'It's all in the mind. It does no harm. It's just a little natural dirt,' and deliberately rubbing his hands along the wet mossy boards he had started making greenish prints of his fingers on her breasts, on her stomach, pulling the lower half of her bikini down to rub cobwebs and slime in between her legs.

With agonizing cramp she had stretched out under him, fearful of splinters. 'What are you doing?' she'd cried out, struggling.

'Soiling you,' he'd whispered. 'You need soiling, you need, once in your life, to be and look impure.'

He'd said it gently, with a smile, all the time holding both her wrists with either one hand or the other, then he had slowly released her and had straddled her.

She had forgotten the cobwebs across her neck, the ooze all over her, and she had watched him unzip his jeans and had realized he was wearing nothing underneath, was totally naked, and though her immediate thoughts had been of the million dangerous sperms that would invade her, she had said nothing, had not resisted, but on the contrary had reached up to help him off with his shirt.

Had that been the time of conception?

Who can tell?

So many occasions had followed during the next few weeks when she had sometimes been careful, sometimes, stupidly, not.

And what did it matter now?

She slowed the car down to light a cigarette, then concentrated on her driving.

Tonight she would take a sedative to help her forget everything and she hoped she would sleep as deeply as Alexander.

chapter six

Alexander awoke when Tante Louise came into the room.

She was carrying a small tray on which there was a glass of steaming milk and a plate of hot buttered toast.

'I thought you might be hungry,' she said.

'What time is it?'

'Nearly nine. You have slept more than twelve hours.'

That was extraordinary. He had never thought the drug would have any effect.

'Where is everyone?'

'Your grandparents went home and your mother went to London last night shortly after you fell asleep, but she is coming back for you this morning, soon. You are to stay with her for a while.'

'Is that what the committee has decided to do with me?'

Tante Louise laughed. 'Yes that is what the committee has decided to do with you.'

'And what will happen to me in London? Are they going to send me to doctors and psychiatrists?'

'Why do you ask that?'

'I sometimes feel they think me sub-normal.'

'Your grandparents have never had contact with a young boy of your age, nor has your mother. They are not used to children. The English aren't. They send children off to boarding school and this is what happens. They don't understand you, Alexandre, it is no more serious than that.'

'I don't think I understand them.'

He ate the hot buttered toast and felt much better, could have done with some more, but drank the hot milk instead.

'Why are they lying to me all the time? I know my father isn't dead, but they won't tell me who he is or where he is. They're hiding something from me as though they were frightened. My imagination is probably worse than the truth.'

'What do you think is the truth?'

'I'm probably the son of an Irish labourer or something. A dummy they can't be proud of, or, more likely, a married man whom I mustn't go and bother.'

'I can't play guessing games with you Alexandre, I do not know the truth myself.'

'I think you do. I think you know but, like them, you can't tell me because you've been sworn to secrecy. I won't ask you because that wouldn't be fair, but you could drop me a clue now and again. I'd pick it up.'

Tante Louise reacted to a noise downstairs which he hardly heard. Used to her house she knew the tell-tale sounds.

'Your mother. I'll go and tell her you're awake.'

He fell back on the pillows and breathed in deeply. There was still a pain in his lungs and he had to make an effort to block out the memory of that dark green water and the ominous shadow of the motor launch above him.

He had been pretty close to drowning.

He stretched out naked under the starched sheets and closed his eyes, pressing his head deep into the soft pillow.

Layed out like the dead he was, like the sculptured effigy on his own tomb. He could imagine it, all white with a lily-of-the-valley across the chest, surrounded by black marble, with a headstone behind.

HERE LIES THE BODY OF ALEXANDER SARANSON
(?)
DROWNED WHILE IN HIS PRIME

Hooker would photograph it and stick it in his album.

The door opened and his mother came in, definitely concerned, but more for herself he sensed, than for him.

She had some of his London clothes in a plastic Harrods' bag which she started to take out. His beige corduroys, blue sweatshirt, socks, his black Amhurst shoes.

'Did you sleep well Alexander?' she asked. 'I'm taking you to London. I've got quite a bit to do, so am in a hurry. Could you get dressed?'

He sat up, pushed the bedclothes back with his feet and swung his legs to the floor.

His mother started leaving but then stopped at the door with an afterthought. 'You are feeling all right? Not sick or anything?'

'I'm fine,' he said.

She left.

He quite liked her sometimes, when she was herself, natural, as she had been just then, nervous as hell. Pity she always had to put on the act of being what she wasn't. A mother.

She was still quite good looking, the blonde bobbed hair that always gave her trouble, the grey-blue eyes under the surprised eyebrows, the slightly snub nose over the large mouth that could smile winningly, but more often than not pouted. A bit heavy under the chin. 'It's the gin dear,' he'd heard her say often enough, because it was.

'I can't stand my son,' he'd also heard her say, knowing he could hear her. 'He knows how to add and subtract and spell.'

Silly cow.

She could never bring herself to kiss or hug him in public either. It wasn't done, or something.

He got dressed, felt a bit nauseous when he bent down to tie his shoelaces, but otherwise was OK. There was still that stagnant water smell up his nose, or was it just lodged in his imagination?

He thought of making the bed, then decided to leave it and went to the bathroom, then downstairs, where he found Mother with Tante Louise waiting for him in the kitchen.

'Are you ol-right, mon petit? Your cheeks have more colour.'

He smiled in way of an answer.

'Do you know a newspaper reporter has just rung to ask about what you did yesterday?' Tante Louise said. 'I told him it was only a pantomime.'

He followed his mother out of the back door and up the steps under the wysteria to the gate. She'd left her Ford Fiesta in the Swan Hotel car park. It was a pretty basic car, and she was over-cautious, but it was fun enough driving with her.

She smoked the inevitable cigarette, was not too relaxed as they left Pangbourne on the Theale road to get on to the Motorway, so he decided to wait till he was spoken to, say nothing unless she asked him questions, but then she was silent for so long and he sensed her tenseness so acutely, that he thought it best to help her out.

'Was Grandpa very angry?' he asked.

'He wanted to send you straight back to Amhurst. That's how angry he was.'

'But it's holiday time.'

'Exactly.'

'Is that what's going to happen?'

It was something he hadn't thought about. Parminger had stayed over the Easter holidays because his parents were in Australia and he had apparently had a wonderful time. The whole place to himself, no boundaries. He had got to know some of the resident masters and had even gone to Brighton and places with them.

'I wouldn't mind,' he said. 'Amhurst in the hols is terrific.'

'Well, he decided against that. Instead you're to stay with me, out of his way for a while which, you will realize, is more of a punishment for me than it is for you.'

'Thanks Mum.'

'And don't call me Mum. Mummy, or Mother, but not Mum. It's not nice.'

'Sorry Mother, sir.'

They were now on the M4 and he checked his annoyance at the way she stuck behind a van on the inside lane instead of overtaking.

'Was Grandma angry?' he said.

'She was hurt. You made a fool of them both, Alexander, and people don't like being made fools of.'

'You've been making a fool out of me all my life,' he said.

'There is a reason,' she answered through a sigh.

'But that's all I want to know, the reason.'

She hesitated, looking into her rear-view mirror unnecessarily so often that he decided she was working up to something big.

'I don't want to talk about it till we get home, Alexander, I don't like talking while I'm driving, you know that.'

It wasn't true. She talked incessantly with her friends when she was driving. She never stopped.

She took a few drags at her cigarette and puffed out great clouds of smoke.

'What I can't understand, Alexander, is why you went to such lengths. I thought we had a deal, I gave you the Spectrum, and in exchange you agreed not to bring up the subject of your father again. Then . . . this pantomime, as Tante Louise called it.'

'You lied to me again. You said the General married you after I was born because I was the son of his friend and he took pity on you and wanted to give me a name.'

'That's right.'

'But you married the General in 1971 when he was a Major. You were married in Mapledurham Church.'

She slowed right down, drove on to the hard shoulder and stopped the car.

'How do you know all that?'

'I saw it in Grandpa's files, down in the cellar.'

She closed her eyes for a moment, flicked her cigarette-end out of the open window and immediately lit another.

'Is my real father dead?' he asked.

'He died about six weeks before you were born, Alexander, if you insist on knowing. I had an affair with him while Geoffrey Saranson was in Northern Ireland, and the reason we have kept it from you, kept it from everyone, is that he was married.'

She started the car up, glanced backwards out of the window and drove off.

After a while he asked, 'Did he have other children?'

'No.'

The question clearly unsettled her.

'What was his name?' he asked.

She looked in the rear-view mirror before answering.

Delaying tactics?

'Young,' she said at last. 'Richard Young. He was an actor, not a well-known actor, but a working actor and he was making a film on location near Pangbourne when I met him.

He didn't finish the film because he died of a heart attack. He was thirty-one.'

He'd known it all the time. And Tante Louise had known it too. That was why she had always encouraged him in amateur theatricals. Acting was in his blood.

'Was he in *any* films?'

'No. He was not very successful. Which doesn't mean he would not have been had he lived. But you can understand why your grandparents don't want him mentioned – apart from the scandal it would cause, actors are not respectable in their book.'

He loved it. He could see himself telling Hooker and Pitts. 'I'm an actor's son.'

The identity crisis was over!

'Was he ever on stage?'

'In repertory, yes.'

'On television?'

'I don't know.'

'Did he use his real name when acting?'

'I think so. You see Alexander, I never got to know him that well. The affair did not last very long because of his illness.'

'You said it was a heart attack.'

'It was, but brought on by pneumonia.'

It could be true, he'd be able to check. Old programmes, old stage magazines, theatre books. Hooker would help him on that.

But the joy only lasted till the Hammersmith flyover when the lorry that had been following them and bothering his mother, shot down the side road on his left, and he saw the name blazing out at him in large letters: YOUNG'S OVEN READY SEAFOODS.

It registered with him immediately, as immediately as it had obviously registered with his mother.

YOUNG'S.

She had read the name backwards in the mirror or had recognized the well enough known gothic lettering with its mascot shrimp. Unable to think up another name quickly enough she'd used that.

So she was lying again.

He wouldn't say anything now, he would just give her plenty of rope to hang herself by, a good deal more rope than he had given himself in the canoe.

As they turned down the Earl's Court road, sandwiched between the inevitable articulated giants, she said 'I'm afraid you won't be able to have your room for a day or two. I have a new lodger.'

That, then, would be the punishment without anyone realizing it. Living in that house was constraining enough with nowhere to sit down alone to read, let alone spread anything out to play, but having to sleep downstairs on the bunk seat in the kitchen was something he really didn't like.

'Does he go to work early?'

'Yes. He goes off at about seven-thirty.'

Which was exactly what he didn't want to hear. It meant that someone would be plodding around the kitchen making boring coffee and breakfast for themselves and waking him up with some banal conversation to be polite.

'Male or female?' he asked.

'His name is Elliot Warder. He is a student doctor at St Thomas's, and just settling in. I also should tell you that he's black, from Grenada.'

Well that was a surprise, a black man in the all white-painted house.

'Do Grandpa and Grandma know?'

'Not that he's black, no Alexander, and I'd be grateful if you didn't tell them, they wouldn't understand.'

'Like they don't understand that I want to know who my father is.'

'Well you know now, and we'll go into all that in greater detail before you go to bed, I promise. But please don't press me. Elliot is quite sensitive about how welcome he is in other people's houses and I don't want us to go storming in having an argument about family matters as though he weren't there. I want you to be nice to him. You'll like him, I'm sure.'

He'd heard that one before.

They turned left into Fulham Road, then left again into Blake's Garden Mews, and she took ages in parking the car in the cul-de-sac of pastel-coloured bijoux houses.

'He's obviously still here,' she said noticing that the light was on in the sitting room. 'He has one day off a week, but I never know which.'

'How long is he staying?'

'I don't know. A month, maybe more.'

As she was about to insert the key in the lock, the door opened and Alexander found himself staring up at a giant of a black man with a great grin on his face, bouncing up and down in a white track suit. His immediate impression was of a magnificent human being, a born athlete, and someone very likeable.

'Saw you parking, through the window Sarah, come right in, got coffee on for both of you.'

The inside of the house had been cleverly designed by some famous interior decorator and had a large number of cupboards and sliding doors and windows between rooms to give it the maximum feeling of space. Alexander, however, had always felt you couldn't swing a cat in it.

Elliot thundered down the narrow stairs to the basement kitchen and thundered up again with three mugs of coffee. He ushered them into their own sitting room and put the mugs down on the coffee table in front of Sarah who sat herself on the edge of the sofa to light another cigarette.

'I'm going to sleep downstairs on the bunk bed, Sarah, I don't want Alexander here to feel homeless.'

'You'll do no such thing. You're paying me rent for a room and that room you'll stay in.'

'I'm paying you rent for a roof over my head. It'll suit me and it'll suit him. That way I won't disturb anyone in the morning and I won't stay any longer than I need, anyway.'

'I don't want you to move out on my account,' Alexander said.

Elliot sat down cross-legged on the floor and beamed at him. 'Well, OK. But if you want to exchange, I'll exchange.'

He had incredible white teeth.

'I've been reading some of your books: Arthur Ransome, Rider Haggard. Good stuff man!' he said.

'Oh, those are my old books. I read other kinds of things now.' He wanted to prove himself more mature, wanted to impress.

'Just bought myself a Walkman,' Elliot said. 'Want to try it?'

The man was up on his feet, standing so tall his head nearly touched the ceiling. He glided out of the room.

Alexander sipped his coffee but didn't enjoy it. The after effects of the sedation followed by the drive made him feel a little sick.

'Will he really let me have my room?' he asked.

'He might, but I won't. I need the rent money.'

It wasn't true. Elliot was her lover, staying in the house free. He'd be curious to see them in bed together, black and white, in that white bedroom of hers, all lace and frills. No wonder she didn't want him home.

Maybe his own father was black. Was that it? Not black black but dark, a foreigner. An Argentinian? From the Falklands perhaps. Someone Grandpa and Grandma would really object to.

Hooker was responsible for making him more observant about his mother. 'Is she on the pill?' He hadn't had the faintest idea. He hadn't even understood what the pill was until Hooker had explained it to him. On the first day of the holidays, when he'd been alone in the house, he'd quickly looked in her bedside cabinet drawer and, sure enough, had found the packet, just as Hooker said he would. Little yellow pills in a special plastic envelope with dates and numbers.

'No woman is on the pill unless she wants to get laid,' he'd said, 'so just keep an eye on them.'

When he'd checked, two days later, two of them had gone.

'There are so many give-aways if she's having an affair,' Hooker had gone on. 'The pill, the drinks in the cupboard, drinks she herself doesn't like, cigarettes she doesn't smoke, or pipe tobacco, foods she doesn't eat herself. Toothbrushes of course, toothpaste brands, you can always find evidence that's been thrown away. And look under the bed. You might find a pair of dog-eared slippers or something.'

He'd looked under the bed, had found nothing, but in the dustbin outside he'd found two medical journals and a quantity of empty fruit-juice cartons and an empty after-shave bottle in the kitchen bin. It had confirmed a man around, but he would never have anticipated someone like Elliot.

'Alexander will sleep in the kitchen tonight because he and I have many things to discuss and I won't have time to talk to him till this evening,' his mother said authoritatively when Elliot came back. He was wearing a small pair of earphones and plugging a second pair into the Sony Walkman hanging round his neck.

'Right Sarah.'

He fixed the spare earphones on Alexander's head and switched on.

It was reggae, beautifully clear with an incredible bass beat, then suddenly, magically, Elliot broke into a body-popping routine, disjointing his arms, his legs, the length of his spine. It was terrific.

After a moment he switched off, took the earphones back, dropped to his knees and drained his mug of coffee. Then he was up again.

'See you guys. Got to buy myself some new medical books today and study.' And he was gone.

'He's an extraordinary mover,' Alexander said, when the door was closed.

'Yes,' Sarah said wearily. 'I expect he is.'

He noticed her checking his reaction to the remark, but he didn't alter his expression. The longer she thought him young and innocent, the better.

Maybe they hadn't slept together.

'I have a lunch appointment I can't cancel today Alexander, so you'll have to feed yourself,' she said. 'And this afternoon I must open the shop for a while.'

The shop was a drag.

An expensive second-hand clothes boutique his mother had opened with Tante Louise's help. It seemed to drain her of all her energy, and she hated working anyway.

He watched her finish her coffee, then reluctantly she got up and eventually left the house.

Alone, he went out into the small paved patio and decided he still disliked it. It was in the shadows all day long, was cold and damp and pointless.

He sat himself down in front of the television and watched the midday programmes, then studied the instructions of his Spectrum booklet, regretting that he had left the computer back in his bedroom at Hernmead.

At six, his mother returned, tired out, complaining about the lack of customers, and went to have a bath as she always did.

He took her up a customary cup of tea on a tray which he slid along the carpet through the open bathroom door till she could reach out for it. The idea was that he shouldn't see her in the nude, but he caught glimpses of her; enough to be able to report to Hooker that his Ma had a fine pair of boobs with very large brown nipples.

'Sign of good quality milk,' his friend had pronounced.

They had supper together watching more television, then just as he thought she was going to suggest having their 'talk', Elliot came bouncing back in, finger to his lips in way of apology for interrupting their evening.

'Change of schedule. I have to be on duty at first light tomorrow and have been told to go to bed early. I'll feed myself, take no notice.' And he was gone.

'I'm going upstairs to get something I want to show you Alexander,' his mother said. 'Unless you're too tired and would prefer to leave it till morning?'

'I'd like to know everything now,' he said.

She left the room and he waited a long time. He heard her and Elliot upstairs, directly above in her bedroom, then on the top floor, in his own room. Was she tucking him up in bed or something? Kissing him goodnight?

'I need the rent.' She didn't need the rent, she needed company. Why couldn't she be honest about it?

She came back down carrying the black deeds-box he had often seen in her cupboard but had never been able to open because she hid the key somewhere in her bedroom and he'd never found it.

She put the box down on the coffee table, knelt in front of it and opened it up. It was full to the brim with letters and documents, his passport, hers, their medical cards.

She took everything out, piling legal papers and certificates on bundles of letters held together with variously coloured elastic bands.

From the very bottom she brought out a large brown envelope and put it on her lap. 'I don't know how much of this you're going to understand, Alexander, somehow I feel I don't really know you.' She was terribly nervous, so much so that he noticed her hands were shaking uncontrollably.

He didn't want that. He didn't want her to feel uncomfortable because of him, but then he felt that she had something quite awful to tell him and he had to know.

She stood up and went to pour herself a glass of whisky, then returned to sit down next to him on the sofa after lighting a cigarette.

'I don't know where to start . . .'

'Just tell me everything about him.'

She took a deep breath. 'I lied to you in the car. About him filming on location and dying. I said he was an actor to make you happy, and I don't know whether he's alive or not.'

'Why don't you?'

It seemed a reasonable question to ask but somehow it upset her even more. At least she was trying to be honest now, and perhaps his name was Young and the seafood lorry had just been a coincidence.

'I haven't been in contact with him since you were born. He may be anywhere, perhaps in Australia. I just don't know.'

'Does he know I was born?'

'I don't think so.'

She looked terribly concerned at the thought.

'I'm sorry Alexander . . .' She moved as though she wanted to reach out for him, squeeze his hand perhaps, but it didn't happen. She didn't go far enough and the moment of possible affection passed.

She took another deep breath and forced herself to lean back on the cushions.

'Let me start from the very beginning Alexander. It's the only way I'm going to manage this.'

She took a puff at her cigarette, a gulp of the whisky, then faced him and looked him in the eye.

'When I was nineteen I was a bit of a rebel. I didn't like the way Mother and Father lived, their values. They weren't strict, but the things they cared for, their snobbery if you like didn't appeal to me.'

'I know what you mean,' he said. 'Like not wanting me to talk to Tom Northey or play with Mary Northey.'

She hesitated, as though she didn't really think them wrong about that, but nodded agreement.

'I met this very handsome army officer at a hunt ball and Ma and Pa were immediately enamoured with him. He was well off, with money of his own, a future, but most important he was about to be posted abroad, and I wanted to go abroad to get away from home. So, believe it or not, I married him.'

'That was Geoffrey Saranson?'

'Yes.'

'Where did you go?'

'Germany, then Northern Ireland, then I came back and we only saw each other when he was on leave.'

She stopped, looked at the carpet, at her feet, thinking back. He wanted her to get on with it, felt that somehow she would never get to the truth.

'We didn't get on, really. I didn't agree with his values any more than I agreed with Mother's and Father's. Money, prestige, society came first for the three of them; they don't for me.'

'What does come first?' he asked.

'Freedom, I suppose. Freedom to do what one wants when one wants.'

She seemed unhappy about it and got lost in thought again, and he realized that if he kept interrupting she might never get to what he wanted to hear.

'Anyway,' she went on,' I was staying for a few weeks at

Hernmead while Geoffrey was in Belfast and Grandpa decided to have the house re-painted. To save money, as always, he hired a local handyman to do the whole house, the whole house mind you, all the gables, all the window casings; a massive job for one person. The man wasn't a workman as such, not one of your common or garden labourers, if you know what I mean. Well, he read the *Guardian*, which I found interesting. Father, instead of sharing my curiosity that he wasn't reading the *Sun*, just said that the *Guardian* was a pink rag. I mean, it's impossible to communicate with Father sometimes.'

He was surprised to see her shaking again, with a sort of anger. 'Oh, Alexander, the man was intelligent. He was painting houses because he was broke and couldn't get any other sort of work. He was an actor, an artist, he was creative and above all he was a free-wheeler, he didn't care about all those things I was taught to care about. And we talked. We talked so much. He was quite good-looking too.'

'This was Richard Young then, my father?'

His mother looked up, annoyed that he was jumping the gun.

'Let me finish Alexander, it's important for me to get everything in the right sequence.'

She paused, then said, 'Yes, he was your father, I fell in love with him.'

'So you went to bed with him?'

'I went to bed with him.'

Why was it so hard for her to admit it? She went to bed with lots of other men.

'I went to bed with him and became pregnant, Alexander, because I was stupid, and he was impatient, and we didn't take any precautions. Do you understand what I'm talking about?'

'The pill,' Alexander said.

She turned to stub out her cigarette and stared at the empty fireplace.

'I don't know you at all, do I? I have no idea how much you understand. I leave it all to the school. Did you learn that at school?'

'I suppose so. Hooker told me.'

'Did he?' she said into the void.

She didn't know who Hooker was. He had never mentioned Hooker to her. He had never mentioned Hooker or Pitts or Wilcox or Goodall, or any of them, because she had never been interested.

'Richard and I had a summer affair,' she continued. 'No one knew of course. When your grandparents were out I used to invite him in to tea and we went off together on the river, and once or twice we went to London. I didn't have the house then so we stayed in cheap boarding-houses. It was wonderful.'

'Where did he live?'

'He had a bedsitter in Reading. We went there as well. It was quite awful, very poor, but it was a haven for us. We spent a long time in that room. He talked well, very clearly. He was eloquent. He loved talking, and had a marvellous voice.'

'Did he paint many houses?'

'No, I don't think so. I think Hernmead was the first one. He'd worked on the cottages over by Gifford's Lane. Anyway,' she said taking another cigarette out of the pack, and lighting it, 'Geoffrey came back from Belfast and we went off hunting for a house, and found one.'

'Thakenham?' Alexander asked.

'No, it was a small place in Surrey, near his parents. We lived with them for a while, then I moved back to Hernmead to have the baby . . . you.'

She laughed nervously at the way she had not connected the two.

'It's strange, isn't it, but I had such a bad time in those days when you were born, and after you were born, that I've tried to forget it all.'

A familiar look came into her eyes that was so overwhelmingly sad that it seemed to draw her eyelids down as though to hide her distress.

He hated that look, it made him feel so uncomfortable.

'Your arrival in the world upset a lot of people, Alexander. Nothing to do with you, but I have to tell you because it explains why the whole subject of your father is so taboo. I decided not to have an abortion you see. I decided, against everyone's advice except Tante Louise's, to have you and get a divorce from Geoffrey. You became the reason, the excuse, for me to get free from a man I didn't love, very much against Mummy's and Daddy's wishes.'

She watched the smoke of her cigarette curl up in the still air of the sitting room.

'What did Richard, my father, do?'

'Oh, he buggered off.'

She opened up the buff envelope on her lap and dug her hand deep into it.

'Once Geoffrey had come back Richard and I only met once to say goodbye, temporarily I thought at the time. It seemed wise for him not to be around. But I never saw him again. He went abroad, travelled, wrote to me several times, but I never saw him again. The last letter I received from him was from Sydney.'

She brought out a bunch of letters, each letter in a separate envelope with different stamps from France, Spain, Morocco, Egypt, India and a dog-eared photograph.

'That's him,' she said. 'It's not a very good picture, but it's the only one I have, taken when he was about your age.'

It was a black-and-white photograph of a boy dressed as a harlequin. His face was not made up, it was not white, nor did he have arched eyebrows or a spot on the cheek, but the young boy had a mop of black hair and looked uncannily like himself, three years back when he sat across the cardboard moon for Tante Louise's village concert.

'It looks like me,' he said.

'I know. You are very much like him, more and more every day.'

She handed him an envelope which contained a postcard and a letter. The postcard was of a medieval tapestry depicting flat-profiled soldiers marching with banners outside the massive walls of a castle. The letter, dated 2 March 1973, had been written from the Hotel de l'Etoile, Montreuil-sur-Mer.

My Darling Sarah,

Fate, it seems, did not want me to leave you. I have had a terrible journey and, as you can see, I have not got very far. This strange little town is no longer on the sea as its name implies. It was built to repel the British army, which seems to dog my footsteps wherever I go. I never gave a second thought to the British army before I met you, but now I tremble with rage whenever I see a Union Jack. I hope this letter gets to you without causing you problems. Tante Louise is trustworthy, I am sure. My aged Fiat broke down at Dover, overheating. It needs a new radiator which will set me back the amount I had calculated would take me to the Italian toe. I shall journey on, of course, with little enjoyment while you insist on staying in my memory, which will be for ever. I hope you are not as pained by the parting as I am, but I fear for you. The one who is left behind with nothing to do usually suffers the most, while the traveller can lose himself in the new surroundings of petty daily adventures, for some moments at least. Should you change your mind and want me back beside you – write to me c/o my Italian friend whose address you have. Au revoir. My love to you and the life within you.

Alexander put the letter and the Montreuil postcard back in the envelope and gave it to his mother, and took the one she handed him.

It was another postcard, from Venice, a much shorter message but still significantly romantic.

Mi amore. An error to come here for you are in every gondola and on every bridge, especially the Bridge of Sighs. We should have escaped here together. I have found a hostel with a room overlooking the fish market. The smell in the early hours of the morning is quite appalling. Last night I dreamt of my friend the freckle on your left breast. I love you. R.

He couldn't help it, but glanced at his mother and tried to see her left breast, but it was well covered by her dress.

She was sitting back now, staring at the painting over the

fireplace, a hay field which apparently reminded everyone of something similar that Van Gogh had done for his brother where he had later committed suicide. He quite liked it. It had a stormy sky above a sun drenched corn field, with an impression of black clouds brought out by stark white and very dark blue brush strokes. There was a dash of scarlet in one corner, representing nothing in particular except, perhaps, blood. The eye always went there.

'He gave me that painting,' she said. 'He did it for me. Five Acre field from the Hernmead steps.'

The next card had a very short message. It was of the Taj Mahal and the message read: 'Shah Jehan built this for the woman he loved. How well I understand him'.

And the next was longer, from Sri Lanka, a beach scene that looked more like Hawaii.

> I have run out of money and am beach-combing down here. I have a job selling non-existent property. I am a real estate agent with no real estate. A rich Australian comes here every autumn in a large yacht to hire a crew for the return trip. So I wait. Thinking of you, but in all honesty . . . less. So write to me. Love R.

He was surprised by this and looked up at her. He wanted to ask whether it had hurt, but he didn't know how, and he was embarrassed, and she smiled because she understood what could be going on in his mind.

The next envelope with an Australian stamp franked 1974 did not contain a postcard but two short notes. The first was in the now familiar sloped handwriting.

> Her name is Melinda and she is nothing like you. The ideal beach-girl advertisements tell you to dream about. She is of mixed Indian and Chinese parentage. She is helping me forget you since you refuse to write. It has taken me seven months and three weeks and two days to forget what you look like. Should I phone your home for news? Are you well? Was it a boy or a girl and when?

The second note on different paper was written in bold

blue ball point which had smudged.

> Dear Sarah, I thought I should let you know that Richard Young died last week in hospital following a surfing accident. I know he would have wanted me to tell you. He did not suffer. Regretfully. Melinda.

So he is dead?' Alexander said.

'I've never known what to believe. Perhaps that note was genuine, perhaps not. Either way I felt the message was a goodbye.'

chapter seven

Alexander put the two pieces of paper back in the Australian envelope and picked up the photograph again.

It was so like looking at himself.

'Did Tante Louise get the idea of my Pierrot costume from this picture?'

'Probably.'

'She knows about all this, then?'

'Yes. Tante Louise was very supportive. She's a very good friend.'

He handed the photograph to his mother and watched her put everything back in the box, close the lid and lock it.

'Why didn't you tell me all this before?' he asked.

'Because Grandpa and Grandma didn't want you to know that you were illegitimate. It matters terribly to them. Much more than to me. In fact it doesn't matter to me at all. I'm sorry I didn't tell you before. I just didn't think you were old enough to understand.'

'You think I'm old enough now?'

'Yes, Alexander, I do.'

And she leaned right over this time to plant a kiss on his

forehead, pulled him towards her, put her arms round him and hugged him like he could not remember her hugging him before. Then, to his horror, he realized she was crying.

He tried to ease himself away, but she didn't want him to see the tears. Eventually she released him and stared at him, wet eyed.

'It's very silly of me . . .'

It made his eyes water.

He hadn't seen his mother cry since a Christmas day, a long time ago, when Grandpa had given her a second-hand Mini.

'I'm crying because I've been in such a muddle for so long over all this. Not knowing whether to tell you, not to tell you. Grandpa and Grandma are so stupid you know, but they're old and one must try to accept their point of view. It's my fault for being so weak.'

She looked at the clock on the chimney piece.

'It's very late Alexander. I think we should go to bed.'

She helped him make up the bunk down in the kitchen and he went upstairs to the bathroom to brush his teeth and put on his pyjamas. They kissed goodnight on the landing and she hugged him again, dry-eyed now, happier.

Content, he snuggled down into the sleeping bag and lay there looking up at the familiar patterns on the ceiling, light from the street lamps filtering through the Venetian blinds.

Wanting to pee, he got up and tiptoed to the stainless steel sink, trying to make as little noise as possible. It wasn't that he was too lazy to go upstairs, it was that he didn't want to hear if any noises were coming from her bedroom. That would spoil everything. It would spoil the warm feeling he now had about his mother and his romantic dead father who had been a vagabond actor and artist. He had been wrong to suspect dishonesty again, jumping to the wrong conclusions about Young's Oven Ready Seafoods, but that was the frame of mind they had got him into. All they had tried to do was protect him from a truth that mattered only to them. So he was a harlequin's son, a fantasist, an actor, an artist. It explained why he liked to make people laugh, entertain.

Gone would be the struggle he had fought against to discipline others because he was supposed to be of military stock. Gone would be the thoughts of uniforms, of decisions as to which regiment, of false love for the Corps. He would join the dramatic society, the Open Theatre Club, and put his name down for the school pantomime. His father had a marvellous voice, Mother had said. Wasn't he a solo singer in the choir? He would take that more seriously, he would listen more to classical music, opera. Pitts liked opera, as much as Hooker hated it. There was a great range of choice ahead of him now, a very great range. Somewhere within him there was an artist; whether actor, singer or painter he would have to find out. He'd never regarded the art classes as anything but a break from the more tedious subjects. He would concentrate on mastering oil on canvas, water colour on cartridge paper.

He sighed out loud and, on such happy thoughts, allowed himself to drift into a euphoric sleep which he had not experienced for very many weeks.

He was woken up, as he had expected to be, by Elliot making himself breakfast.

He opened his eyes slowly and watched the tall man dancing about the kitchen eating a grapefruit. He was wearing a sleeveless vest and white underpants, and his muscles were flexing and un-flexing. Abandoning the grapefruit he bent completely double and touched his toes as though he were made of rubber. He was incredibly fit.

Then Elliot started jogging on the spot and turned to look at him.

'Want to join me?'

'What's the time?'

'Seven.'

'No thanks.'

'Sorry to have woken you man, but now's the finest hour to run round the park.'

'What park?'

'Battersea Gardens man. Just across the river.'

It was miles away!

Elliott jogged off, up the stairs and out of the front door, which he closed very quietly.

Alexander remained in bed, deep in the sleeping bag realizing he had hours, days, weeks ahead of him to daydream about the interests he had inherited from the Harlequin.

Maybe he would go to a theatre for a matinée, or go to Waterfords and buy books on the theatre and painting, start a collection of his own, or he would go and see a film connected with art, he didn't want to waste time on anything that was not directly connected with his future.

Perhaps he should go to drama school.

Would Grandpa allow? Would Grandma approve?

Hardly.

He didn't even have a paint box. He'd get one and when next at Hernmead he'd try his hand at reproducing Five Acre Field, Gorse Farm, Mary Northey's cottage.

His mother came down, bleary eyed, at eight o'clock to make her first morning cup of coffee.

'Did he wake you?'

'Yes.'

'Sorry. He jogs. He won't be back.'

'Ever?'

'No. Today! He gets back late though. Do you mind? Just for a week. I need the rent.'

It really irritated him the way she went on about that all the time.

'Are you going to work?'

'Of course.'

'Can I have money for the cinema, or the theatre.'

'The theatre? That's expensive you know. I haven't got that much with me. Why don't you come over to the shop, lunchtime, and we can have a sandwich together. I may have sold something by then; if not I'll go to the bank.'

She wasn't admitting it but he felt she was still in love with him, with Richard Young, his father. He was Alexander Young. Alexander Saranson-Young? Alexander Saranson was a better stage name. Maybe he'd use it in homage to the late General who was now dead and buried, as far as he was concerned.

His mother spread some horrible slimy margarine on a piece of toasted bread and dipped it in her coffee. She was worried about getting fat.

'What theatre did you want to go to? What's on that interests you suddenly?'

He shrugged. 'Not sure, just thought I'd like to go.'

'Because I told you your father was an actor?'

He nodded.

She finished her coffee and washed up the cup. On her way out she came over and tousled his hair.

'Going on the stage then, are you?'

'Maybe.'

'Well I'd rather that than have you in the army.'

She gave him a kiss and shuffled off in her old slippers up the stairs to get dressed. It would take her ages before she was ready to leave. She'd read the paper, open her letters, have a bath and spend about a year doing her face.

He turned over and went back to sleep.

At least Hilda Kelly wouldn't be coming in and pulling back the sheets as she too often did, irritating bitch.

He came out of a pleasant slumber when his mother bent over to kiss him goodbye. 'You'll make your own breakfast. You know where things are. I'm late.' She was wearing one of those flowered dresses that made her look rather plump and with her flat shoes and straw basket she might just as well have been going out to prune roses in some country garden.

'I'll see you lunchtime then. You remember how to get there?'

'Of course.'

The door slammed shut and he was alone.

He eased himself out of the sleeping bag without unzipping it and swung his bare feet on to the cold white tiles which was a good way of getting a sore throat, or so he'd been told. Not that he'd ever had one.

He went to the cupboard above the freezer, reached for

the cornflakes, spilled a quantity out into a soup plate, and added the sugar and milk.

As he munched, he caught sight of himself in the small kitchen mirror.

Perhaps, somewhere along the way, he *was* related to Oven Ready Seafoods.

He went up to the bathroom on the top floor, which smelt strongly of some new perfume. It was pleasant but rather overpowering, and his own room, right next to it, was the same.

He went down to his mother's room, the bed wasn't made. No particular evidence of two people having slept in it, the usual bolster and the usual one pillow. He sniffed around, couldn't detect Eau de Elliot anywhere. Maybe there was no relationship.

He looked around her little dressing-room with its own wash-basin and lavatory. No male trousers or anything significant in the waste-paper basket. She was probably behaving herself.

He went back up to his room which overlooked other people's gardens. Small, with a narrow bed, the counterpane drawn creaselessly and more tightly than he had ever managed, from foot to pillow, everything in its place, his books on the shelf neatly arranged in order of height, nothing on the desk except three ball-point pens, blue, red and black laid out like surgical instruments. He opened the drawer. Tidy. Writing paper, envelopes, a desk diary. He pulled that out, carefully, opened it up, flipped over the pages. SUNDAY. Read *Myocarditis*. MONDAY. Cancer ward. Mr Howes. Op. Geriatrics. TUESDAY. Transfusion. Pharmaceutics. Geriatrics. WEDNESDAY. Mr Howes. Op . . . then it struck him, unpleasantly, a sinking feeling.

He had seen the handwriting before. That bold blue ball-point writing. It was the same as the note he had read the night before, the one announcing his father's death.

He placed the diary on the desk and went down to his mother's room, slid open the cupboard where she usually kept the black deeds-box, found it on a shelf next to a set of jumpers. No key. She had to keep the key somewhere, unless she carried it with her in her handbag. But that was unlikely. It had a short red ribbon on it.

He opened the bedside table drawer, the pills, the tell-tale pills, half a packet. So she was still on it. A box of Tampax, a face-pack, no key.

The dressing table? He opened the top three drawers. Make-up in the middle one, pots of the stuff: pan sticks, rouge, lipsticks, bottles of nail varnish, all mixed up. In the left the knickers and stockings, hundreds of them, squeezed in tightly. In the right her jewellery, three velvet-lined boxes. No key.

He tried the other bedside cabinet, the one with the telephone and the shelf for her address book, cigarette packets and sleeping pills underneath. He opened the small cupboard usually reserved for jerries. Three old pairs of slippers, two pairs of sandals all jammed in on top of each other. Inside a white rope shoe he found it. He'd never thought of looking there before.

He quickly put the deeds box on the bed, opened it up, found the envelope and the note. He smelt the paper, detected a hint of fresh ball point ink, but that could be imagination.

He took the note upstairs to his room and compared it with Elliot's writing in the diary. It was too similar to be a coincidence, the vowels were identical, the style.

So his mother had come up the night before when Elliot had just come in, begged him to write the note which he would have had to do quickly, and in order to agree he must have known the story and was therefore probably her lover.

Total deception.

A complete lie.

Christ! What was all this about?

Who *was* his father?

An important politician perhaps? Like that Conservative MP who'd got his secretary pregnant and who had to be protected from a public scandal for fear of the Government falling?

Was he the son of a cabinet minister?

More his mother's style than a down and out actor.

A married industrialist perhaps, someone really rich who was keeping his mother. All that rent crap was just a cover-up. The whole story of Grandpa owning the house a story?

She was lying to him, really lying, but why?

The letters from abroad had seemed genuine enough.

Who was he? Alexander what?

He absolutely had to find out, and it wasn't stuck here in this small house in London that he'd manage anything. He was committed to meeting his mother for lunch. He would think about questioning her again, but there was an anger building up within him now, which he knew would have to be tightly controlled.

He stood there for a long time looking out of his bedroom window at the gardens belonging to the larger houses behind. Patio with white iron furniture, colourful umbrellas and overgrown cyclamen, a pretence of Spain, as someone had said.

He heard the front door open and met Elliot on the stairs seconds after he'd slipped the diary back in the desk drawer and slipped the Melinda note up inside his pyjamas top and behind the elastic of his trousers.

'Hi man! Just come to collect my things. Found another place to stay. You can have your room back.' It took him two strides to get from the first landing to the second. One to bound into his room.

Alexander didn't say anything but sat down on the top step of the stairs wondering how he could get Elliot to reveal something.

'When my mother asked you to write that note last night, how did she get you to do it?'

Elliot was now in the bathroom relieving himself, the door half open.

'What note man?'

'The one about Richard Young dying in a hospital after a surfing accident. She told me you helped her out.'

It was a long shot.

Tall, wide-eyed Elliot came out zipping up his flies, and hesitated in the doorway.

'You having me on, man, eh?'

'Did she tell you who Richard Young was?'

Elliot couldn't answer he was so confused, which was a real give away.

'What did she ask you to do?' Alexander pressed on.

'Why don't you ask her?'

'I did, but I don't believe her.'

He watched Elliot move across to the bedroom in an attempt to get away.

'My mother lies to me, continually. I don't know my real father, you see, and I'm trying to find out who he was, or is. She was trying to palm me off with some story that he was dead, through you, but I don't believe that. I think he's alive and somewhere secret she doesn't want me to know about.'

'You best ask her man, nothing to do with me.'

'Have you slept with my mother?'

'Man, that isn't any of your business.'

'It is my business. She is my mother and I live in this house. Did you sleep with her?'

'No sonny, I did not.'

He was getting tetchy, it was beginning to be fun.

'Well don't because she's got herpes.'

He'd never seen anyone pack so fast. Elliot opened all the drawers, the cupboards, thrust everything in a plastic holdall that grew bigger and bigger like a balloon. He slipped on his leather jacket, shoved two pairs of shoes in a canvas bag, and that was it.

'Tell your mother I'll send the rent money I owe her. Better still, tell her nothing. I'll ring her myself.'

Half way down the stairs he paused and looked up.

'Nice knowing that people like you are around.'

And he was gone.

Alexander went down to his mother's room and looked out of the window. Elliot was OK, but dispensable. From now on it was going to be all-out war. A campaign of intimidation. With a little cunning, adults could be manipulated by the sheer terror of their own imagination and guilt. He'd use that.

He took his time dressing, wandering around the house, looking through all the drawers in his mother's room, the cupbards downstairs in the sitting room and in the kitchen. There was nothing new, nothing he hadn't seen before, nothing that gave anything away about his birthright. He examined the papers in the box again, the letters seemed genuine enough, the stamps alone proved that, but had they been written by his father or just some other lover his mother had had? Was his father called Richard, even?

Who would know? Who could he ask?

Someone in the village who would know whether a Richard Young had existed, a Richard Something who had painted the house? He needed to get back there. He needed to be back in Hernmead where there would be more information. There was still six weeks of the holidays to go. He had the time.

As he was combing his hair through with water because bits kept sticking up behind, he heard the front door open.

Elliot back having forgotten something?

'Alexander?'

It was his mother, and she didn't sound too pleased.

'Yep?'

'What happened? What did you say to Elliot?'

She was coming up the stairs quickly.

'How do you mean?'

'What did you say to Elliot?'

She was there in the bathroom doorway, tight lipped, mortified. 'He just rang to tell me he was leaving for good. He said he didn't want to stay while you were in the house.'

She gripped him by the elbow and squeezed his arm. It didn't hurt.

'What did you say to him?' she repeated.

'I asked him why he wrote the note.'

'What are you talking about?'

'Richard Young, my father's death note. He told me. You asked him to write it. You're still hiding things from me and

I'm going to find out why, and until I do I'm going to make life hell for everybody.'

She spun round, her heel leaving a dent in the beige pile of the carpet.

Then she swivelled round again.

'Did you tell him I had herpes?'

'It was a joke.'

'Do you know what herpes is?'

'Of course. Jackson Minor's got it at school, all round the lips from kissing the head prefect's arse!'

'This time it's me who's going to ring your House-master!' She was incensed.

'He's in the Channel Isles studying the sex life of bees,' Alexander said.

'Christ! I can't stand it!'

She was off, down the stairs to her room, slamming the door behind her.

He knew the scene well. Two holidays ago she had gone out to a party leaving him alone in the house. She had come back late with a man and hadn't even bothered to check whether he was all right, so he had gone down to the sitting room and had found them mauling each other. He'd coughed, and she had been so furious at the intrusion that she had turned him round, pushed him out of the door and had slammed it behind him.

After that she'd come up and said sorry, had tucked him up lovingly, kissed him goodnight, and had closed the door.

He hadn't gone to sleep. For quite a time he had listened to the thumping and groaning going on, not sure, in those days, what it was that adults really did.

He went downstairs to the kitchen and switched on the television. Open University or cookery. She'd come out of her room eventually and they'd have a talk. Another series of lies.

He heard the telephone click.

Who was she ringing?

He reached out for the kitchen extension, held down the

button, lifted the receiver gently then let go. It clicked but she was still dialling.

The number rang, a familiar tone, but he wasn't sure whether it was Hernmead or Tante Louise.

''Allo?' the funny french voice answered.

'It's me,' Sarah said sounding really down. 'It didn't work. I muffed it. He found out, somehow, that Elliot wrote the death note. And yet it seemed to have worked so well last night.'

'He is very astute Sahara.'

'Too bloody astute, and dangerous. He comes up with such astounding things sometimes . . .'

'He is like a bubble of mercury that boy, Sahara, you will never be able to catch him because as soon as you get hold of him he splits up into several personalities.'

'I'm not sure I can cope right now, could I take you up on your offer?'

'Of course. Send him to me today. Put him on the twelve-thirty and he can be here for a late lunch.'

'Are you sure?'

'I will look forward to his lively company.'

'Thanks. And good luck. I'll put him on the train, he can walk down.'

'Of course he can.'

The phones clicked. Alexander didn't put his end down, but let it buzz.

He was going to stay with Tante Louise. He was going to be free around the village. Without lifting a finger he had managed to get exactly what he wanted.

He put the phone back on the hook.

He was astute, and dangerous and like a bubble of mercury.

Sarah took Alexander to the station and put him on the train to Pangbourne. She gave him his single ticket, bought him a 'Test Your Own I.Q.' paperback which he asked for, and a bar of chocolate. She watched him settle in a window seat and waited for the train to leave.

As soon as it started moving off and they waved to each other, she felt a terrible sense of relief. She was free, free of Alexander and free of Elliot. Whatever fearful things Alexander had said, making poor Elliot want to leave the house, she was delighted at the outcome. Elliot with his vegetarianism and super-hygiene had proved to be a pain.

She turned the corner in Praed Street expecting to see the car papered over with parking fines or, worse, the clamp, but the traffic wardens had not been around.

It felt good, a minor victory, to have parked on a yellow line in broad daylight and got away with it.

She drove straight home.

What would she do without Tante Louise? Did everyone have such friends to turn to? Probably not. Yet Tante Louise had not come to mind as an immediate saviour when she had faced the first real obstacle in her life. She could still make herself feel sick over it, the vacuum in time, the draining of the whole being when she had realized she was pregnant. It had needed confirmation and the twenty-four hours of waiting for the test results had been fearful enough, but nothing like the moment when she had realized she had not had her period for well over a month. Oh God! The panic! tryig to remember when she had last had one, unable to calculate, her mind obsessed with the memory of that afternoon with Alexander's father.

'What you need, of course, is a lover.'

She had always imagined it would be a handsome foreigner, immaculately dressed and frightfully rich, who would take on all the responsibilities, but then the idea of letting herself be wooed by a married man who was bored with his wife had become irresistible, partly because he was the last person on earth either her parents, or Geoffrey, would imagine she could be attracted to.

Instant thoughts of abortion of course, but she'd had one already and it had gone wrong. A seedy doctor visiting her in a seedy flat, fever for days, the probable father only just managing to borrow the necessary cash to pay for it and avert a family scandal. Eighteen and in the heyday of her life as an eligible debutante. She'd slept around but only with subalterns or supposed members of the aristocracy under twenty-one.

So she had run to Tante Louise who had convinced her that she should use this natural event, this 'gift' from nature, to become independent of everybody. It was then that those long discussions at Weir House had taken place during the winter of 1972, with a view of the river in flood through the windows of the drawing room, as they sat by the fire eating garlic bread and slurping onion soup downed with a rich red wine.

Tante Louise, her 'analyst', who had made her think for the first time in her life.

What did she want for the rest of her years? An ambitious army officer of a husband, her life to continue very much as it was now, entertaining military wives, shooting parties in Scotland, officers' quarters in Germany, Cyprus, Belfast and eventually, when she was in her thirties, a brood of kids which would anchor her down to some country town? Or something of her very own to cherish and bring up? How independent did she want to be? She had only married Geoffrey to please her parents and get away from them at the same time; but hadn't that operation proved to be jumping from the frying pan into the fire?

She had made no decisions. She had allowed time to go by experiencing an unexpected satisfaction at the thought of defiant motherhood.

It had been pleasant visualizing herself leaving Geoffrey, and shocking her parents with the news.

'Mother, I'm going to have a baby.'

'Oh darling, how exciting. Geoffrey will be so pleased.'

'It's not Geoffrey's.'

Wasn't that more or less what had happened? Those dreadful expressions of reproach on their faces. How could she do such a thing to them? What would their friends say? Eventually they had asked the unaskable. Who? Who was the father? And they had found it impossible to believe that their daughter could associate with such a dreadful man.

Then, *then*, she had learned his full history and the endless nightmares had begun, because it had been too late.

Tante Louise had held her hand during all that.

Tante Louise had held her hand during the whole pregnancy, the birth and the divorce, and apart from visiting her at the hospital and settling the inevitable expenses, neither her father nor her mother had helped her emotionally. They had not wanted to be part of it and she, to be honest, had not wanted them around. Nor the real father, who had escaped the uncomfortable situation by going abroad. She had learned, later, that he had also escaped his wife who had given birth, after great difficulties, to an unwanted daughter.

One day, when shopping in Harrods, she had met Geoffrey Saranson by accident. He was with his new wife in the furniture department buying a sofa for their country house. She had been with Alexander who was in his pushchair looking horrible. He was crying and kicking, and instead of feeling proud of him she had wanted to disown him, and that had been terrible.

She got home, closed the door knowing she had the place to herself for as long as she wanted. She kicked off her shoes as she went down to the kitchen, not caring where they landed, undid her tight dress and let it slip to the floor and made herself a large cup of coffee.

Up to her room to her glorious unmade bed.

Oh how she loved the freedom of living decadently.

She picked up the telephone and dialled the Hernmead number praying that her mother, not her father, would answer. Get the duty bit over and done with.

Her prayer was answered.

'I've sent Alexander off to stay with Louise Rimbaud for a few days, Mother. I thought I'd let you know just in case you saw him in the village. It's to give me time to work things out with my new lodger.'

'I don't think we should tell your father, dear, he'll be rather angry.'

'It's because we never tell father all sorts of things that he's always angry, Mummy. You've wrapped him up in cotton wool for so long that the poor man just isn't used to everyday family problems.'

'Who?' Her mother asked, 'Alexander?'

'No . . . Daddy!'

She closed her eyes. She would have to learn that both her parents were getting old and were sometimes unbelievably thick. She could not rely on either of them to be intelligent any more. The problem she now had to face was that Alexander was getting brighter and her parents were getting dimmer, and she was caught in the middle.

'I'm going to see a psychoanalyst friend to talk things over as well,' she said.

'Oh I should be careful what you're doing, dear. If they get their hands on Alexander . . .'

'Mummy. *I'm* going to talk to the analyst. I'm not taking Alexander with me, that's one reason why I've sent him to Louise's. He is suspicious and gets his nose so much into everything that I thought it would be safer.'

'Why didn't you send him to us?'

'If you remember, you sent him to me. We have to admit it, Mother, Alexander has become a handful, mostly due to our lack of understanding or realization that he has suddenly grown up. Also we've all told him different stories and he's not stupid.'

'I don't know what your father's going to say.'

'He told me I should be responsible for my son, so responsible I am being. I only rang you to let you know what I was doing.'

Reluctantly her mother thanked her for that, and the conversation ended.

Sarah put the receiver down, highly satisfied with her own performance. It was the first time in ages that she had been so positive, the first time since Alexander had been sent to boarding school, that she had taken back the reins.

From now on it would be thus.

chapter eight

It was simply a question of showing no emotion whatsoever. His mother was managing it, but then she was very good at that.

Alexander looked at her through the dusty window, she looked at him, her anger had gone, they exchanged meek smiles and both tried to find something else to do but just wait.

Railway station partings were always dreadful, but this one was beginning to be as painful as it was pointless. He wasn't going away to school for three months, she was sending him away for a few days to Tante Louise, so why pretend it saddened her.

Perhaps what saddened her was that she had failed to deceive him.

A whistle blew, the train moved off and his mother waved him goodbye.

She surprised him sometimes, the way she got rid of him the moment he became a problem. It was as though she was forever waiting for an excuse. Her show of affection last night had nearly been embarrassing, it was so rare, but it had brought tears.

The trouble was she lacked warmth, or was unable to show it, like five years back when Hobb's boat-house had caught fire. He had seen the cloud of smoke from the garden and had ridden over on his bicycle. He had stood in the lane leading down to the boat-house frontage where all the punts and skiffs were moored, and had watched the old timber-repairs shed being engulfed by fierce red flames thirty feet high, the roof collapsing, the hull of a brand new cabin cruiser split open, its white paint blistering, popping, exploding. His mother had been shopping in the village and, like many others, had stopped on the way home to look at the blaze, and he had felt her hand on her shoulder as they stared at the holocaust, and he had burst into tears.

She had only been concerned that he was eight and should

not cry. She had not asked him why he was crying, only reproached him for doing so. That had been a point in time when he had felt estranged from her. She had not seemed to understand that such fearful destruction was new to him and frightening, that it was his first experience of violence. He had followed her swervingly on his bicycle, more tears blurring his eyes because he felt misunderstood. In a way he had thought the inferno quite beautiful; then he had caught sight of the old boatman's expression and that had shocked him. The utter despair which no one could do anything about. It had been a terribly strange experience; one of those experiences that had made him feel years older afterwards, and wiser, and annoyed that he could not reach his mother to talk about it. 'You're a grown-up boy now; you shouldn't be afraid of things like that. What about all those people who get killed in wars? And those who are dying now in Afghanistan. He's only the boatman, it's not even his business.'

It had been as bad as Grandma telling him to eat Hilda's awful porridge because children of his age were dying of starvation all over the world.

The only person who had had any sympathy had been old Tom Northey who, like himself, had gone on his bicycle to watch the fire. He had found him after lunch on the other side of the walled garden by the rubbish tip sitting on an old beer crate smoking his pipe. He always wore the same greasy felt hat, his streaky white and yellow hair sticking out from underneath like the Straw Man in *The Wizard of Oz*. He always wore the same trousers, the same waistcoat over a faded blue shirt, his gnarled, cracked hands etched black with earth. He had puffed and looked at the ground, then had looked up as Alexander had walked towards him.

'Saw the fire then, Alexander?'

'Yes,' he'd said, kicking a stone with his sandals.

'I suppose you thought it exciting?'

'No I thought it was awful.'

Old Northey had reached out, for a second, to squeeze his arm.

'You're too sensitive lad, for the world you're growing up

in. You mustn't let things like that upset you.'

The train was stopping at Slough, after that Maidenhead, Reading, Tilehurst and Pangbourne. The scenery would change from hot, dusty back gardens overlooked by open rear windows with grey curtains hanging heavy in the draughtless air, to beckoning summer meadows carpeted with cornflowers, peaflowers and buttercups, and his beloved Thames with its wild banks of purple loosestrife, cow parsley and flowering nettles.

The canoe was moored at Weir House he presumed, so he'd be able to paddle around in it, down the weir streams, though the waters would be as still as they had been two days ago.

It would be interesting to hear the latest news from Tante Louise, what people had said of his suicide attempt, what gossip there had been about it and about his grandparents' reaction.

Mother had said nothing about it at all.

But Tante Louise would.

If not her, then Mary Northey.

He'd have to get to her somehow, which, without his bicycle, would prove a jolly long walk, circumnavigating the great Hernmead estate so as not to be seen by Grandpa.

The railway embankment ran parallel to the river for a mile or so and Alexander pressed his forehead against the glass of the window to get a panoramic view. He hadn't done this journey by train for years, and from up here you could see into the river, two or three feet down if the water was clean, especially round the edges of the islands where shadows suggested improbably large fish.

There were a few motor boats cruising up and down, the occasional skiff, the water looked incredibly inviting and he longed to swim. He'd go out in the weir pool and swim across the spot where he had nearly drowned. The experience hadn't put him off, though he could still taste the nauseous river at the back of his throat if he thought about it.

Had Mary Northey been worried, he wondered?

She was so self-effacing that only a handful of people were

aware of her existence. Whenever he asked any of the locals if they had seen her, they'd invariably answer 'Who?' and he'd have to explain, 'Connie Northey's daughter,' or 'Old Tom Northey's grand-daughter' or 'The girl who lives up at the Hernmead cottages,' and even then a blank look would settle on their faces.

The thing that he liked most about her was that he could never hurt her feelings. She was used to being pushed around and asked to do things by everyone that she genuinely didn't seem to mind. He had never seen her cry, she laughed quite a bit and generally she was happy. She was, as his grandmother liked to point out at least once a week, simple.

She was thin with darkish skin, brown eyes and rather thick eyebrows. She wore a constant bow which flopped over one ear, held to a fistful of mousy hair by an elastic band. She only seemed to have two dresses, summer frocks which she wore with or without a matted wool cardigan that had once been bright green but now reminded him of faded pea soup. She had mended it herself several times at the elbows with different coloured wools. She never wore socks, but always had her dark, sometimes dirty feet stuck uncomfortably in stiff, black leather shoes tied with laces. She was poor, and looked it.

She could knit and sew and did both competently. Her main pastime was making rag dolls with no faces which she gave to the hospital where her father worked. It was called a hospital, but in fact everyone knew it was a loony bin, like they knew that her father didn't work there, but was a patient. She was the daughter of a nut.

Mary had been his first playmate. Ever since he could remember she had been around whenever he stayed at Hernmead. Three months older than himself, she had first made an appearance in the gardens as a toddler with her grandfather. Nanny, with his grandparents' permission, had allowed them to play together providing she didn't come into the house with her muddy gumboots. He remembered her gumboots, black and frayed at the top while his were a shining bright red. But he couldn't remember the Nanny. He'd had several.

As he grew older and went to school he saw less of Mary, but when he was given permission to ride his bicycle beyond the estate boundaries, he had started going out for long rides with her, because she knew all the lanes and paths through the woods, and the interesting places to go to. She'd been given a bicycle for Christmas by Tante Louise, which everyone had thought terribly generous.

One summer, when they were nine, she had kissed him on the mouth and forced her tongue between his lips which he'd found disgusting. That was one of the times she had laughed hysterically. The other time had been when Damian Thomas had fallen through the roof of the derelict outhouse at Gorse Farm and broken his arm.

He never thought of Mary during term time. When she was not there to be seen, she was totally forgettable. Even when his mother drove him to Hernmead at the beginning of the holidays and he made mental plans as to what he would do and who he would see, Mary never came to mind. He'd quite look forward to meeting the Simcock brothers and Damian, but he'd never think about her, until, having crossed Hernmead meadow to go to the woods, he'd see her sitting there on the wall outside her cottage, her presence causing no more surprise than the twisted iron gate that had hung unmoving on its rusty hinges for so long that weeds had grown in and out of its bars.

The flint and brick semi-detached pair of cottages had once been part of the estate but his grandfather had sold them off to the council when they'd become too expensive to maintain, and they were now rented to the Northeys. Old Tom, Mary's widowed grandfather, in one, Mary and her mother in the other.

The train drew into Pangbourne station seven minutes late and Alexander got out, ran down the subway steps, up the other side, down the short hill and across the main road to Weir House.

At one time a small railway cottage stood between the old

Victorian station and the Thames lock, trains had unloaded goods on to barges in the pool. A major road had then been built between the railway and the river, the river traffic had disappeared and the pool had become a beauty spot. The cottage had been sold by the railways and someone had built on to it, not once, but four times, so that now it was a big rambling house with nooks and crannies. The kitchen and the room above which Tante Louise used as a laundry and ironing room, were terribly old, dating back, it was thought, to Queen Elizabeth I.

He went in through the tradesman's gate, down the little step past Tante Louise's vegetable garden to the bright green door at the back. It opened before he could ring the hanging bell.

'*Hamboorgeur* and french fries, ice cream with chocolate topping, just like McDonalds!'

Tante Louise leaned forward so that he could give her a kiss. The skin on her cheeks was always smooth, smelt pleasantly of powder but was a bit floppy. It was rather like kissing a bloodhound, he imagined.

He sat down to his lunch, hungry as ever, and lifted the corner of the top bun. She had stuck a huge slither of blue cheese in there which he didn't like, but couldn't remove. Her cooking, though terrific, was always a bit overlush and she always insisted on him eating what *she* liked.

The ice cream, he knew from experience, would be loaded with Cointreau or apricot brandy or something not at all to his taste, but her french fries were terrific. He decided to eat the cheese first.

'Don't you like the meat Alexandre?'

'Yes, but I like eating the cheese first.'

'You should eat it all together.'

'OK.' So he ate it all together and she sat across the table from him to watch, leaning heavily on her strong cook's arms.

'I understand Elliot has left,' she said.

'I didn't know you knew him.'

'I don't, but your mother told me about him. Was he nice?'

'Very nice. Very tall, athletic. He break-dances.'

'Is she in love with him, do you think?'

He shrugged his shoulders.

'Would you mind if your mother were to fall in love with a black man?'

'And marry him? It would take some getting used to, specially at school. She's supposed to come to my confirmation next term.'

'It would upset you if she turned up with someone like Elliot?'

He thought about it, imagined his mother with a silly hat, all in white, Elliot on her arm, grinning wide eyed, shiny black, coming up the aisle of the school chapel. 'It would be great, actually.'

He finished the meat and had to please her by eating up all the bun. She thought him thin.

'Your canoe is at the end of the garden but full of water. Can you bail it out?'

'Yes, I think so.'

As he was wiping his plate clean with a piece of bun, a French custom not allowed at Hernmead, she got up to go to the larder for his dessert. He wondered what it would be.

'You like *meringue glacé* with *purée de marrons*? Chestnut cream?'

It looked delicious, providing she didn't go and pour *crème de menthe* or something like that over it.

She set it before him and gave him a spoon, then busied herself cleaning his hamburger plate at the sink.

The minute he'd finished the meringue she took that plate and spoon away too. 'You have eaten well?'

'Very well, thank you.'

'You will digest it all?'

'Yes, thank you.'

She was always on about digestion. She filled him up with rich food that made you feel sick, then seemed to wonder if you would survive.

'Even if I tell you some bad news?' she said over her shoulder.

He wanted to be one step ahead of her so that he could be ready to take on the impact of the imminent disaster.

'The canoe's got a hole in it?'

'No . . .'

'The police want to talk to me about last Saturday?'

'Not the police.'

'Grandpa?'

She nodded. 'Your grandmother rang.'

'How did she know I was going to be here?'

'I expect your mother told her. They don't want you to stay with me. She did not say so, of course, but this is what she meant. They want you to stay with them.'

It didn't surprise him, a few days of total freedom with Tante Louise would have been too good to be true.

He sighed, resigned. 'When do I have to go?'

'Mary Northey is coming over with some raspberries from the farm, I thought you could go back together in the canoe.'

'She can't swim,' he said.

'So don't rock the boat again.'

He liked that.

'I have a box full of oddments for her doll-making; you could take that with you too.

'Sure,' he said. Then sighed again. 'I was really looking forward to staying here with you, Tante Louise.'

'Thank you, mon petit. Unfortunately in life, and specially when you are young and other people are responsible for you, you cannot always do what you want.'

He got up feeling really testy.

'Why did mother have to go and ring them?'

'Because you have frightened her and she needs support.'

He was about to protest, question what she meant, but he understood perfectly.

He had frightened his mother.

He had been deliberately obscene knowing that it would unsettle her and that there would be repercussions. He had nobody else to blame but himself.

'Did Grandma say anything about last Saturday?'

'Of course not. She would not talk to a foreign lady like me about a private family problem.'

She was always funny about his grandparents' attitude towards her.

'Has anyone else mentioned it?'

'We are in Angleterre, mon petit, your performance sent a few ripples of curiosity round the village, but such unacceptable behaviour is quickly swept under the carpet. I think you should expect your grandfather to castigate you sooner or later. But, in answer to your question, no one thought it was anything more than a childish prank that went wrong.'

He was about to ask her if she could cast more light on his father, when he saw Mary coming through the gate. She was carrying a small straw basket covered with newspaper.

'Here is your friend with my raspberries,' Tante Louise said. 'You are friends, aren't you?'

Alexander shrugged his shoulders. Tante Louise was always trying to pair them off together. She liked doing that with people, coupling boys and girls together, men and women. She was a matchmaker.

'She could be quite pretty if she looked after herself, but she does not live among people who care.'

Mary came in, unbearably shy, biting her lower lip. She was wearing one of her two dresses and her old shoes but, for the first time, he noticed her ankles, how slim they were.

'I am making a *gâteau-au-framboise* Marie, and you must help me top it with the raspberries. After that, Alexandre, like the gentleman he is, will take you home by boat.'

Tante Louise took the basket from Mary and poured the fruit into a cullender, Mary watching her every move. Tante Louise taught all the local girls how to cook.

Alexander sat down in a ladder-back chair in the corner of the kitchen to wait patiently and think things out. It was funny, but there was something he quite liked about Mary this time. The way she tossed back her hair to keep a strand out of her eyes, and her long thin arms, nut brown.

Tante Louise laid out the washed raspberries on a clean piece of cheesecloth spread on the table and started to dry them, then she and Mary picked out the unripe or damaged ones, placing the good ones in a bowl.

He'd been pretty nasty to Mary in the past, had rather enjoyed hurting her.

During the Easter holidays, when he had thought himself a soldier's son, he had organized the Simcock brothers, Mary Northey, Damian Thomas and others, into two separate teams and had called them Saranson's Army and Simcock's Guerrillas. It was a game he had played at Clairmount, his prep school, an elaborate war game during which one side had to capture the enemy's headquarters. The Simcock HQ had been the old barn in Five Acre field, while his had been the chalk pit in the middle of Hernmead woods, half a mile away. Both could be equally well defended by posting lookouts, but victory was achieved by stealthily setting up ambushes and kidnapping opposing men. A game could take up a whole day, and sometimes it meant staying in one hide-out for hours.

Mary Northey had first been allowed to play as a nurse who ran the field hospital up by the cottages. He had gone up there once as a ruse to attack the Five Acre barn from the North and had asked her to bandage his arm because, he claimed, he had been shot. She had gone along with the pretence, but not fully enough to satisfy him, her imagination not stretching that far. Then, a few days later when she had joined the Simcock Guerrillas and had been stationed at their HQ to guard it, he had crept up behind her when she was standing at one corner looking vacantly across the field towards the river, had grabbed her and had pushed her into the barn. He had told her she had to do as she was told because she was his prisoner, and though she had put up no resistance whatsoever, he had held her in a half-nelson and had frog-marched her up to the old oak pillar in the centre of the barn and had tied her up with her hands behind her back.

Because he could not stand her docility, her inane expression because he had wanted some reaction of fear, some semblance of drama in the game, he had lit some straw with forbidden matches, and had held the blazing torch very close to her eyes, so close that he had singed her eyebrows and she had screamed. For a moment it had excited him terribly, the power he had over her, then he had been very frightened, not by her screams, but by the madness that had overtaken him. He could well have blinded her, set her alight, even burned down the whole barn. He had released her immediately and said he was sorry and had got her to promise not to tell anyone, and she never had. Rubbing her eyebrows, she hadn't looked all that different, no one had noticed, or if they had she had apparently told them a story.

Tante Louise brought out a sponge cake from the larder and showed Mary how to fill it with the raspberries, then she put it in the larder again.

'I have some pieces of material for your dolls and some buttons, if you'd like to come upstairs,' she said, reappearing. 'Why don't you come up too, Alexandre, there is something I would like you to try on.'

They went upstairs, past the guest room where he had slept, to Tante Louise's sewing room. She was the tidiest person he knew, cupboards and drawers could be opened and everything was in its place neatly folded or arranged in boxes. Everything was in order, always.

There was a cardboard lid on her work table and in it were various pieces of material: velvets, silks, satins; he didn't know what the others were called, except the bubbly seersucker. She opened a tin full of buttons and another of ribbons.

'You could use these for the eyes, Marie, and I thought this gold length of lace could be made into a crown. I don't know how, but you'll find a way.'

Tante Louise then opened a wardrobe and brought out two matching blazers and two little straw hats. 'I was thinking of producing another village concert this Christmas and wondered if you two could do an act together?'

Hardly likely, Alexander thought, Mary trying to remember lines. Tante Louise asked them to put on the blazers and he was embarrassed by the way Mary was shy putting on hers. He just got on with it to please.

'I thought you could sing a little Maurice Chevalier number . . . "Every little breeze seems to whisper Louise . . ." ' she sang out suddenly.

He'd never heard of Maurice whoever . . .

She stuck the straw hats on each of their heads at an angle.

'I think it could work. What do you think?'

And she opened up a mirror that he had not realized existed. It was a large, flat, triptych hanging on the wall.

Tante Louise took Mary and Alexander by the shoulders and moved them into position, side by side so that they could stand and look at their reflections, wearing the bright pink-and-yellow striped blazers and the straw hats.

He smiled at himself. He wasn't bad-looking at all in the outfit. Then he looked at Mary's reflection and was surprised. With her hair tucked up under the straw hat, she had a boy's face, his face, the same shape, similar nose, the full lips, the same line of eyebrows. It was uncanny.

Mary looked at herself, then at him, waved her hands, palms up as they do in dance routines on television, he did the same and they giggled.

'You should be a brother and sister team,' Tante Louise said from behind them, and looked strangely at Alexander as though she wished she hadn't said it.

He was puzzled for a moment, then saw Mary staring at herself, pulling the straw hat down over her eyes, then pushing it to the back of her head, tilting it to one side, then the other and finally taking it off and placing it on her heart and giving herself a little bow.

It was delightful. She was so involved in what she was doing, in being herself, that it was clear she had forgotten she was not alone, then, again, he caught Tante Louise looking at him in the mirror, and this time he understood, and blushed. She was matchmaking and she had perceived his interest in the girl.

Mary handed the straw hat back to Tante Louise and he did likewise, then took off the blazer.

'I'll go down and get the canoe ready,' he said, thankful

that he had an excuse to go.' It may take a while if there's a lot of water in it.'

'Take your time,' Tante Louise said, 'Marie and I will sort all this out and pack up the things she wants and bring the box down to the river steps.'

Tante Louise and Mary were waiting for him at the docks. He lined up his ship to come in close to the steps, timed it beautifully, back-paddled just at the right moment and stopped the canoe alongside without a bump. Excellent seamanship which neither women, of course, appreciated.

He stood up, tied the painter to the post and held out both hands for the box of rags and buttons which he placed in the bows.

'Put your left foot in the middle of the canoe, there, then your right, and sit down facing the front. It won't overturn,' he said to Mary getting hold of her wrist.

She did it all wrong, put her right foot in first and sat down facing him. He would never understand why girls had no idea of fore and aft.

He settled down in command at the stern and they set off, both waving to their hostess who watched the departure from the bank.

Terrified, Mary clutched onto the side for dear life, and with a few strokes Alexander swung the canoe round and headed for the tip of Otter's Island, gliding past the wild-mint-scented banks and the monster willow with its silver-leafed branches arching way out over the water.

As he paddled he looked down. Mary was sitting with her knees apart and he could see right up her dress. She was wearing pale blue knickers and it embarrassed him, so he looked away and she caught the blush and made a face as though saying 'whoops' and put her knees together.

They didn't talk. There was nothing to say, but Alexander had a sense of pride in his canoe and enjoyed the gallantry of taking her down river. She forgot her fear and dangled her hands over the side. He had never noticed it before but she had very long fingers and she trailed them in the water and watched the feathering they made on the surface.

A cabin cruiser was coming upstream so he prepared for the inevitable waves and steered the canoe into the wake. Mary had no idea what was happening and when the boat started bobbing up and down, she clutched onto the sides again.

He navigated into the still waters as soon as he could. Not long ago he would have deliberately sought the rough ride just to frighten her, but he didn't feel like that towards her any more.

She looked up at him suddenly, and grinned. She was enjoying the ride.

'Why did you do that the other day?' she asked.

'Do what?'

'Do that falling into the water, all dressed up, with the rope round your neck?'

How could he answer her? How could he explain?

'Was it supposed to be funny?' She had a lilt in her voice which was attractive in its way.

'I was trying to frighten my grandparents into thinking I wanted to drown myself.'

'Whatever for?'

'So that they would give me something I want.'

'Why didn't you just ask?'

'It wasn't anything tangible,' he said, knowing she wouldn't understand.

There was no sign of anyone near the boat-house, but he decided to avoid it by keeping to the opposite bank then crossing over to moor by the woods. As he drew level with the boundary fence he cut across the river and glided in among the reeds to the little creek where a meadow stream rippled into the Thames. Digging his paddle deep into the mud, he pushed the canoe well up on to the bank and jumped out.

'It's safe, it won't wobble, just hand me the box.'

Mary stood up and gave him the box then jumped out herself.

'We'll go through the woods. I don't want them to see me from the house. Not that keen to go there yet,' he said.

Mary smiled. He pulled the canoe up a foot or so more, tied the painter round the trunk of a sappling then lifted the rag box to place it on top of his head.

As Mary led the way through the woods, stepping high over dog roses and violets, forget-me-nots and yellow pimpernels, he decided he had been relegated to the inferior position of native carrier, trudging through the jungle following the Memsahib.

When they came to the stile giving on to Gifford's Lane, she stopped to help him with the box, then gave it back to him as they walked along the hedgerow to the Cottages.

The front door, under the little green gable, was always locked because they only used the side door which led straight into the kitchen. Though neither of them were tall enough to have to stoop, Alexander felt he had to, the beams were so low, the room so small.

Mary's mother was at the stone sink, washing clothes. She just managed a smile in way of greeting, a cigarette stuck in the corner of her mouth.

'Keep quiet, won't you,' she said. 'The babe's only just gone to sleep.'

'I didn't know you had a baby,' Alexander said, astonished.

'I haven't,' Mary laughed. 'My mother has. My new kid brother. Two months old.'

He'd had no idea. There was no reason he should, but it was a surprise.

'His name's Timothy,' Mary volunteered without being asked, 'but we call him Timmy.'

She led Alexander into the next room.

The cottage was only two-up, two-down, the kitchen untidy with piles of washing and baby clothes, and this room worse with a broken down old sofa covered with a faded tartan rug, a small television set in a corner by the narrow stairs, the centre dominated by a huge, brand new, spotless pram in which there was a neatly wrapped bundle, apparently a living human baby.

The whole place smelt of soap powder and rancid nappies

and he would have been quite pleased to get out and away from it all, but Mary asked him to follow her upstairs to the back room, her room, where there was a bed and an old chest of drawers painted dark blue. It was very tidy, much tidier than the rest of the house, and on the floor under the window he was astonished to see a toy theatre. It was quite beautiful, with a little row of stalls in front, boxes on either side, a red and gold proscenium arch, foot lights and a red velvet curtain. Mary wound a little handle round at the back and the curtain bobbed up to reveal a little stage and scenery depicting a ballroom.

'Cinderella,' she explained. 'My Dad made it. I made these.' Around the room, hanging over her bed and from a shelf were various puppets. Not Punch and Judy puppets, not as ugly as that, but rag doll puppets which stared down with blank eyes and vacant smiles.

But he was more intrigued by the theatre.

'It's only got two changes right now. The enchanted forest and the ballroom.' She showed him how to slide the different bits of scenery in and out and he loved it.

He sat down on the squeaky bed, the thin hard mattress reminding him of his bed at school, and he stared at the little theatre. It was really a superb piece of workmanship.

'He's making a bigger one now,' Mary said. 'About half the size of that wall, with everything working electrically.'

'Does he make them to sell?'

'No,' Mary laughed.

'Where does he make them?'

'In hospital,' and she tapped her head with her finger. 'He's at Mileswood. A bit of a loony is Dad. They let him out now and again to come and see us, but not often.'

So it wasn't being kept a family secret.

He knew Mileswood. It was up beyond Streatly way. He'd cycled past it a few times. It was like a prison with flowers in the front to make it look better.

'I've got a picture of him, if you'd like to see it.'

He didn't particularly. He actually wanted to get away from the smell of nappies and the feeling that he wasn't wanted in the house by Mary's mother. But he was polite and feigned interest.

Mary got down on her knees, reached for something hidden under the bed and pulled out a plastic zip-case, bright blue, a Christmas present from the Co-op or Woolworth's, he guessed.

She opened it slowly as though it contained the Crown Jewels and brought out some letters and a quantity of snapshots.

'He writes to me sometimes,' she said, more to herself than to him, and as he watched her looking through the letters he sensed that she was very fond of her loony Dad, which was sad.

'That's him,' she said, proudly handing him a photograph, 'when he was a boy.'

The picture was of a harlequin, about thirteen, and he had seen it before.

'Looks a bit like you,' Mary said.

And giggled.

chapter nine

The walk to Hernmead Court took seconds rather than the timed five minutes.

It was all a question of permutations. He had so much information in his head, which could now be pieced together to make an astounding pattern, that he wanted to put off the incredible revelation till he was ready to absorb it totally. He needed to be alone and secure in the knowledge that he would not be disturbed till he had had time to check all the available facts carefully, and what he wanted to do most was sit in front of his family tree in his secret room and work it all out.

As he reached the door in the walled garden which old

Tom Northey sometimes forgot to lock, he realized that that very man, old Tom, might be his grandfather.

The gardener, his grandfather!

He lifted the catch, pushed, it was open, he went through.

Rows of tomatoes, beans, carrots, onions, lettuce.

He glanced up at the windows. No one standing by them looking out, no one around. He made his way to the old stable yard and the back door. If Hilda wasn't in the kitchen then she'd be up in her room, which would prohibit his plans for a few hours of peace.

But she was in the pantry, doing something with raspberries, preparing a tasteless jelly or raspberry fool which would be nothing like Tante Louise's gateau.

'You're back young man, are you?'

'Yes,' he said. 'Grandpa around?'

'Sleeping lunch off in his study, I expect.'

'Grandma?'

'She's in the rose garden, killing greenfly.'

He went through the old butler's pantry and up the back stairs to the first floor, second floor, paused on the landing to listen and, sure that the coast was clear, tiptoed down the short corridor to Hilda's room, opened the door and stepped in.

Neat and tidy and smelling of lavender, the crucifix above her bed with a bleeding Jesus making him aware that he felt guilty at the intrusion.

He tiptoed to the curtain, stepped through her coats and dresses and over her shoes to open the tiny door of his sanctuary.

Once in there he felt released from the anxieties of the outside world. Kneeling down on the straw mattress he faced the square pigeonless light of the opening, then turned to sit cross-legged before his family tree.

The grandson of a gardener.

How much of the jigsaw could he now piece together?

He traced the ascending line of his known ancestors.

Himself, ALEXANDER SARANSON, his mother SARAH SARANSON neé MIDLEY married to

GENERAL SIR GEOFFREY SARANSON (divorced), daughter of RALPH GEORGE MIDLEY and HELEN MIDLEY (neé CRANE). Ralph George Midley the son of ARTHUR GEORGE MIDLEY. Helen Midley the daughter of BERNARD CRANE. It went on up to his great great grandparents, mixtures of Scots, Irish, Welsh, east Anglians and Huguenots.

Now he could start on the other side.

Illicit union between SARAH SARANSON (divorced) and RICHARD NORTHEY, married to CONNIE NORTHEY née . . . what? He could forget her, though there was his half-sister, MARY NORTHEY and her little brother TIMMY.

Then he remembered, as though it had been in a dream, Mary and himself standing in front of Tante Louise's mirror looking at themselves with the straw hats on and the look in Tante Louise's eyes when she had said . . . and she *had* said, 'You could be a brother and sister team.'

Did she know?

He looked back at the chart.

RICHARD NORTHEY son of TOM NORTHEY and who?

Who was his grandmother? Old Mrs Northey who had died several years back in the cottage one winter's night. He had watched the coffin being slipped into the hearse with all the wreaths, and Grandma dutifully attending the funeral.

Hooker country.

He understood now why there had been all the secrecy.

He had a lunatic father.

Is that what they were all afraid of, then? Him being insane as well? With his behaviour he had probably given them reason to think so.

He would have to meet his father, he would have to visit him in that hospital and find out just how crazy he was, and Mary was the only one who could help him do that. She went to see him at least once a week, taking her rag dolls. He could offer to help her make them or pretend a passionate interest in model theatres and ask if he could go along. He'd think of something clever, but now he needed to get out of his secret room before Hilda Kelly came up. He needed to plan a campaign, make absolutely sure that he would be staying at Hernmead for the rest of the holidays so that he could go to Mileswood without anyone knowing.

Suddenly the dread of having to meet up with his grandparents disappeared, to be replaced by an intense desire for acceptance within the family.

He would be a good boy, repentant, remorseful, contrite, and he would do exactly as he was told, even play croquet with the silly old fool if he absolutely had to.

He eased back the lock, opened the door and stepped through the curtain of clothes. The bleeding Jesus on the cross was the first to forgive him his trespasses and he left the lavender room with a lighter heart.

Down the corridor, down the back stairs to the first floor then to his own bedroom with his framed prep-school photographs and school shield, the crossed naval sabres and the Zulu spear. A boy's room, dull cream walls, oak furniture, bookshelf of ancient children's encyclopedias and five volumes of British heroes, Scott of the Antarctic to Lawrence of Arabia. Comics were allowed. Superman and Spiderman were in there somewhere, and his favourite, *A Life on Stage*, with its thick hardback and glossy illustrations, the very smell of the printed pages still exciting him as they had when he had first been given the book for his birthday by Tante Louise. Model theatres would not be hard to be enthusiastic about. Had his father been an actor before going mad? Maybe just an amateur.

So much to find out.

'Alexander?'

His grandmother's voice from along the hallway.

'Yes?' He managed to convey contriteness with just the one word.

'I didn't know you had arrived.'

She was in the doorway, unsure whether she should be pleased to see him. 'When did you get here?'

'Just now. I came down by boat from Madame Rimbaud's. I collected the canoe.'

She managed a little smile.

'I am sorry Grandma,' he said straight away. 'About the way I behaved. I'm not really sure why I did it. Something just made me, in my head, you know?.

He could milk it, couldn't he? He could suggest madness. It would frighten, but it would bring sympathy and understanding and everything would be forgiven.

They would have to forgive.

'Grandfather was very upset you know, and he wants you to go and work on the farm for the rest of the holidays. He's spoken to Mr Simcock about it and you're to help with the harvest.'

'Of course.'

That surprised her, his acceptance. She'd expected a face, a sneer, a refusal. She was grateful and checked her watch.

'It'll be tea-time soon, maybe you could go and talk to him now. He's in the study. But let me tell him first that you're here.'

Admonition by appointment.

Standard procedure.

The boy's got to be made to understand that it's serious. Ask him to come in and see me once I've the authoritative stance by the fireplace. Like the Head at his prep and The Buzz at Travellier's, like Wilcox and Goodall; traditional reprimands just became a big joke with repetition.

'I'll call you, Alexander,' Grandma said.

Even she had been taught how to play the game. Make him wait a little while outside the study, it'll give him time to think over what he has done and fear the punishment.

He jumped on to his bed and lay down full length with his arms behind his head.

Yes sir, no sir, three bags full sir.

The inherited madness would allow anything.

The gates were open, the curtain was up!

Another major step in the awareness of how other people would treat him and how he could respond to advantage.

When had that last happened? When had he last experienced that moment of clear self-knowledge which had made him realize he was suddenly a hundred years wiser? The first day at Amhurst on the train from Victoria when the tall, smiling prefect came down the carriage and took off his felt hat, shook out his mop of ginger hair, and sat down next to him. 'The day of Awakening is nigh!' he had said. No one had warned Alexander about what his new school would teach him. He was going there to learn more Latin, more French, more maths, more history. He was going there to play football and cricket and swim for the House. He was going there to please his grandfather, his grandmother and his mother. But nobody had told him what else he would learn there.

'New boy then?'

'Yes . . .'

'What Prep?'

'Clairmount.'

'What House are you going in?'

'Travellier's.'

'Shit! And you?' he'd asked a blue-eyed, fair-haired boy opposite.

'Travellier's,' the boy had answered without blinking.

The ginger-haired prefect had got up and walked down the aisle of the carriage looking at the other new boys in their respective seats.

'Wilcox! Your luck's in,' he'd shouted to another senior.' Window seat left, five back, brunette and a blonde opposite.'

Alexander had instinctively counted the rows. There were five.

He hadn't understood, exactly.

'My name's Hooker,' another boy opposite had said, a rather pimpled youth with glasses, 'I'm Travellier's too.'

'Saranson.'

My name's Pitts,' the one with blue eyes had joined in.

The two seniors who had been addressed by the first had come along, one with fiery eyes, the other with dark, knitted eyebrows.

'Travellier's you two?' they'd asked.

'We three,' Hooker had said.

'No one asked you.'
'Sorry.'
'What are your names?'
'Pitts.'
'Saranson.'
'My name's Goodall, I'm one of your house captains, this is Wilcox, your Head of House. Report to us after Hall tonight.'
And they had gone back to their seats.
Saranson had been bewildered by the aggression, and Pitts had smiled at him. Hooker had sighed deeply and had pushed his spectacles up his nose.
'You're either going to have a great time or a terrible time, you two.'
'Why?' Alexander had asked.
Pitts had made a face conveying he couldn't bear ignorance and had looked out of the window.
'I'm the brains, he's the bum,' Hooker had said, and Pitts had winded him with a vicious elbow punch.
Alexander had not known what to do.
'Were you two together at Prep?' he'd asked.
'Fernbanks,' Hooker had said, regaining his breath.
'Would you like to join us?'
Pitts had frozen Hooker with a stare.
'You're clearly going to be with him Pitts, it'll make the team stronger. Two of you can work them beautifully; they won't know.'
Pitts had shrugged his shoulders, crossed his knees and had looked at his nails. He'd reminded Alexander a bit of a girl, the way his hair had a curl falling over his forehead.
'Do you sing?' Hooker had asked.
'Yes.'
'Treble, in the choir?'
'Yes.'
'You see Pitts, you could both lead the processions and have them all eat out of the palms of your hands.'
'I don't understand,' Alexander had said.
And Pitts had deliberately looked out of the window again.

'Little boys are half a crown, standing up or lying down,' Hooker had chanted. 'In the gym?'

He'd tried to look intelligent about it, had imagined himself in the gym, standing up, then lying down. He didn't really understand it at all. Was it to do with taking bets on boxing?

'He doesn't know what you're talking about, Hooker,' Pitts had said. 'He's a million light years from knowing what you're talking about.'

'A virgin then?'

'Intacta,' Pitts had added.

'Boy Scouts?' Hooker had asked him.

'No.'

'Ever been to camp, or on an expedition?'

'No.'

'Ever played for an away team?'

'No.'

'You're wasting your time,' Pitts had said.

'I'm not wasting my time. We have prime beef material here. With your help we can own the House.'

Alexander had opened his eyes wider.

'Just look at those eyes. Even matron will love him. Are you frightened he might depose you Pitts? It'll happen sooner or later, we don't want jealousy in the service, we want new blood. Were you a prefect at Clairmount?'

'No.'

'Captain of any sport?'

'No. I didn't do very much.'

'What's your hobby?'

'I'm not sure.'

'Jesus!' Pitts had turned and looked up at the ceiling.

'You're so impatient Pitts. Where do you live?'

'London and a place called Hernmead, on the Thames.'

'*Both* places?'

'Yes. But I live mostly with my grandparents.'

'Small house, big house?'

'Big house.'

'How many bedrooms?'

'Fourteen.'

'You're joking!'

Pitts had turned round to look at him, more interested, then he'd glanced up at the luggage rack.

'Your luggage?'

'Yes. Well, my mother's suitcase.'

'Gucci,' Pitts had noted. 'The kid's rich.'

'Are you rich?' Hooker had asked. 'What's your grandfather do?'

Alexander had shrugged his shoulders. 'He's just rich.'

'How many servants do you have?'

'Just two . . . If the gardener counts.'

'Does the gardener count?' Hooker had asked Pitts.

'Our gardener counts,' Pitts had said, 'up to ten, just.'

He had sensed that they would poke fun of him forever if he didn't make some impression, so he had tried harder.

'Why does that House Captain want to see us after Hall?'

'Tell him,' Pitts had said.

'They're going to feel how ripe you are, I expect.'

'For God's sake Hooker, the boy's a complete innocent.'

'Well it's better that he should learn it from us than from them. You're pretty, Saranson, right?' Hooker had said turning and looking at him intensely. 'You've got a pretty face, great big beautiful eyes, a pretty little mouth and big boys eat little boys like you.'

'You'd better explain what you mean by eat,' Pitts had said, laughingly.

'I can't. That's your department.'

Alexander had felt very unsettled. There was something very unpleasant waiting for him, and he hadn't been warned.

'Does the name Oscar Wilde mean anything to you?' Pitts had asked him in a slow, deliberate way as though talking to someone who was really dim. It had reminded him of the way he often spoke to Mary.

'I've heard the name,' he'd said, 'but no.'

He'd known that he had to be honest. Lying about knowledge of any sort could get you into immense trouble. He had at least learnt that much at Clairmount.

'Queen, poofter, faggot, fag, queer, twink, kite?' Pitt had enumerated. 'Heard of any of them? Pansy perhaps?'

It was like a crossword puzzle.

'Bugger?' Hooker had added.

It was rude.

'You must have had some experience, a boy like you. For God's sake, didn't any master ever try to touch you up?'

The Clairmount taxi driver had come to mind immediately, in the Vauxhall collecting them at the station. Five of them at a time, four in the back, himself always in the front to the annoyance of the others. He'd never liked it because the driver always squeezed his leg and had complained when he had started wearing long trousers.

'I think I know what you're talking about,' Alexander had said.

'Big boys have little boys upon their backs to bite them, little boys have lesser boys, and so on *ad infinitum*,' Hooker recited. 'Tonight, after Hall in the Prefects Room you two will be auctioned off as fags to someone for the term. If Wilcox gets you I expect that'll be OK. But if Goodall chooses you, I think you're in for a bad time.'

The fear had come back, the fear of saying something stupid, of seeming dumb, of not understanding.

'I'll take care of Goodall,' Pitts had said. 'Goodall won't get near him,' and he had leaned across and squeezed his knee playfully, just as the taxi driver had. 'You know what wank means?'

He'd heard the word 'wanker', of course.

'Yes.'

'What does it mean?'

He hated that. It made him blush immediately, being asked a direct question which he couldn't answer. That was what he hated most about school. People only asked you what something meant directly if they knew damn well you didn't know. He'd fallen into that trap often.

'It means to pretend to do something when you don't really do it,' he'd said.

'It means masturbating, you berk,' Pitts had said.

And Hooker had seen straight away that he didn't know what that meant.

'You'd better show him what that means,' he'd whispered to Pitts who had collapsed with laughter. He'd curled up on his seat and had banged his head against the window.

'It's all to do with your prick, Saranson, that stem of goodness between your legs. Masturbating means playing with yourself, and big boys like to have a little help from their younger friends. So if you play your cards right you can get anything you want in exchange for such a small service.'

Hooker had smiled, then looking at Pitts he'd added, 'It's called prostitution, actually.' And Pitts had kicked him violently on the shins.

Thankfully they had then arrived at their destination.

It was on entering the dormitory, a huge room with six beds down one side and six beds down the other, all covered with bright red blankets, that he'd realized he had suddenly grown up, and become wiser. He was with eleven other new boys and Matron was showing them their respective beds, and cupboards and telling them what to do. They were to unpack, put all their clothes away and she would come and inspect them. They were to stand by their beds and wait until she did so. In the morning they would all go and see the doctor. The matron had then picked on him. 'Saranson, you look fairly intelligent, make sure that they all put their sponge bags in the right cubby hole,' and everyone had immediately accepted his authority.

All he had done was walk in confidently, more so than the others because he was with Hooker and Pitts, had guessed they knew nothing at all and seen that none of them were pretty. 'Sex,' as Hooker had told him on getting into the school bus, 'rules the world. Never forget it. Sex rules, OK?'

In Hall he had sat with Hooker and Pitts. Goodall, like a demented vulture, his long nose seeking trouble, his curly eyebrows twitching with anticipation, had then made Alexander change places with another new man so that he could be closer. Though this had initially made him feel good, he had been embarrassed at the way the House Captain had stared at him continually while slurping his soup, and even more embarrassed when Pitts had impudently asked, 'Do you find Saranson sexy, Goodall?'

Goodall had turned his attention on Pitts with an amused look.

'That's a very insolent remark for a new boy. You'd best come and see me after Hall in my sanctum.'

'Yes Goodall,' Pitts had replied with a pouting of the lips followed by a very gentle smile.

Five weeks later there had been the Grand Inquisition.

'The Buzz wants to see you in his study after breakfast Saranson, so stand by.'

Just as now, he had waited for the call, for the regal summons, knowing he had nothing to fear.

'Ah, Saranson,' the nervous Housemaster had said, standing by the chimney flapping his black gown and scraping his pipe on to the carpet. 'Settled down have you? Made some good friends with your contemporaries?'

'Yes, thank you, sir.'

'Any problems with House Captains or anyone? You can always tell me you know.'

'No, sir, thank you, sir.'

'Good, good . . .'

And that had been it. The backing down, the inability to break the code of honour which had been so resolutely implanted in him at preparatory school. Hoisted by their own petard the establishment had not been able to check the spread of rumoured decadent behaviour.

'Buzz is probably terrified of an AIDS epidemic,' Hooker had remarked, a disease he had then started to describe in detail with great satisfaction. 'Frightfully good news for the undertaking business.'

'Alexander!'

His grandmother's voice cut across his day-dreaming from half way down the stairs.

'Can you come and help me take tea into the study?'

The excuse was to make sure that he would enter the lion's den like an innocent and well-behaved lamb.

She handed him the tray at the foot of the staircase and opened the study door for him. Only two cups, he noticed; she was staying well out of it.

'Ah, Alexander, there you are.'

Standing by the fireplace, one hand in trouser pocket, holding the folded *Times* in the other; standard stance for those in authority.

He put the tea-tray down on the desk.

'Alexander, I want to talk to you about the rest of your holidays.'

It had been rehearsed a hundred times and was spilling out too quickly to convey the severity of the situation.

'I thought it a good idea if you went to work on the farm. I've spoken to George Simcock about it and he'd be pleased to have a helping hand with the harvest, which is jolly good fun anyway, and he'd pay you, not much, but something, so I think you should, don't you?'

'Sorry Grandpa, I can't remember whether you take sugar in your tea or saccharin.'

'What? Ah, sugar; just one spoon, thank you.'

He handed his grandfather the cup of tea with a ginger nut on the side of the saucer.

'I think it's a lovely idea, Grandpa. When would I start?'

'Next Monday, I should have thought,' the relief was hardly contained.

'Do you know what sort of hours?'

'Hours? No, why?'

'I have this homework to do; you know, the computer programming. Only it takes time.'

Confusion. The modern age invading Hernmead.

'I can't remember Alexander. I have so much on my mind these days what with one thing and another. What computer?'

'Computer programming is in the new maths curriculum for next term and we have to know how to use cursors and modes and print outs and how to programme calculations by the end of the holidays.'

'You have to read-up on all this you mean?'

'And work on the computer.'
'What computer, where is the computer?'
'Upstairs in my room.'
Panic. Terror. 'In your room?'
'Mother bought it for me. It's a Spectrum ZX 16 K RAM.'
'And it's in your room?'
It was registered on his face, the fear that something insane had been allowed to happen behind his back, that millions had been spent and that the floors of the house would not be able to take the strain of vibrating machinery.
'How did you get it up there?'
'I carried it.'
Disbelief. How could a young boy carry a computer?
'And your mother *bought* it?'
'It wasn't very much. I expect she got it with her credit card. It's only small, plugs into the TV.'
Relief again, the heart attack averted.
'Only I was going to spend a fair time doing the homework, so if I go on the farm, which I'd much rather do, could you write to the school explaining?'
It was, of course, too much for the poor old chap; new technology, his daughter buying expensive equipment without clearance, his grandson involved in something he didn't understand, George Simcock's harvest to be gathered and now a letter needed to excuse the boy from his homework.
'Maybe you'd best get on with what you have to do, Alexander. School comes first.'
'Yes, Grandfather,' a touch of disappointment.
'I trust it will keep you busy and out of mischief.'
'Yes, Grandfather.'
'We don't want a repetition of last weekend, do we?'
'No, Grandpa. I'm very sorry about that. I don't know what came over me. A sort of summer madness I expect. I get these strange ideas in my head when there's a full moon sometimes.'
'Well we won't talk about it any more. Have your tea, then you'd best get on with whatever you have to do.'
He'd have to ask for the use of the TV set, of course. He'd

have to master the Spectrum so that at a touch of a key whatever game he was playing would convert into something unintelligible.

He drank his tea and nibbled a biscuit, leaning against the red-leather-covered mahogany desk. Grandpa sat himself down in the winged-back chair and unfolded his *Times*.

'How was your mother?' he asked.

'Fine.'

'When did she buy you this computer?'

'Last week. I'd brought it down with me the first time.'

Grunt.

Case dismissed.

He left the study, sauntered into the drawing room, out of the open French windows and into the Dutch garden where he sat on the wooden bench to stare at the pond with its stone statue of a nymph watching the goldfish darting about under the water lilies.

He felt good.

He was winning.

He had calculated the way his grandfather would jump correctly, and now he could put Phase Two of his plan into action. The Seeking Out of Father!

But he didn't move. The sun felt warm on the top of his head and along the length of his arms. It was all a question of moods. His and theirs. He liked moods, the self-imposed moods, the mood he was in when in London, the different mood when he was at school, and this mood now, the Hernmead Court mood in the gardens and the countryside, with the moon at night, the sight of the silver ribbon of river from his bedroom window, and Mary Northey, his own sister, over there in her small cottage.

That was a new mood. That feeling of not being alone anymore. He belonged there, in the cottage, as much as he belonged here.

He would visit his father at the asylum very soon. She would take him along. It wouldn't be difficult to programme her. It wouldn't be difficult to programme any of them, now that he knew his goal.

★

At lunch the next day he announced his intentions when his grandmother asked him how he was going to spend the afternoon.

'Mary Northey's making rag dolls for the church fête, and I said I would help.'

'Are you going to bring her over here?' The smell under her nose seemed to become unbearable.

'No, I'm going to the cottage.'

'Well, don't spend too much time over there,' she said, and might have said more if Grandpa hadn't glanced at her across the table. They shouldn't keep telling the boy what not to do.

'Mrs Northey's very busy with the baby and you mustn't get in the way,' she finished.

Hilda came in with the sweet, plonking the plates down because she was in a bad temper.

'What's the matter with her today?' Grandpa asked when she had left the room.

'I told her Sarah would be coming down this week-end, possibly with a new boyfriend.'

'The black one?' Alexander asked, spooning up the trifle.

'What black one?' If it had been a bad smell under the nose for Mary Northey it was a stink bomb now.

'What black one?' his grandfather echoed.

'Well, perhaps he's not a boyfriend. Elliot something, the lodger.'

'No dear,' Grandma covered up quickly. 'This young man is called Charles and he's in the diplomatic corps. I've never heard of a black man. You have it wrong.'

She was sending signals; don't elaborate, don't contradict, you'll only upset Grandfather.

He could do that; upset him, and her.

'Do you know,' he said, 'I think I want to be a gardener when I grow up. I think I've got green fingers like old Tom. Please may I leave the table?' And as he left the room his grandfather got up to help himself to a brandy.

A pattern was clearly emerging.

chapter ten

TIME IMMEMORIAL.

Without any help from her family she had done it all.

Well nearly all.

She had chosen the name, had found the premises, repainted them, refurbished them and had opened the shop without her parents knowing because they would not have understood.

Tante Louise's money of course, the sleeping partner giving invaluable advice from a comfortable distance away.

'What are you doing with your life these days Sahara?'

'Nothing very much. Existing, surviving, waiting, I suppose, for Mr Right to come along.'

It had been one of those marvellous lunches in the Weir House kitchen one Saturday after shopping in the village. She had dropped in casually to see Tante Louise and had instantly been invited to eat.

They had sat at the large scrubbed kitchen table on which a Basque table cloth had been spread and plates of piping hot *Soupe de Poisson* had been served.

'You like your job?'

'I'm a temp., a menial secretary. It's all right for some, but not for me. On the face of it my life is wonderful. I have my little house in Chelsea, parents with a manor on the Thames to escape to at weekends, I'm the envy of everyone I meet; but I'm also forty and I can't stand having to work in a typing pool with girls half my age who speak a different language.'

'So you would like to get out of it?'

'Yes, but I have no talents.'

The soup had been delicious and she had thought of asking for the recipe but had known it wouldn't work with her. Somehow recipes weren't enough. A pinch of salt was not a pinch of salt through her fingers, a clove of garlic or two bay leaves were not just that, there was the magic of knowing when to put them in, the instinct of cooking. She had tried Tante Louise's *Pot-au-Feu* and it had come out as a watery Irish Stew. 'Northern Irish Stew' her guests had kindly called it.

'Why don't you open a shop of second-hand clothes?' she had suggested. 'I have come back into fashion Sahara. Because I have such a large house I have never thrown anything away, believing that one day it would all come in useful, and maybe that day has come. When we have finished lunch I will take you upstairs to show you what I mean.'

It had been quite incredible. She had never been right upstairs, though she knew that an attic existed. There were two sizeable rooms and they were filled with clothes and hats and shoes, a mountain of stuff, and all of it unbelievably valuable. Molyneux, Chanel, Balmain, Dior, Balenciaga, Worth. 'My husband was not only rich but very generous you know. He was not altogether patriotic. He cooked for the Germans in Paris during the war, and made a fortune. So why don't we sell it all and start a business?'

They had discussed names, 'Tante Louise' and 'Sarah's Seconds', but she had eventually come up with 'Time Immemorial' which had worked. She'd put small expensive advertisements in *Harper's & Queens*, *Vogue* and *Country Life*, and *Time Out* had given her a mention. 'NOSTALGIA WITH MOTHBALLS. The 1930s, 40s and 50s spill out of ancient wardrobes in this small Chelsea boutique at bargain prices.' For three months it had been wonderful; friends and acquaintances dropping in, wine always available in the small basement office for the improvised party. Then she had found she couldn't replace the good stuff, that once Tante Louise's own wardrobe had been emptied and those of her mother's friends, the clothes she had left to sell were tatty.

Now the whole thing was boring and beginning to be expensive. She wasn't a good business woman. She wasn't anything.

Someone had once said to her, 'the more you do the more you are able to do,' and she had found this to be true. She had worked terribly hard over a period of several weeks, had found herself to be happily exhausted by the end of the day and stimulated by having achieved something. It was only after the three initial months, when she had found herself alone behind the counter with nothing to do and no customers coming in, that a fearful depression had overtaken her, and Alexander had chosen that moment to start asking particularly awkward questions.

And where was she now, only one year later? She was in a rather musty basement at the wrong end of the King's Road surrounded by dirty second-hand clothes that she couldn't sell. She was nothing more than a rag-and-bone man, or should it be 'person'? Whenever there had been a choice of roads to take she had always managed to pick the wrong one, and this one was sometimes quite painful because it allowed her to view the decline of a way of life, her parents' way of life, and that of her own childhood.

Her mother and father and their small coterie of cocktail friends were so unaware of what was really going on. They were pretending to be rich, ignorant of how much richer the truly moneyed people were and how poor most of their acquaintances had become. She knew, for God's sake. Four people had come into the shop yesterday, desperate to sell clothes, and she had bought them at ridiculously low prices. Two people had come in to buy jackets and trousers and bits and pieces for next to nothing because they couldn't afford anything better. They were living in a second-hand world. England was now a second-hand country and nobody wanted to admit it. She could see the faces of the impoverished rich selling their bits of tat, somehow managing to kid themselves that it was the OK thing to do.They were doing it because they were all poor, poor, poor; an Argentinian couple had come in by mistake one day and had made her realize it. Incredibly stylish, the two small women with fiery eyes, and heavy with gold and crocodile, had come in, chattering away in Spanish, when one of them had realized it was a second-hand shop. 'De segunda mano!' they had screamed, and had run off as though the place were swarming with fleas.

Maybe it was the fault of the young Royals. They were rich

and everyone else was trying to keep up and finding they couldn't. The future King had his court but because of the media everyone thought they could join in and be part of the set. They couldn't. It was only for the few. And the insults kept hitting her. A vicar had come in, cassock and all, bald, pale translucent, carrying an old suitcase done up with string. 'We've had a clear-out at the church crypt,' he'd said. 'Thought you'd like some oddments to sell for your charity.'

She'd started to explain that it wasn't that sort of shop, but he hadn't listened. So she'd let him leave the suitcase in a corner and when she'd opened it up she had just found a whole lot of dirty socks, men's socks, about forty pairs of them. Then Tante Louise had visited and had not liked what she had seen. 'You will have to do something about the window display, Sahara, I think it needs to be more stylish. It needs to arrest the attention of the type of customer we want. Find one of those gay window dressers to do it for you.'

She'd rung up Steven who worked in an estate agency and was as charming as he was smooth of face, a face that hinted of creams and make-up at night. Who knew? 'Sarah, long time . . . what can I do for you . . . do you want to sell your house?'

'Yes,' she'd said, 'But it's not mine to sell. I need a talented young boy to do something for me.'

'Don't we all sweetie. What sort of thing?'

And she'd explained.

'If you can put him up for a week he'll do it for nothing, he's from Liverpool, name of Jack, frightfully clever, worked in the theatre for Lloyd-Webber, costumes.'

It had been an unsettling experience, partly because Jack had been far more feminine than herself, but much more because she had suddenly been thrown by the thought of the dreadful disease. It had been a joke so far, with certain people, but to have someone in the house who might be a carrier had made her unbelievably nervous. She knew it was ridiculous and grossly unfair of her to even think of him in connection with AIDS but she couldn't help it. It had all been in the mind and she hoped to God that he hadn't been aware of her feelings, but she had found herself being very cautious about the towels he used, the glasses he drank from, the forks he ate with. He'd smoked a great deal and had drunk her whisky and had sat for hours looking out of the window, rather than at it, when he'd said:

'Your shop is the wrong colour, the black and white and the "Immemorial" gives it a funeral feeling. You are emphasizing the end of something – making the people who come and sell their clothes feel worse, and probably alienating those who might come and buy. You need a feeling of the past, but a happy past. I think you should add some red, and maybe a hint at the great Atlantic liners, the Cunards, that sort of thing. *Vogue* 1934, or Scott-Fitzgerald. It's not original I know, but you are in a rather un-original trade, and you yourself should dress differently and have your hair cut in a Vortex-Coward style. I know exactly who can do it for you.'

She'd returned from the cinema one evening and all his stuff had gone and in the kitchen she had found a note, 'Invited to Hamburg by a new-found friend. Can't refuse. Thank you for your hospitality. Jack.'

She'd got an estimate for re-painting the shop front, found she couldn't afford it and hadn't dared mention it to Tante Louise.

So here she was still in her funeral parlour.

Two weeks ago her morale had been lifted when a middle-aged woman, barely older than herself, wearing a fantastic long dress of no particular period, hair everywhere, dark glasses pushed back on top of her head, and a clutter of stuff in a massive basket, had hurled herself into the shop demanding anything of the 1960s. She had bought £120 worth of rubbish apparently for a film, then had suggested, 'My dear, you should display things by period. It's a frightfully good little shop, and you have immense taste, but people are into periods now. You've got enough room here to do that. Concentrate on the fifties and sixties, even the seventies, buy anything of those decades and change the name to "Period Pieces". I'm sure you'll make a bomb.'

It had turned out that the woman was a frightfully famous costume designer and needed clothes for 700 extras.

The next day Sarah had started dutifully moving her stock around and had labelled it by decades only to find that most of what she had left couldn't be said to belong to any period at all. It was all drab, jumble sale left-overs, nothing more, and she had wondered why she wasn't in the film business with a basket of active addresses and note books, and telephone calls to make and high blood pressure due to a busy-busy life.

No connections. No energy.

She sat all morning smoking too many cigarettes and getting irritated by two very stupid girls who came in looking for leather mini skirts. The irritation was not so much due to their high-pitched giggles but more to the fact that she really wanted to be alone to sort herself out.

Again.

Geoffrey and Alexander were haunting her, not to mention her parents. Even Elliot had joined the line of her accusers. And Tante Louise.

Once upon a time, like ten years ago, she had really got it together. She had enjoyed Alexander because he had been pretty and controllable, he could talk just enough to tell whether he was hungry or thirsty, or where it hurt when he felt unwell, she could leave him in the care of babysitters, and the dreadful routine of nursery schools hadn't imposed itself on her. She had also made peace with her parents.

She had received a call from her mother, out of the blue, at her flat in the North End Road, which she had liked because it was a cosmopolitan and cockney area because of the market, and her mother had said, 'Father is very ill and wishes to see you.' It had been a very unexpected message.

'How ill?'

'Very ill.'

'Do you mean he's dying?'

'Yes,' and her mother had burst into tears over the phone. This woman who had spent all her life claiming that she longed for the man to die because he swamped her life with his pettiness, had suddenly been faced with what his death would mean. Hadn't they all?

So she had returned to Hernmead with Alexander, spotlessly fitted out because she had realized how important it was to show her parents just how much she had achieved without their help.

And her father had been stunned.

'This is your little bastard grandson, Daddy,' she had said, finding her father sitting up in bed and not at all as ill as she had been led to believe. The bastard grandson had knelt on the edge of his grandfather's bed and had reached out with both hands to stroke the elderly face and had said, through a joyous gurgle and for no explicable reason, 'You're the good man.' After which it had been instant recovery time for everybody. The fears of death had changed the old man anyway, and he saw Alexander as the angel of life. 'You must give up that filthy place in London, give up your secretary job and come and live here.' It had been an order.

The best years of her life had followed. Helping mother look after father who was convalescing with Alexander, the fulcrum of all their lives.

Then his schooling had come on to the horizon. Name down for Eton, Charterhouse, Winchester, Amhurst, a trust fund set up, money here, money there, and that was when she had begun to find being an exemplary mother tedious. The routine of the infant school, the need to hide that she was a single parent for the family's sake, the start of the undefined lies had built up an unbearable feeling of claustrophobia and she had told her father she wanted to work again. She needed to mix with people her own age, she had said, so that she might have the chance of finding a new husband, a kind soul, a bachelor perhaps or a childless widower who could give the boy a name. And Daddy had come up trumps.

He had bought her the house in London, the ideal house where she could behave like the rich divorcee she was, never mind a job, and they had all embraced the lie that Alexander was a Saranson and that she had been the unfortunate victim of a failed marriage due to her military husband devoting himself entirely to his army career.

Alexander, at six, had been sent to prep school, Clairmount in Oxfordshire, and she had found total freedom for the first term with only one letter a fortnight to write to him and a tuck parcel every six weeks, as recommended. But when he came back for the holidays, he was a boy, with knees to scrub and a temper, and a will of his own and an expensive uniform to buy out of her allowance, and then he went to Amhurst and he was a little man, a dangerous, bloody-minded little man.

She heard the shop door opening and closing upstairs.

A customer?

'Sarah?'

It was Phoebe coming in for a chat, which would depress her even more because she was a reflecton of herself. The menopaused middle-class woman gone to seed.

'I've brought a vino blanco!'

She came down the stairs looking like an amateur theatrical version of Mary Poppins, a quite stupid black hat stuck on her abundant unkept auburn hair.

'It's pissing outside, thought you might need cheering up.'

'I do.'

Phoebe was as much a failed shopkeeper as herself, country kitchen-ware over the other side of the river for homesick country wives stuck in the big city.

'Apart from three wooden spoons, I haven't sold a thing all week. How are you doing?'

'A moth-eaten musquash coat, £8, and a green feather boa, 95p.'

'Success is all to do with energy,' Phoebe said sitting on the bottom step. 'Energy, not talent. We've all got talent, somewhere, but we need the energy to bring it out and use it. Look at people like Peter Hall or Maggie T, they never ever stop, from one thing to another to another . . .'

'My problem is that I can't stand people,' Sarah said, finding two glasses next to a carton of curdled milk under the desk. She was a loner who hated being alone.

'Are you trying to tell me something?'

'No. It wasn't personal.'

'There's so much hate in you Sarah,' Phoebe pointed out, 'why don't you try liking someone for a change?'

'Any suggestions? Lovable people are a bit thin on the ground right now.'

'Why not try your son?'

She didn't need that.

'I love my son, more than I can bear, but I just can't get to grips with him. He's like an adorable purring kitten who quite suddenly hisses and scratches you viciously.'

'What do you feed him on?'

'Lies.'

'Rod for your own back then, sweetheart.'

The conversation changed to the banalities of Phoebe's sexless life. Sarah managed not to tell her of her own domestic trauma with Elliot, then Phoebe had to go, the bottle empty.

'A terrible urgent appointment dear. I'm pretending to myself that I'm needed. Nobody will care a fig if I'm late, it's a try-out aerobics class. We're alike, the two of us. Failed marriages and failed spinsterhoods. The only difference is that you at least have produced a child. I've failed in motherhood as well.'

Sarah stayed on at the shop for half an hour more, then closed at four deciding that no one would come by because of the rain. 'I am actually bone idle' she said out loud, not for the first time. 'But I haven't learned to live with it. I should be in bed, enjoying guiltless sleep.'

All Alexander's fault. He made her feel guilty about everything. But at least he wouldn't be at home tonight and she would have the place to herself.

What a way to think about her little boy.

She'd have to ring Hernmead tonight to learn of the latest fearful developments.

And she shouldn't drink in the middle of the day.

She turned round the corner and could not believe her eyes.

She had been clamped.

There, on a perfectly good parking space was her Fiesta with a bloody great card stuck on the windscreen together with a hundred other bits and pieces forbidding her, on pain of death, to use her own totally taxed car!

The fury started to mount at the unfairness of it. She had a valid parking permit, so why were they penalizing her? But when she checked she realized the permit was out of date.

Three days. She had forgotten, despite the reminder. Her fault entirely, no one else to blame, so the fury got worse.

She couldn't stand it. She suddenly could not stand anything any more and she started banging both fists on the roof of her car so hard she hurt herself. 'You silly bloody cow! Fuck! Fuck! Fuck!' she screamed, not caring, not caring about anything or anyone, weeping through closed eyes at the hopelessness of her whole life.

Somehow she managed to get herself home. They'd unclamp her within the hour. She'd have to go back to the car later. As she walked in the telephone was ringing.

She reached for it but let it ring for a moment to guess who would be calling. Please God let it be a super invitation to a dinner party.

It was her mother with her crisis voice.

'We've got Alexander back with us, darling. Father thought it best, you know he doesn't like having to be grateful to Louise.'

'The idea was to give us all a break from him,' she said, sounding petulant.

'He seems to have calmed down but of course Father is concerned about you having bought that computer for his school work. Was it very expensive? These things generally are.'

'For his school work?'

'That's what Alexander told him, that he had to do a great deal of work with the computer during the holidays as part of his maths curriculum.'

'Oh yes . . .'

'Father was going to have him work on the farm with the Simcocks, to keep him busy, but he seems to have this homework to do.'

'I know. They're pushing children very hard now.'

Into another lie.

Protecting him, or herself?

The thought came to her that dear Daddy might fork out for the expense if he thought it was more than just a toy. Was she so totally obsessed with money?

'Anyway, we'll see you at the weekend.'

'Looking forward to it.'

'The boyfriend you're bringing down, what did you say his name was?'

'I didn't mother. I never said anything about bringing anyone down.' She was imagining things again.

'Not your lodger, anyway?'

'I haven't got a lodger right now.'

'No dear. Best really. See you on Friday night anyway.'

She was going off her head.

She could imagine the scene, telling Hilda she was coming down with a friend and Hilda going on forever about it, not knowing which room to get ready, and complaining that they didn't have enough linen for guests anymore.

How long could it go on? There would have to be a breaking point. Alexander, alone, was going to enmesh them all in their own falsehoods. He was growing much faster than time itself and the idea that everything might be resolved by a death in the family and the resulting inheritance, was quite unrealistic. People didn't die when it was convenient. One day, oh, one day of course, she would inherit Hernmead with the proviso that it would in turn go to Alexander and Alexander's legal offsprings. It had been discussed. But what did that mean today? Now? It meant waiting.

One answer to the dilemma might be marriage.

Re-marriage.

She should find herself a man who could get her out of this hell-hole, who would persuade her stupid father to give her the deeds of the house as a wedding present, as her dowry, and a man who could somehow control Alexander.

Marriage had been the answer once, it might be the answer again.

Her new month's resolution? She would, by the end of August, find herself a husband even if it meant facing a fate worse than death several times, with demanding, but not necessarily exciting executioners.

Alexander needed a father, she would find him one, with an estate as far from Hernmead as possible, maybe a foreigner, a Frenchman with a château in the Loire, or an

American with a ranch in Texas. Forget the contemporaries, go for the sugar daddy.

Next week she would throw a dinner party and invite all the awful people she had discarded over the years, all the successful ones. She would ring up Howard, and start with him.

Why not Howard?

He had rung up several times declaring his love. 'I think I'm in love with you Sarah.'

Who else had said that to her other than sex-hungry subalterns when she was eighteen, and Geoffrey, twice. Had Alexander's father ever declared himself? Howard would be older now, richer, and it would please Mummy and Daddy enormously. A member of Lloyds, a member of the Atheneum, close connections with the Conservative Party and some ambitions to become a Member of Parliament.

How far away was the next election? Would she enjoy that life? Canvassing? Helping him to win some Northern constituency. An MP's wife? She had absolutely the right credentials, the rich little poor girl who had never wanted for anything except freedom. Burnside Girl's School for daughters of gentle folk. She had been adequate at sport, adequate at studies, she had dabbled with art but had never mastered anything to her own satisfaction, so she was humble. Divorced, which was the one black mark against her, that and her illegitimate son, but would that matter to an MP?

He wasn't one yet anyway, and he had a beautiful flat in Mount Street and a farm in Kent.

She went quickly down to the living room and helped herself to a vodka and tonic, drank it down rather quickly while looking up his number, then knelt on the floor and placed the telephone before her, the God of Communication to which she was once more offering herself as a sacrifice in return for hope.

She would ask Howard to dinner, invent a party, and build it up after that if he accepted. It would be wrong to ask him to come round alone straight off.

Once she had replaced the receiver she would be

committed; she would not go back on her word, she absolutely had to get out of her present, hopeless way of life.

She did not recognize the voice that answered.

'Howard?'

'No, this is his wife.'

She put the receiver straight back in its cradle.

Howard was married and had a wife who sounded like a fog horn.

Christ!

She would take some Mogadon to get her through the night and hope to God that in the morning she wouldn't feel so desperately alone. She'd take the next man who came along *whoever* he was.

chapter eleven

Alexander waited at the bus stop.

It was not the bus stop outside the Three Horseshoes where Mary would get on, but the request stop further up the hill on the Streatly road where it was unlikely that anyone who knew him would pass.

It was a pleasant summer's afternoon and he was happy, if a little impatient. Everything had gone according to plan so far, but it only needed one person to see him, and report what he was doing to his grandparents, for things to get complicated.

He'd managed a good story. He was going to Reading with Michael and Keith Simcock to see the new Superman film which was on, he'd checked, at the Odeon, and the Simcock brothers were actually going because he was paying for their seats in exchange for an alibi. He'd told them that he was going to meet a school friend his grandparents didn't like, a tale they had accepted, not caring anyway.

He pulled at a long piece of grass from the abundant

rosebay willowherbs along the hedgerow and stuck it in his mouth. The patterned shadows of overhanging beech leaves on the hot grey tarmac of the road suggested a coolness away from the sun which was beginning to burn his arm. From where he stood he could see the bend round which the bus would appear, and waiting for buses was about as engaging as fishing, without the excitement of knowing whether or not you'd catch one.

At least he had got away after a lunch that had taken for ever. Nearly as bad as breakfast when he'd wanted to get over to Mary's to double check that this would be the day that she'd be on the 2.10 bus. They hadn't let him get away that easily and he'd fallen back on counting the seconds his grandfather took to stir his coffee in the hope that it would make time pass more quickly. It hadn't. One hundred and thirty-five seconds he'd taken this morning, with the first cup, and he knew he could count to between five hundred and three thousand before the opening of the mail was finished and he was allowed to get up.

Letters could never be opened before the clock on the chimney-piece struck nine, even then Grandma might interrupt with something she was reading about in the newspaper and a pointless argument might follow. This morning she had found a bit of gossip about Robert Graves and a lost poem and Grandpa had exploded – damned poets! – as though they had directly offended his life. It had made him wonder whether the soon-to-be-encountered father was a poet too. Was it possible that the anger generated by the mention of poetry was brought about by the fact that his real father had written verses to his mother? Grandpa hated them nearly as much as left-wing politicians. Maybe his father was a socialist as well.

He didn't see himself as a politician's son. Too boring. Standing up on soap boxes and holding the lapels of your tweed jacket and brandishing a fist. Not him at all. Much more a poet, or dramatist. He'd written a play, not a very good one, and not very long, three pages. He'd written it for himself and the Simcock brothers to act out on a tape recorder. A radio play it had been, with lots of sound effects, which hadn't worked too well. The explosions on the sinking submarine had sounded exactly like Keith blowing into the microphone, and then Mary Northey had proved to the world that she couldn't actually read. Well she could, but jolly slowly. Nor could either of the Simcocks, come to think of it. Education, lack of, he supposed.

'What are you doing today Alexander?' his grandfather had asked after complaining about a bill.

'I'm going to check with Michael and Keith Simcock about this afternoon's film and then I have to work on some computer data.'

'Be careful on the farm . . .' and the regular warning about being run down by a combine-harvester or a tractor had inevitably followed. 'Farms are not what they used to be in my day, you know. They're factories now. Factories with dangerous machinery.'

It was the same every day, it never changed.

The sky was blue,
The trees were green,
The moon as pink as floss.
The little pig curled up his tail
And didn't care a toss . . .

He could write poetry standing on his head – a gift inherited from his father, the Poet Laureate, you know . . Percy Bysshe Taylor Coleridge Taylor Saranson, or Northey, rather.

What would he be like?

And a shiver made the hairs on the back of his neck bristle.

He was launching himself into this adventure quite blindly, avoiding even a second of anticipation. He didn't want to imagine what his father would be like, he simply wanted to meet him, find him in a dark corner of the lunatic asylum curled up in a pre-natal position maybe, and just look at him. That was all. Perhaps, deep down, he hoped to be disgusted so that he would never have to think about him again. He'd be unshaven, frothing at the mouth and waving long arms about like a caged baboon.

Who knew?

The bus still didn't come.

Maybe he was violent, or just cruel, as *he'd* been cruel to Mary by burning her, or mentally cruel, exposing other people's secrets to cause calculated distress as he himself had that memorable Sunday lunch, last holidays.

Poor Grandpa with his meanness. He could spend a fortune on his special brand whiskies and brandies and cigars, but when it came to others it was another story. And when it came to saving scrap paper or other useless things, he went quite mad.

He collected corks, for one thing, always used the inside of old envelopes to write notes, finished off stubs of pencils and collected elastic bands off the pavements in London, which was quite amusing. 'The streets of London are paved with postmen's rubber bands,' he'd declared with glee one day. He had picked up five outside the RAC club. The fact that he had then spent something like £50 taking a friend out to lunch was never mentioned, except by his daughter who liked repeating the story.

One day he had heard Grandma tell his mother a secret. 'When we first married and I moved into this house, I started tidying up his cupboards and do you know what I found? A shoe-box marked "PIECES OF STRING TOO SHORT TO USE", and inside it was full of just that: little bits of useless string. But never ever breathe a word, because I didn't stop laughing for weeks, and he hated that.'

He'd used it at the end of the memorable lunch with Grandpa and Grandma and Mother eating Hilda's acid rhubard and custard.

'I found two rubber bands for you today, Grandpa,' he'd declared.

'Did you my boy? Did you? Good, good, put them in the box.'

'What box is that?'

'I have a box where I keep rubber bands Alexander, you know that.'

'Oh, is that the one next to the PIECES OF STRING TOO SHORT TO USE?'

The silence had been impressive.

Gandma had frozen, mother's mouth had dropped open

and Grandpa had looked from one to the other and his face had become red from embarrassment. He'd been so vexed that he'd got up and had left the room, mumbling some excuse about needing to wash his hands.

Grandma had looked at Sarah accusingly, and his mother had turned on him.

'Where did you hear about that, Alexander?'

'I don't know. Is it important?'

'We must be more careful what we say in front of him,' his grandmother had then whispered to her daughter so loudly that Hilda could have heard it in the kitchen. Why was it that adults always reminded each other in front of children not to talk in front of the children? Mother had once gone as far as saying '*Pas devant les enfants*' nearly in his ear, and he had corrected her, 'Don't you mean "*Pas devant l'enfant*", in the singular?' which hadn't gone down too well.

The top of the Thames Valley bus suddenly rose up above the dip in the bend and its full red frontal flatness with its small crab-eye headlamps accelerated towards him.

He held out his hand, it stopped a few yards from him and the automatic doors swung open.

There were only three people in the vehicle; two elderly ladies huddled together on one seat, both wearing summer frocks and Women's Institute hats, and Mary, all on her own, sitting at the very back.

He paid the fare to Mileswood Hospital and joined her, grabbing hold of anything available to keep himself steady as the bus lurched off up the hill.

She moved to one side and patted the place next to her, all smiles. She had no idea, of course, of the real reason he was joining her. As far as she was concerned he was just coming along because he wanted to see the new model theatre her father was making.

They didn't talk.

There wasn't anything to say.

Alexander stared out of the window at the woods, the fields and the cottages that they passed. Mary had brought Tante Louise's cardboard box with her rag dolls inside. It was badly tied up with loose, white stranded string. She'd give them to

Matron who'd give them to needy children or sell them on behalf of the hospital charity fund.

The bus eventually stopped outside the hospital and they got off. It was an immense dark-grey stone building with green railings all around, the gates were wide open though, and they walked in, holding the box between them.

They went up the entrance steps and through a pair of glass and stainless-steel doors. Inside, the smell of carbolic soap, with pastel-blue walls, fluorescent lighting, paintings and murals everywhere. It was more like an exhibition hall than a hospital.

Mary went to the reception desk and just stood there, her shyness forbidding words to come out.

'Hallo Mary, come to see your Dad?' The woman took the cardboard box from her and put it behind her desk.

'Yes please, Miss.'

'And who's your friend?'

'He's come to see Dad's theatre.'

'You know the way, he'll be there.'

He had expected a security check, white-coated male nurses flanking them, but they were on their own, walking down long corridors with dark blue doors on either side. He wasn't tall enough to look through the small square-netted windows, but when one of them opened he saw that it was just an office. He had half expected padded cells with some lunatics tied up in chains or in straight jackets, but it wasn't like that at all.

They passed through a lounge with sofas and a large television set. Several patients in their dressing gowns were watching cartoons, bizarre looking people with vacant smiles, uncombed white hair, toothless gums.

Mary led the way on through more double doors, then down some stone steps and out into a beautiful garden laid out to lawn with abundant flower borders. There were people everywhere, sitting on benches, walking along paths, lying on the grass. It could have been a garden fête.

Mary led the way to a set of wooden huts tucked out of sight behind two huge cedar trees. Over one of the doors the word WORKSHOP had been painted in bright yellow letters.

They went in and the smell of sawdust and glue now filled Alexander's nostrils. The din of hammering and sawing and the whining of electric drills hurt the ears, but they went through yet another door into a comparatively silent room where a tall, round-shouldered man, with puffy eyes, wearing jeans and a denim shirt with rolled-up sleeves was painting two thin pieces of plywood in gold. He wore old suede shoes and had a cigarette in the corner of his mouth which wasn't lit.

Without turning round to look at them, he said, 'Hallo Mary, let me finish this then I'll be with you.'

Was this him?

He had expected worse. He had imagined someone demented, someone with a twitchy face, with pebbled lenses perhaps and mad hair, but not a perfectly normal sort of man who seemed to be totally in control of himself.

'Who's your friend?'

'Alexander,' Mary said. 'I told you about him last time.'

'Oh yes?'

He didn't remember, obviously. He didn't have a memory and therefore wouldn't remember anything.

The man turned round rather suddenly and stared at Alexander, lowering his head a little as though he were wearing spectacles and had to look over them to see properly. It was a strange mannerism to emphasize what he was doing.

'Alexander Saranson of Hernmead Court, is it?'

'Yes, sir.'

'Sir, is it? I haven't been called "sir" for a long time.'

He smiled engagingly.

'You, of all people, don't have to call me "sir",' he said.

Did he know then? Did he know he was his son?

'What do I call you then, sir?'

The man painted some glue on the two pieces of gold plywood, slammed them together, placed them in a vice and spun the bolt round.

'Good question. What do you call me, after all this time?'

He glanced at Mary and ruffled her hair.

'Alexander doesn't remember but I met him a long time ago, a very long time ago. Shall we go and have tea?'

'He came to see the theatre,' Mary protested.

'Of course he did. I'd forgotten.'

The man leaned over to kiss her lightly on the forehead at

the same time feeling the length of her arms, then squeezing her waist with both hands. He was gentle with her, so gentle, and amused by her concern.

'It's at the other end of the workshop,' he said, ushering them out of the small room and pointing them in the right direction.

When he could, Alexander glanced back up at him. There was a look in the man's eyes he couldn't quite gauge, but it was very warm, whatever it was.

The model theatre, set up on its own stand, was much bigger than he had expected, and quite beautiful.

'This is a model of the Teatro La Fenice in Venice, designed by Antonio Selva. Have you ever been to Venice?'

'No,' Alexander admitted.

'I wanted to be an actor, you see, but never quite made it. Then I wanted to be an artist, and didn't quite make it at that either, so I've combined the two. I'm a bit of a failure, actually Alexander, a bit of a failure.'

He didn't want to hear that. He didn't want the man to denigrate himself.

'Do you go to the theatre Alexander?'

'Not much. But I wanted to be an actor too.'

'Wanted? You've given up the idea?'

'No, but . . .'

'You don't get much encouragement? You're at Amhurst aren't you? They don't encourage the arts too much in those establishments. You have to get marks you see, pass exams and be good at sport so that you can get a job at IBM or ICI or some corporation or other where they can be proud of you and where you will show no signs of individuality whatsoever.'

The man put his arm round Mary's shoulders and led them out of another door.

'I expect Matron will have got us some tea and biscuits. Worse, it'll be someone's birthday and we'll have to eat a bit of their cake. But you might like that.'

The three of them walked out into the garden passing the cedar trees where a man was sitting on his haunches rocking himself.

'He thinks he's a dwarf. He is in fact six foot five inches tall, but he thinks he's a dwarf. No one can work out why.'

Alexander walked behind father and daughter, Mary hugging her father, the father toying with her hair.

'And that woman there,' he said pointing to an eccentric looking lady lying full length on a bench, 'thinks she is Greta Garbo's daughter, if the name means anything to you. Garbo was a Swedish film star. They're the only two real lunatics here, and we love them dearly. All the others are just cases of schizophrenia, paranoia and manic depression.'

'Is anyone dangerous here, sir?'

He felt it was rude to ask, but it came out.

'Call me Richard, I'd prefer it. No. Well, maybe one or two, but they're drugged up to the eyeballs. The only really dangerous person is Matron. I call her the Hell Hag.'

No allusions were made to their relationship during the tea they had in the canteen along with a lot of other visitors and patients. Richard was very affectionate with Mary, who stared at him with admiration throughout while he prattled on about building another model theatre when he had finished La Fenice, though he wasn't sure why he should bother except that the authorities left him in peace when he was doing something pointless. Maybe his model theatre would serve someone in the end. Maybe he would make a whole series of them: La Scala, Drury Lane, the Olivier; though he liked proscenium arches. Once, he'd destroyed one by setting fire to it. The Royal Exchange, Manchester. They had punished him for that, in a cell with bread and water for a hundred days.

'Not true, Alexander, I'm joking. I've never set fire to anything more inflammable than a relationship.'

Is that where the dottiness was? Lying for effect, rambling on without making much sense? It wasn't too bad, in fact Alexander wanted him to talk more, but the visitor's bell sounded and they were told they had to leave.

'Come again, Alexander, and we can have a chat. And take care of Mary. She's been much happier since you helped her with the dolls. It's good to help fellow creatures. We're all sisters and brothers, one way or another, aren't we?'

The first direct hint that he might be trying to find out whether he knew.

'Yes, sir . . . Richard.'

The look lasted a long time, pensive, doubting, concerned. It was the look of a father who did not know his son, but wanted to. Alexander was sure.

'Come again soon,' Richard repeated, and saw them to the canteen door.

There was only one thing that Alexander needed to do now and that was to go up to his secret room, to think about the meeting undisturbed and make plans to go and see him again.

He needed the privacy, he needed to be alone, he could take the canoe out and go to one of the islands, but the evening had turned chilly and there was a wind and he preferred his hideout.

He now belonged to someone else, someone who had seemed to care, and he wanted to swear allegiance, desperately wanted to show that he would be loyal, and if he couldn't do it publicly, he would do it privately, by writing 'RICHARD NORTHEY' in big and elaborate letters on his family-tree board.

The bus ride was uneventful, Mary sitting in the back corner seat looking out at the passing scenery.

If someone saw him around the house when he got back they would ask him about the film, so he had to get ready for those sort of questions, but six o'clock was a good time: Hilda would be cleaning up the tea things and getting supper ready, and he could probably make his way up the back stairs without anyone seeing him.

He left Mary at the end of Gifford's lane and cut across the orchard, over the fence into Hernmead meadow then through the door into the kitchen garden.

No one around.

Up the kitchen steps, across the deserted scullery, slinking through the empty kitchen and up the back stairs. Hilda was in the pantry clattering about with jam pots.

So intent was he on getting to his hideout that he was not cautious enough before opening Hilda's bedroom door, and she was there, sitting on the edge of her bed, darning one of her stockings. It must have been Grandma down in the pantry.

Hilda had one stocking on and the other off, her bare white leg and naked foot spotlighted in a patch of sunlight.

She looked up, surprised.

'Don't they teach you to knock on doors at your posh school, young man? What is it you want?'

He was so taken aback by her presence that he had no answer.

'Come in and close the door and I'll tell you what you want. You want to go into that attic room of yours don't you, believing, like the innocent you are, that I don't know about it.'

He closed the door and leaned against it.

'How long have you known?' he asked.

'A long time, and I'm thinking of telling your grandfather about it. All those names on that board. Is it a form of black magic you're practising? Casting evil spells on all your family?'

She was totally dotty.

'If you tell, Hilda, I'll do dreadful things to you.'

'I don't think you can frighten me young man.'

'I have ways . . .' A fearful frustration was building up inside him. She had no right to be there imposing a barrier. 'By tomorrow night,' he said, 'I'll get you into terrible trouble, just to prove it.'

'You're a very conceited boy, Alexander, much worse than you used to be, and goodness knows you were bad enough.'

She removed the wooden egg from down inside the stocking and threaded her hand inside the foot to examine her work.

'I've not told your grandfather about you sneaking into my room to go into that place because it's suited me not to, but if you're not nice to me and you don't say your prayers regularly, I may do so.'

She rolled up the stocking and stuck it over her yellowing toenails, pulled it up her white leg, then got to her feet.

'Turn around young man, I don't need to be watched while I'm dressing.'

Alexander turned around.

'What sort of trouble do you think you could get me into anyway?'

'I could get you the sack,' Alexander said.

'And how do you think your grandmother would manage without me? They're as frightened of losing me as you are of me telling them about that room.'

It was true, his grandmother lived in terror of losing her, but then Hilda herself couldn't risk getting the boot because she had no one else in the whole wide world but this family, and if she left Hernmead she would have nowhere to go. Her dream of going to Australia to live with her niece, a threat which upset Grandma often enough, was complete fabrication. Hilda did not have a niece, nor did she have any sisters or brothers. She hadn't even been married. She was Miss Hilda Kelly, spinster, but for some reason, best known to herself, she had invented a drunken husband who had left her, probably to get sympathy. He knew all this because he had read through her diaries one boring winter afternoon. 'Confessed to Father O'Byrne about my never marrying and never having brothers or sisters.' He had known that such knowledge would come in useful one day.

'I'll get you into trouble Hilda, just you see, and in the next twenty-four hours,' he promised.

Dinner the next night afforded him the chance to prove his power. Denied access to his sanctuary, he spent most of the day in the drawing room playing with the computer and mastering 'Horace on the Ski Slopes', switching over to a jumble of meaningless figures whenever anyone came near. He went out in his canoe, and sat on the banks of Otter's Island looking at the river enjoying the warmth of his newly found filial affections. But the thought of Hilda telling his grandfather about the room stayed and an anger built up inside him. When he learned at lunchtime of the dinner party Grandma and Grandpa were giving that night for a boring old couple visiting from the Cotswolds, he knew he could have his revenge.

And when his grandmother told him that he was to have supper in the kitchen with Hilda then make himself scarce, an evil little plan came into his head.

While he ate a tasteless watercress and potato soup alone in a corner of the kitchen, Hilda, vexed and stupid, made a big production about ignoring him. The twenty-four hours were virtually up, so when she was busy in the skullery, he crossed the kitchen, opened the oven door and poured a vast quantity of salt over the roast, and even more into the bowl of fruit salad.

After eating a banana, he disappeared, making himself scarce as requested, and took up a position on the steps of the back stairs where he could listen to the muffled dinner conversation coming from the dining room and the clattering of dishes from the skullery.

'Hilda, I'm afraid you've put far too much salt in the meat, it's quite unpalatable.' It was Grandma with her mortified voice only just held in check.

Silence while the meat was tasted by the head cook, then a fearful rush to heat up a not very good canned stew. Then, again, Grandma coming back into the kitchen with the dessert.

'What has been happening Hilda, you must have mixed up the salt with the sugar . . .'

Hilda found him on the stairs.

'The salt, is that your doing?'

'Of course.'

'Then as soon as the guests have left I'm going to tell both your grandparents about your quite horrible behaviour Alexander and I'll tell them about the attic as well so may the good Lord help you.' Her fury made the sinews down the length of her neck stand out in red and white streaks. He had never seen her in such a state.

'You won't,' he said, 'because if you do I'll tell them about your niece in Australia who doesn't exist and about your brothers and sisters who were never born. I've read your confessions to Father O'Byrne you see, *Miss* Kelly!'

'Go to your room you evil boy, go to your room before I take the broom to you!'

The ruction that followed was extremely satisfying. It started with the shattering of one glass, then another, then several, then, apparently, the whole dinner service being hurled against a wall. There was a moment's silence, and a saucepan was obviously thrown high into the air to hit the ceiling and ricochet against another wall.

Tiptoeing his way on up the stairs, Alexander, well pleased, went to bed.

The next few days were spent peacefully sitting in front of his computer working out cursors and modes, key words and graphics, or paddling around in his canoe.

The fact that Hilda Kelly refused to speak to him was not noticed because she was refusing to speak to anybody, and Grandpa and Grandma munched away at the hardly tolerable food set before them, unaware of the bond of silence based on exchanged secrets that united their grandson and their excitable Irish cook.

Twice he went over to Mary's cottage to help her with her rag dolls, sewing small buttons as eyes on to the white linen circle, while she stitched in a mouth with crimson cotton.

On the Friday he waited for the bus as he had done before, this time more excited at the prospect of meeting his father again, and when he entered the hospital with Mary, and walked through to the workshop, he realized that the smell of sawdust and glue would forever remind him of that lyrical moment when high expectation had been realized.

Richard Northey, his father, was sitting on a stool in front of the model Fenice theatre, flicking the tiny switches on a light control gadget he held in his hand.

'I think you might both like to design the sets of the first production. It can either be a pantomime, or a musical, an opera or a play. What do you think it should be?'

Alexander liked the way he spoke to them as though they had always been there. Without turning round he addressed them as though they had never left his side.

'Perhaps a ballet?' he went on. 'Do you like ballet, Alexander. Have you ever been to one? Mary has never ever been to the theatre.'

'Yes I have, once.'

'*Babes in the Wood*, in Oxford, of course. I remember. How could I forget. You were about eight then, weren't you, and I was sane.'

He swivelled round on his stool and faced them both.

'We live in a mediocre world, Alexander, and if you're a perfectionist, or worse, an artistic perfectionist, you have three choices. Overcome all the mediocre odds of which there are many, by gaining power and therefore be allowed, indeed *begged* to do what you want. Sail along with the undistinguished flow and hope for survival. Or ignore it all and bury your head in the sand. I tried the first and failed, was incapable of surviving the second and have ended up here, where I am unknown and where nothing is expected of me, but where I do spend a good deal of my life in beautiful, sometimes outrageous fantasy. Shall we go outside and sit on the grass?'

He ushered them out of the workshop, a heavy hand on Alexander's right shoulder, the other on Mary's left.

They walked in silence down a path, then Richard manoeuvered them across the lawn to a secluded corner surrounded by rhododendron bushes and hundreds of other shrubs.

'You see, Alexander,' he said, sitting down cross-legged, 'the big difference between people like your mother and her parents, the rich, the well off, and people like Mary's mother and myself, is that they are born in an artificial world and are completely unaware of it. They do not know what it is to be poor. "Labouring people are poor because they are numerous", they say, quoting Burke, or, "There's no scandal like rags, nor any crime so shameful as poverty", quoting George Farquhar. They say these things without understanding them. To be poor is to care about money, not bolster up what already exists, but to help survival. And I'm not talking about real poverty which, of course, I know nothing about. I'm not talking about hunger. I have never been hungry in my life, but I have needed money badly to survive the life imposed on me by others, their false life. Some people can never get over this simple hurdle; the hurdle, for instance, of buying a motor scooter to make it easier for them to go to work. People like your grandfather have no idea about such things. He was born in a position where it was all already there. He has never had to save. He does save, his type is obsessed with saving, but only to protect a security that already exists.'

Alexander was hardly listening. It had got beyond him. He wasn't sure why his father was telling him all this, whether there was a point to it.

'Mary, why don't you go up to the canteen and see what they're doing about tea?'

Alexander thought the request a bit abrupt, but Mary, apparently delighted, quickly got to her feet and ran off up towards the main buiding.

'She gets bored with my rambling, Alexander. Besides I wanted to talk to you alone. Are you worried about going mad, like me?'

It took him aback.

It had never been established between them that they actually were father and son, it had never been admitted that the other knew.

'You needn't be,' Richard went on. 'You're not tainted by me. It's a mental disease that can be inherited, of course, and I fear that little Timmy may have it, but not you. He's not well you know. Your little half-brother.'

Alexander said nothing.

'I wish something could be done about it because Connie, Mary's mother, is poor you see. Have you ever paid attention to her daily life. Observed the paucity of it? She never stops. Can't afford to stop. She only gets a certain social benefit and that leaves her nothing at the end of the week, so she has to work very hard. If she didn't she would not have a television or a refrigerator and other such things which are considered luxuries by the rich, but which the poor *need* to survive. There are no more neighbours to help out with the babysitters you see, we have become a society of loners. The community has gone. Those cottages should be full of people, crowded yes, but somehow a family. Who is there next door? My aged father, and that's all. Mary is the only one who can help her. It's Mary I feel sorry for. If the baby wasn't there she would have a chance, for she is a sweet child, not too bright, but a sweet and willing human being. I want to do something for her Alexander. It's the only thing I really want to do in my life.'

He stopped talking and stared into the distance at nothing in particular.

'A set for *A Midsummer Night's Dream* might be fun. Do you know the play?'

'I was Puck in an excerpt at my prep school.'

'Puck? Yes, you'd make a good Puck, I can see that.'

Alexander watched Mary come back, skipping lightly across the lawn in her worn leather shoes, smiling at the various visitors and patients to her left and right.

'Mary's coming back,' Alexander warned.

His father stared at him with affectionate pride.

'I'm pleased you came,' he said. 'I heard from the doctor today that I may not have very long to live. I don't mean that I'm going to die tomorrow, but sometimes I feel very, very tired, weary. I won't mind a bit.'

He looked up as Mary stopped just behind him.

'Ten more minutes, Matron said.'

'Did she, the old bat. Shall we go and look at the goldfish?'

There were no goldfish because there was no water in the pond, but it didn't stop his father pretending there were.

'Pretty aren't they? The ones with the white fluff on their backs are diseased,' he looked over at Alexander for a reaction.

Did he really think that he would be frightened by such an act?

'Some visitors believe I see goldfish you know,' he said stroking Alexander's hair. 'I go through a whole routine for their benefit. But the only thing I've ever done that was unbalanced was try to kill Mary's mother.'

He was quite serious now, which was unsettling. Alexander glanced quickly at Mary.

'Oh, she knows about it, she was there. In fact if it wasn't for Mary I dare say poor Connie would be dead. I attacked her with a poker; standard procedure for a maniac enraged by a petty misdemeanour on his wife's part. I can't remember what angered me so much, but I lost control and still lose control now and again. Which is why I'm here.'

He tweeked Mary's cheek because she was looking at him rather sadly. It made her smile.

The relationship between father and daughter was rather peculiar, but endearing, so much so that Alexander sensed a sort of envy at not being able to share the bad times her father had obviously put her through.

After the empty pond, Richard took them to look at the empty aviary and, for the benefit of another lunatic's visitors, he pointed at several non-existent birds admiring their colourful plumage.

'Green-and-purple turtle doves are very unusual Alexander,' he said, glancing a little too obviously to see the effect, 'but I do like that yellow warbler.'

It seemed to amuse him. Maybe if you were stuck in the same place week after week, anything would be fun. Didn't he himself feel like that at Amhurst – an intense desire to fool people into thinking he wasn't quite well in the head?

Hooker would like his father.

They went up and had tea, then the visitors' bell ended the afternoon and he and Mary said goodbye and went off to wait for the bus outside the hospital gates. Half a dozen other relatives waited with them, some pensive, some sad, one elderly woman wiping her eyes unable to hide her tears. Mary nudged Alexander and whispered, 'He's up at the window again, watching.'

He turned to look up at the sinister building and, on the first floor above the main entrance, saw his father at a large window flanked by two other patients, one in a dressing gown, all holding on to the iron bars that were there to prevent accidents.

'He always goes up there to watch me get on the bus. All the loonies do.'

'He's not a loony,' Alexander protested.

'Of course he is. He wouldn't be in there if he wasn't.' She said it quite seriously, then added, 'I don't mind. I've got used to it. Sometimes I think it's quite funny.'

That hurt.

chapter twelve

Breakfast at Hermead Court.

Saturday.

His grandfather at the head of the oval Regency table, his grandmother at the other end, his mother, bleary-eyed, one side, himself opposite her.

On offer, courtesy of Hilda who was in a better mood, scrambled eggs on soggy toast.

Alexander waited politely for his grandmother to start eating hers before he cut into his. His mother winked at him because she knew he hated the ritual as much as she did, then they all dug in, only the sound of chewing breaking the oppressive silence.

'Anything interesting in the paper Daddy?' his mother asked.

Daddy scanned the front page of *The Times* and grunted.

It could mean anything.

Then Alexander noticed the envelope in the pile of mail next to his grandfather's napkin ring. It was long, white and bore the school crest in one corner.

His second Amhurst report.

It could mean anything. A good day, a bad day, a complimentary pat on the head, peeved looks for the rest of the holidays.

He had no idea. He had no idea of how well he had done, or how badly, what the masters thought of his work or their opinion of his character. The masters had hardly entered into his school life; it had all been house captains and prefects, Parminger, Bowles, Marriott and Dougal, Wilcox and the dreadful Goodall.

Goodall and Pitts.

Would that episode be mentioned in his report.

Three weeks into the term and one warm Saturday afternoon he had gone to Goodall's study to tidy things up thinking the House Captain was playing cricket. Appointed his fag, he had been promised an easy time if he did what he was asked, and so far had managed to please without being hassled. Goodall, to his surprise, had been there.

'Ah, great, Saranson, just what I need. Look!'

And he had sat well back in the chair and unzipped his flies and it had popped out like a white and pink snake.

'Want to have a feel?'

'No thanks.'

'You know what a blow-job is?'

Alexander had backed away.

'Draw the curtains, Saranson.'

Alexander had hesitated.

'Draw the curtains, man!'

As he had gone to draw the curtains, Goodall, with his flies open and his penis sticking out, had got up to bolt the door. Bolts were forbidden, but he had fitted one. He'd then turned and said, 'Take down your trousers.'

'I don't want to.'

'I'll have you lynched you little tart. Take down your trousers. I don't want to touch you, I just want to watch you do it. Do you come yet?'

'No . . .'

'I bet you do. I bet I can make you.'

It had been humiliating. He'd taken down his trousers, had stood in the middle of the study while Goodall had knelt before him and had grabbed him and had moved him up and down till he was raw, and it had hurt, but Goodall had come, disgusting white spew all over the carpet and he had made him wipe it up with a filthy handkerchief.

'I'll turn you into a faggot yet, Saranson. Pretty boys like you shouldn't be allowed. You're too bloody dangerous.'

He had got as far as The Buzz's door after being allowed to go before deciding he couldn't tell. How certain could he be that The Buzz wouldn't just shrug the business off as 'part of life's rich tapestry'? Telling was the worst offence of all.

Goodall had been more pleasant after that, swearing at him less, not giving him lines on occasions he could have done, then one day, in the changing rooms, after a game of Fives, the House Captain had sat there, naked, watching him take a shower, watching intently, his bunched-up towel held tight between his legs, and Pitts had come in from squash and had stripped and displayed a proud prick larger than most boys of his age, had eyed Goodall and had got into the shower with Alexander and had started soaping him.

Goodall, in a sudden state of nerves, had slammed the door, put a chair against it, had grabbed hold of Pitts by the balls and had forced him to his knees.

To Alexander's horror Pitts had then got hold of Goodall and had started licking him like a lollipop. At that moment, the door had burst open and Wilcox and Parminger had stood there, staring at Pitts and Goodall with expressions of utter repulsion.

'You bloody fool, Goodall!'

Alexander had stayed under the shower while Pitts and Goodall had rushed for their clothes. He had stayed under the shower, open-mouthed, seemingly paralysed, until Wilcox had turned the water off and had handed him a towel. When asked what he'd been doing, he'd pretended to be unable to answer and later, much later, during evening prep, Wilcox had summoned him to the Prefect's Common Room and had advised him to go and talk to The Buzz about what had happened.

'You were humiliated, Saranson, by those two, and I can't have that going on in Travellier's. It's your duty to talk to our housemaster about it for your sake as well as for the rest of us.'

He'd known he was being used for some devious political advancement of Wilcox's, but he'd had little option because Wilcox had already made an appointment for him.

After supper, sitting next to a paler Pitts, a shattered Goodall and an amused Hooker, he had gone to the Housemaster's study and had found The Buzz in black cape, smoking his pipe, sitting behind his desk correcting Greek.

'Yes, Saranson, you wanted to see me?'

'Yes, sir.'

'So what can I do for you boy?'

'You said, sir, if we had a problem, sir . . .'

'That's right. What problem have you got?'

He was correcting again, not listening, clearly not wanting to hear.

'I was humiliated this afternoon, sir.'

'Were you? Humiliated were you?' He took off his glasses and stood up. 'By whom?'

'I don't want to say, sir, not until I know what it will mean to those involved.'

The Buzz had fished a tissue out of a drawer and had started cleaning his lenses.

'I expected something like this might happen to you, Saranson . . . "When a man, starting from this sensible world and making his way upward by a right use of his feeling of love for boys, begins to catch sight of that beauty . . .". Plato, Saranson; you don't do Greek. The *Symposium*. Good stuff. So, tell me exactly what occurred.'

'I'd rather not sir.'

'I'd rather you did, Saranson. That's what you came to me for. Where, for instance, did this humiliation take place?'

'In the showers, sir.'

'Cleanliness is next to Godliness . . .' The Buzz had mumbled to himself. 'An older boy molested you, I presume?'

'Not me, sir, someone else, sir.'

'So you were not directly involved?'

'Not directly, sir. I was an involuntary witness, sir.'

'Were you now?'

'Had it not been for an intervention, sir, I think I might have become involved.'

'Of your own free will, Saranson?' His eyebrows were raised in surprise.

'No, sir. Against my will, sir.'

'And this intervention? Someone came in?'

'Yes, sir. Wilcox, sir. It was Wilcox who suggested I should come to talk to you.'

'Indeed. And will you now volunteer the offender's name?'

'I'd rather not, sir.'

'I understand. Good. Right. Leave it to me. And are you all right, Saranson; shocked perhaps?'

'I think I'm all right, sir.'

'The term homesexual is not foreign to you I presume?'

'No, sir. I have heard it used.'

'The term is derived from the Greek prefix "homo"

meaning "the same as" and not, as many suppose, from the Latin meaning "man". Did you know that?'

'No, sir. I don't think I did, sir.'

'Well dwell on it Saranson, and perhaps a visit to the school doctor will do no harm. A little talk about these things.'

And the next day he'd been sent very discreetly to the doctor, an indifferent man who had sat him down and lectured him on humanity and sex between men and women and then had told him that sometimes boys behaved like this but that it had to be stopped. Bad for morale. The doctor had insisted on knowing the names of those involved and eventually Alexander had told him.

He hadn't felt very good about it, had felt quite awful in fact, but hadn't said a word to Hooker or anyone else. That night Wilcox had taken Lights Out, Pitts was missing, all his clothes had gone and rumour had it that he had been sent to the sanatorium with apendicitis, then driven in an ambulance to Brighton for an operation.

The next day Hooker had told him Goodall had gone as well; both had been expelled, no one knew why, no one would ever know the truth, it had happened before, the masters could move swiftly and silently, like the KGB, and cover up when something really nasty happened in the woodshed.

The clock struck nine and Grandpa wiped his mouth, cleared his throat and reached for his letters.

The report was about five envelopes down. Grandpa went through his boring routine, making comments, having arguments with Mother, Grandmother, then he picked the envelope up and, examining the crest, raised his eyebrows and glanced at Alexander.

It might, of course, just be a communication regarding Old Amhurstians.

The ivory-handled knife slit open the envelope and the anticipated report was pulled out and unfolded.

'Your second Amhurst report, Alexander. Let us hope for some improvement.'

His first report had not, in fact, been at all bad, but he was going to have to sit still like a good boy while the missive was read through, read through again, and digested. It would then be handed to Grandma, handed to Mother, then eventually to himself. The ritual demanded silence from everyone while it lasted. It would take at least another half-hour out of his life.

So he watched the frowning and the eyebrows being raised and lowered. It was all a pretty awful act, but then what else did the stupid old man have to do?

'I've seen better,' was the comment that accompanied the request for the report to be passed to the other end of the table.

Grandmother, kinder, adjusting her glasses on the end of her nose.

He didn't dislike her. She was, when he came to think of it, the only really stable person in the family. When he wrote to her from school she always answered, and it was she who sent him whatever he asked for, be it a new pen or a set of stamps or a book, providing it was within reason. He knew that she had to go through the long and tedious process of asking Grandpa for whatever he wanted, but she was protective, and certainly the one who seemed most concerned about him when he was ill.

'I don't think it's too bad,' she said passing the report to her daughter.

Mother read it quickly, as impatient as he to get out of the dining room. She made no faces, did not put on an act, but simply handed it across to him when she'd finished reading it.

'I think it's rather good,' she said pointedly to Grandpa, then got up and left the room.

He read the report, with some fascination, from top to bottom.

A. R. SARANSON	Age: 13.4.	Summer Term.
FORM:	Middle IV.	Average age: 13.11
DIVINITY	He has good background knowledge of the New Testament.	

ENGLISH	His composition is often over-imaginative which does not compensate for his bad spelling.
HISTORY	A very good grasp of dates and lineage. He has a sense of this subject.
GEOGRAPHY	He has worked very well.
LATIN	He does not display a great deal of interest and must apply himself better next term.
FRENCH	He has worked well enough, but could improve his grammar.
MATHEMATICS	Keen at all times, if occasionally muddled.
SCIENCE	His work has been rather uneven.
FORM MASTER	Adequate for a boy who knows he can do better
HOUSE MASTER	His contemporaries might be a little happier if he were a little less curious. But he is a nice fellow, lively and yet essentially serious. A good sense of House loyalty.

The school will re-assemble on 19 September.

Wasn't that an incredible cover up? By forgiving him a manufactured fault The Buzz had glossed over his own appalling inadequecy as Housemaster. It was, after all, The Buzz who had appointed Goodall a House Captain.

But he made no comment, there was no point, his grandfather in fact had already forgotten about the report and was gazing out of the window no doubt wondering what he was going to do.

'What plans have you got for today, Alexander?'

'I'm going to clean out my canoe, then I still have to work out sines and cosines on the computer.' He could say anything, he hadn't an earthly what it was all about.

'Well don't be all day in front of the television, there's a race at three o'clock I want to watch.'

Case dismissed.

The accused found not guilty.

He was free to do as he pleased.

It was a beautiful morning outside, already hot, the smell of the freshly mown lawn reminding him of endless afternoons in the cricket fields.

So his report had been passed as acceptable by the supreme power. Good for him, good for Mummy, it might mean a peaceful weekend which he rather wanted. Meeting his own father had caused him enough emotional tension for a while, that and Hilda's tantrum.

He walked down the garden to the boat house, rather wishing he had company. He thought of visiting the Simcocks and crossed over Gorse Lane to go to the farm, then changed his mind. Today would be a good day to entertain Mary and get to know her better. He walked back across the lane, jumped over the fence and made his way diagonally up across Hernmead meadow to the cottages.

Mary was in the front garden rocking the pram, and when she saw him coming she put her finger to her lips.

'Timmy's just dropping off,' she whispered.

He looked into the pram. A neat, white cellular blanket covered a bundle which only displayed a tuft of light brown hair.

His half-brother.

Somehow it didn't mean anything to him.

'Like to come out in the canoe?'

Mary shrugged her shoulders, smiling. It meant 'yes' but she was too shy to say it outright.

'I'll just tell me Mam.'

He led the way to the boat house and helped her into the canoe, getting the paddle and untying the painter. She sat safely in the middle, holding the side, he positioned himself on the stern Red Indian fashion, and pushed the canoe out so that it glided silently through the wide open doors.

They went upstream under Whitchurch bridge, keeping to the centre of the river, then he crossed over to the lock island and hugged the bank that promised sightings of otters or water rats. It was Kenneth Graham territory. *The Wind In The Willows* had been inspired by these very banks. It was familiar country. When younger, he had often sat with Grandpa fishing from the lock pier, first catching bleak, then using the bleak to catch the crocodile-mouthed pike. Once, Grandpa had caught a brown trout which Hilda had made a fuss about cooking. It had tasted of mud and had been pretty horrible.

They didn't go through the lock but turned around after watching two cabin cruisers coming through, and in their wake Alexander paddled furiously back under the bridge, past the boat house to slip smoothly in among the reeds and beach the bows high on to the meadow shingle of Hearn Creek. Here they were safe from the outside world, a backwater that had become their own.

'Got a swim-suit?' Alexander asked. 'We could have a dip.'

'I don't need a swim-suit . . .'

She was like that, Mary, not a bit shy about her body on certain occasions. He had seen her several times crouching down in a field, not even attempting to hide behind a tree or a bush. A year or so back she had come up to watch him peeing against a wall, she had actually gone round and leaned against it to face him and look at him closely, fascinated.

'You boys are lucky,' she'd said, and giggled.

That was the difference between working class and upper class, he'd decided. No manners. Now, however, he was rather amused by her earthiness. Hooker's influence no doubt. 'You're such a prude, Saranson. My mother took me to a nudist beach once with one of her boyfriends and after a while, I can assure you, all the tits, bums and dicks were just boring parts of the anatomy, like ears and toes.'

Mary got out of the canoe, sat down on the grass and took off her leather shoes, then her dress. He pulled off his T-shirt and hesitated about his jeans, but slid them down. He was wearing his light blue briefs, which would be OK.

To his surprise she slipped her knickers off and stood there in the sun, her eyes shut, completely nude. He hadn't seen a naked girl for ages, not since a friend of his mother's had come to stay and her nanny had insisted on bathing him and her little girl together. She was five, maybe six, himself seven, and he'd hated being treated like a baby, but he had been intrigued by that slit between her legs, which was all he remembered.

Mary was more grown up. There was fair hair down there, not much, but some, and she had slight breasts, which she suddenly squeezed with both hands.

'Come on then. You going in those? Take them off, you'll never get them dry before we get home and they'll start asking questions.'

He thought of Hooker in the nudist camp. His talk about not caring. Why should he care? So he took them off, but felt brave.

Mary didn't give him a second look. She didn't wait either, but waded into the water up to her waist.

'It's lovely and warm.'

Then she launched herself out towards the reeds where it was deep.

'Mary, careful . . .'

She turned round in the water, looked at him and laughed. She *could* swim.

'I've only been pretending I couldn't swim to frighten you, silly. I come here quite often.'

Mary had this strange unexpected sense of humour.

Not to be outdone he dived in, which was risky because all sorts of rubbish might be lying at the bottom and he might carve himself up on an old bicycle or something.

But there was nothing, only mud.

The water was icy, not warm at all, and he didn't like the slime that came off the reeds. He splashed around a bit then got out shivering. 'It's too cold for me,' he said.

She didn't answer, but went on swimming in small circles, stopping to hang on to the side of the canoe, studying the faded name.

'What's it mean, "Xanadu"?' she asked.

'In Xanadu did Kublai Khan

A stately pleasure dome decree . . .?
It's a poem by Samuel Taylor Coleridge.'

She shook her head, embarrassed by her ignorance, but not that much.

She came out of the water and, for a moment, she looked quite wonderful, gleaming wet and white in the sun. Her young body stirred something in him and instinctively he cupped his hands over himself.

It was extraordinary to think that it could go through in there, 'fit snugly' as Hooker had said.

'What would your Granny say if she knew we was swimming naked?'

'I expect she'd be rather shocked.'

'Madame Rainbow wouldn't be. She's French.'

She wiped the water off herself with the flat of her hands then put on her knickers and her dress and threw her shoes into the canoe.

He put on his blue briefs and bundled his other clothes on top of her shoes, and they both got into the canoe at the same time.

He should have known she could swim because he had seen her out in boats before. She'd rather made a fool of him, but that was all right. He didn't really mind.

He pushed out and paddled more vigorously, heading upstream. As his bows drew level with the edge of the boat house he swung the canoe out, then sharply in so that he sailed straight between the old punt and the indoor jetty.

Mary helped him tie up and handed him his clothes and her shoes. When they were both standing on the boardwalk and he was putting on his T-shirt, she quite unexpectedly got hold of his hand and guided it up her dress and inside her knickers.

He blushed as never before, felt himself go puce from his neck to his forehead. She guided his fingers between her legs where it was warm and soft, and then he realized she was reaching for him.

'Have you ever tried it?' she asked.

His throat was so tight he couldn't answer.

'I haven't,' she said, then she pulled his hand away,

turned abruptly and sat down to put on her shoes.

'I'd like to,' she went on, 'but not with you.'

He wasn't sure why, only sure that he was very relieved. His heart was beating so fast he thought he might be sick.

'It's not that I wouldn't want to with you,' she continued. 'But we can't, can we? Not us being who we are.'

He looked at her, uncertain he had understood what she meant.

'Who are we?' he asked.

'Brother and sister,' she answered simply. 'Didn't you think I knew? I've known for years.'

chapter thirteen

Upstairs in her bedroom, where she had grown up and had always felt secure, Sarah sat on the window seat and looked down on the familiar Dutch garden, the neatly trimmed yew hedge, the lawns and the river beyond.

Alexander appeared below, ambling slowly towards the boat house; a small, slight, vulnerable figure, who hardly gave the impression of being a threat to the calm and serene life she so much longed for.

But she had deceived him and lied to him and she felt guilty. That guilt was the threat to the desired tranquillity, not Alexander.

At least he had left her alone for the past few days. She had expected him to ply her with more questions, make things difficult, but he had said nothing.

Nothing at all.

His silence, perhaps, was the calm before another storm, like Richard's calm on the last night they had been together.

Was he like Richard?

Was there instability there?

Ten o'clock in the small Abingdon hotel where they had

gone to escape the world, the bar still open downstairs and the two of them lying in bed in satisfied silence.

That had been serenity.

Then he had become violent so suddenly.

He had leapt out of bed, nude, his body glistening with sweat, and he had hit the dressing table mirror with such fury that it had shattered completely.

'I hate myself, I hate myself . . .' he'd shouted, and, demented, he had torn the curtains down and smashed his fist through the window at his reflection.

She had screamed, and help had come immediately. Two men from the bar had burst into the room and had grabbed him. He was covered with blood, a jagged piece of glass had stuck in his arm just below the elbow. He had fought like a tiger, but one of the men, a burly farmer, had delivered a blow and Richard had collapsed on the floor.

'Are you alright Miss? . . . Mrs? . . .'

She had cowered under the sheets. The police had come, Richard had been taken to hospital and she had gone with him in the ambulance. When he had regained consciousness he had just said, 'I'm sorry. I have these fits. I forgot to take my Thorazine.'

The next day his whole medical history had come to light and she had recoiled, terrified for the child inside her.

She watched Alexander change direction and climb over the fence to cross Hernmead meadow.

Was he going to visit Mary?

Her heart sank at the thought that there might be a bond between them; the girl seemed so dim.

Maybe she should take him right away from here, take him abroad, not just for a holiday, but for a longer period of time.

On Friday morning a grey-haired man, a few years older than herelf, had come into the shop looking for premises in the area. He had been extremely pleasant and amusing, if a little camp. 'In antiques, dear, doing frightfully well. Specialize in art nouveau, art deco. Export to the States, that sort of thing.'

He had taken her out to lunch down the road and had seemed surprisingly interested in her as a woman. By the time they had got to the coffee and brandies, they had mapped out an ideal partnership: her house and her shop in London, his sixteenth-century abbey in the Quantocks, and countless trips to New York, Florida and California.

She hadn't mentioned Alexander, but had admitted to being the divorced wife of General Sir Geoffrey Saranson.

'Oh, I love soldiers,' he'd joked. 'Tin ones, and not sailors at all,' and he'd reached for her hand, not letting go of it till it had come to him paying the bill.

An ideal husband?

She stared into the sun and at the sparkling strip of river and thought she could see Mary and Alexander silhouetted in the canoe.

How could she sell her son the idea of a new father when she hadn't been able to sell him the idea of an old one?

There was a gentle tap at the door and her mother came in.

'Well, Sarah, Alexander seems to have behaved himself at school. I thought his report quite good. It is a very great relief. Father was terribly worried. One just doesn't know what that boy might do.'

'I think he's all right now. He's just been a bit confused. Our fault really, Mummy. We should have told him the truth years ago and then he wouldn't have started asking questions.'

'I don't think he should ever know the truth. I don't think anyone should.'

The wall. The narrow-minded stubborness again.

'Because his father is working class or because he's insane?' She threw the little dart. It helped dampen the mounting anger.

'Oh don't take that aggressive attitude dear, it's so tiring.'

Both fell silent.

'He's gone out playing with his half-sister,' Sarah said, looking out of the window again.

'Who has, dear?'

It was really quite pointless trying to rile either of them, they were so hopelessly lost in their own little worlds.

'Never mind,' she said, and crossed over to the bedside table to get herself a cigarette.

'How many are you smoking now dear, per day?'
'About twenty.'
Mother had been asking that question for the last hundred years.
She ignored it, lit the cigarette and deliberately inhaled a lethal dose of nicotine.
'I'm thinking of re-marrying,' she said suddenly.
This was what she had come down to tell them, but she hadn't meant to put it so abruptly.
'*What* darling? Who?'
Her mother's complete repertoire of expressions displayed themselves as her hopes and worst fears flashed through her mind. Rich man, poor man, beggerman, black.
'He's quite well off, an antique dealer from Somerset with his own business. He wants to open a retail shop in London and we met when he came to look at "Time Immemorial". We've talked of going into partnership, but there might be a little more to it than that.'
'How long have you known him?'
'Six weeks,' she lied.
'That's a bit soon to talk about getting married, isn't it?'
'Yes, of course it is. I just thought I'd let you know what was going on in my mind. We haven't discussed it very seriously.'
'But has he actually proposed?'
'Not in so many words.'
Her mother would now think she had gone to bed with him. It was farcical. Everything she was saying was a sort of desperate need to make her life interesting to her parents.
Did she need attention that much?
'Are you going to mention it to father?'
'Oh, not yet. It's just that I sometimes feel a more stable home life might benefit Alexander.'
'Well we all know that dear, but these things can't be forced. I mean, you can't marry the first man that comes along just for Alexander's sake.'
She might as well be seventeen for the level of maturity that was involved in conversations with her mother. They could never get down to the raw truth. He would hardly be

the first man who had come along. He'd be about the hundredth man who *hadn't* come along!

'What's his name?' her mother asked.

'James Hobson.'

'Oh, that sounds nice and English. Will you be bringing him here to see us one day?'

'Yes, Mummy. I'll introduce you before I actually take the plunge.'

Mother left the room after reminding her what time they would have tea.

Sarah went back to the window and stood looking out at the darkening shadows of the sunset.

A marriage of convenience?

Would James Hobson be at all interested in her, really? Could she imagine herself embracing him even, going to bed? He didn't attract her physically.

And how would he take to Alexander?

'I have a son by the way. Thirteen, at public school. Stays with my parents during the holidays, so you won't see him much.'

A lifetime spent dreaming of being free of the child she should adore.

Maybe the canoe would tip over again and this time he would really drown.

And she shook her head at the thought. The triggering of such images was fearful. From drowned child to ambulance to funeral. Tears welled up in her eyes as she visualized a small coffin being lowered into a dark grave.

Christ, she was losing her mind.

She looked over to the boat house. Alexander was just coming out with Mary, both behaving as guiltily as hell.

Maybe they'd just had it off. And she laughed at such a ridiculous speculation.

Alexander found his father behind the model theatre in a canvas chair, feet apart, hands clasped between his knees, head well back, eyes staring at the ceiling, mouth wide open with a little white saliva dribbling from the corner of his lips.

'Excuse me?' he whispered.

The head turned, the eyes blinked, looked at him vacantly, then recognition seeped into the brain.

It was an unpleasant moment, the first time Alexander had seen anyone so senile.

'Hallo Arthur . . .'

Alexander smiled. Had his father forgotten his name or did he think he was someone else.

'Hallo,' said Alexander gently. 'How are you today?'

'Not well, not well. I have had bad news. Bad news without good news. Usually one has bad news with good news but I have only had the bad.'

He sat up, wiped his mouth, looked down at the floor, then round at Alexander, colour coming back into his cheeks, a smile playing on his lips.

'Your name's not Arthur, it's Alexander, isn't it?'

'Yes.'

'And you're my son.'

At last!

'That's right.'

'That's right,' Richard repeated.

It was very unsettling.

'A friend of mine in another hospital got bad news and good news once. Do you want to know about it?'

'Yes.'

'The doctor came to see him one day and said "I have bad news and good news" . . .' he paused again, shifted in the chair and tried to control a grin. '"Which would you like first, the bad or the good news?" "The bad news," my friend said. "The bad news," the doctor said, "Is that we have to amputate both your legs." My friend took some time to recover from that one. "What's the good news?" he asked. "The good news is," the doctor said proudly, "that I've managed to sell your shoes to another patient."'

He went into peels of laughter then stopped abruptly.

'Humour helps to get over one's own fears you know, one's own anxieties. My bad news is a little bit worse than that. I'm going to die.'

He was obviously obsessed with death.

'I wonder what I will be looking at in a year's time and

whether there will be any windows to look out of? Have you ever thought about death Alexander? What it will be like? Whether one goes on, or whether one stops . . . for ever. It's hard to contemplate, isn't it? Nothingness. It will be like going to sleep but never even waking up to realize that one had been dreaming. One will just not wake up, that's all. I suppose I fear pain. Is that it, do you think? Pain? But then if one is in pain, death must come as a relief.'

He turned and heaved himself up from the chair and in one leap crossed the room and heaved himself up on the work-bench. He dangled his legs watching his toes touch the floor.

'You're too young to think about all that. The only danger you're in is being knocked down by a bus, or getting involved in an accident. Does your mother still drive?'

'Yes.'

'She drives quite well. I don't think you need have any fears in that direction.'

He smiled at Alexander for a long time, trying to gauge what he was thinking, perhaps. But it wasn't that.

'I have a brain tumour you see, which is growing. Brain cancer really. Intercranial neoplasm; an abcess which creates lesions within the skull. I quite like the language used in medical dictionaries, don't you? Ipsilateral retrobulbar neuritis with a central scotoma, and optic atrophy often occurs.'

He sounded like Hooker.

'Objective contralateral sensory changes may or may not appear. I learn these things by heart to argue with the doctors.'

Alexander didn't know what to say, so he didn't say anything.

'Glad you came alone. I'm very worried about Mary. She won't be able to manage without me.'

He stopped dangling his legs and looked straight at Alexander again for a long time. A serious expression came into his eyes; a kindly, serious expression that Alexander could respect.

'I talk too much Alexander. You must understand that. You and Mary are my only visitors I can chat to without feeling I mustn't. My father comes to visit me once every now and again, but he treats me like a demented infant. I am, actually, quite sane. It's only that I get very depressed sometimes and they keep me here so that I won't do anything stupid, like kill myself. It comes in phases, the depression, and it passes with the help of drugs. But I do worry about Mary because little Timmy is going to be a burden on her for the rest of her life, because he has brain damage too. That's the real bad news. When Mary's mother is too old to cope, Timmy will be his sister's responsibility and that really isn't fair. Is it?'

The dark brown eyes suddenly looked at him demanding a response.

'No . . .' Alexander agreed.

'I like Mary, she's a simple girl, but she has a heart and it will just floor her. Unless you can help.'

He wasn't sure how he could help, so he asked, 'In what way?'

'Oh, I don't know. You're intelligent. You can help. I'll think of something, now that I know I can rely on you. What's that school like, the one they've incarcerated you in? Are those institutions as bad as they make out? Or are you enjoying it?'

Alexander shrugged his shoulders. 'It's all right.'

'Is it true they auction little boys?'

'Sort of,' Alexander said, hoping he wasn't blushing.

'Did they auction you?'

'Yes . . .'

'Well, that happens everywhere, one way or another. It's funny though, how curious one is about such things. Public Schools hold so many mysteries for those who have never been. Like wondering whether a Scotsman wears anything under his kilt. It's about as important, too.'

He clamped his feet together and lifted both his legs to look at his worn shoes. 'Weary, aren't they?' he said. 'But comfortable.'

Alexander moved over to look round the back of the theatre, at the tabs, the intricate details behind the curtain.

'What about your step-father, your divorced step-father, the General? Do you know him?'

'I met him once,' Alexander said.

'He did the right thing, that's for sure. Breaking with Sarah immediately like that. It was the honourable thing to do; the conduct of a self-respecting officer and gentleman so that everyone knew exactly where they stood. No lies, no deceptions. That's what's affected you, isn't it Alexander, the deceptions and the lies? Because you have been affected, haven't you, or you wouldn't have come to see me? I never understood why Sarah tried to keep me a secret.'

'I think Grandma and Grandpa . . .'

'Stopped her? Because I was mad? The boy mustn't know his father's mad or he'll have nightmares. They've never even bothered to try and understand the madness. Besides, I don't think it was only that. I think it had to do with me being a common house-painter. Can you imagine what it does to people like that? To learn that their beloved and sacred daughter, heiress to Hernmead Court and wife of a General, a future Lady Saranson . . . can you imagine what it means when they learn that she has bedded down with a common house-painter and that this not only results in a divorce, but a bastard son as well? Such people don't recover. It crumbles the very foundations of their whole life. The sad thing is that your mother never recovered either.'

Alexander looked out of the window at the black branches of the cedar trees, then at his father. He had a good face, a kind face.

'Why are you looking at me like that?'

Alexander shrugged, embarrassed.

'It must be strange for you, but it's just as strange for me looking at you, you know. Blood of my blood. All that. What do you think of me so far?'

'I think you're very nice,' he said. Then quickly added, 'You're more than that, but I can't put it into words.'

A large hand reached out and tousled his hair.

'It must be very difficult for you, and I appreciate you coming here alone. I appreciate that very much.'

Richard got off the bench and dusted the bottom of his jeans. 'Shall we go for a walk?'

It was a warm, windy day with fast low clouds sweeping across a leaden sky. His father put an arm round his shoulders, ushered him out of the workshop door and walked along a path that circled the hospital garden.

'Tell me about yourself. Are you ambitious in any particular direction?'

'I thought I wanted to be a doctor at one time.'

'Did you? But not now?'

'No. I also wanted to be a soldier.'

'Ah! Searching for an identity, was that it? The indispensable need of an identity. I've looked for one all my life and have never found one. Two things motivate man in life, Alexander: a search for an identity, and sex. Some people manage to combine both and live happily ever after. Your mother nearly did, you see, she got very close to it, marrying a General. "I'm an officer's wife and I get screwed regularly on Saturday nights after manoeuvres." Did you know that that was her main objection to the gentleman – he took his military discipline to bed with him? Once a week, then once a fortnight, then once a month and not at all when he was abroad, of course, because then he would have himself an Irish colleen or a German tart. Those sort of men destroy women. But then I destroyed your mother. I was the one who destroyed her. Do you follow me?'

Alexander nodded.

'Has anyone told you the facts of life?'

'Yes, thank you,' Alexander replied.

His father was going on a bit.

'I'm rambling, aren't I? You're very sensitive. But you must forgive me, I am obsessed by the thought of Timmy growing up a monster and plaguing everyone's life. You must help me.'

'How?'

'How? Does the word "euthanasia" mean anything to you?'

'It's something to do with killing sick people.'

'Exactly that. Killing sick people, for their own good, to stop the suffering. I really don't see the need for Mary to suffer, nor Mary's mother; all their troubles could be eliminated so simply. Don't you think it would be easy to kill a little baby before he grows older? No one need know. Babies die accidentally all the time, don't they? Suffocation, a pillow, like the princes in the tower. But Mary will need help. She intends to get rid of her little brother, at my suggestion, with my encouragement, but I don't think she'll be able to carry it through by herself. She will need to be organized, and you are a born organiser.' He stopped, turned Alexander round by the shoulders to study him.

'Do you think you could kill, Alexander?'

Alexander shrugged. He had no idea what to say.

'I nearly killed once,' his father went on, 'but wasn't brave enough to carry it through. That's why I'm here. Had I killed I would have escaped and might have got away with it. Instead, she reported me and I was certified.'

'Mary's mother?' Alexander asked for confirmation.

'Mary's mother. I got it into my head that Mary wasn't my daughter, you see. Jealousy. I need people to be loyal to me. Like sons and daughters are loyal to their fathers and do what they are asked, however crazy it might seem.'

He was putting his message over very clearly. Alexander acknowledged it with a nod, and looked away, needing time alone to sort everything out. Was he listening to the ravings of a madman or was it all logically reasoned out?

'Now, I've talked enough about myself and my fears for one day. What have you been doing?'

'Nothing very much,' Alexander said, as they walked on, and he started telling his father what he had been doing, with Mary, without Mary, but realized he wasn't listening. He stopped talking, and they walked on in silence for quite a while.

'Perhaps Timmy could be drowned?' his father said suddenly. 'A boating accident, something like that. Do you think you could help Mary take care of Timmy? It's the only favour I'll ever ask of you Alexander.'

They reached a garden bench and Richard sat down on it, first sprawling all over it exaggerating a tiredness, then grabbing hold of Alexander's wrist and pulling him closer to sit next to him where he could be hugged.

Alexander found it an effort to relax and allow this huge man to be affectionate.

The bench faced a square of green lawn which had a notice requesting no one to walk on it.

'Do you now know what that is there? It's the old cemetery. They buried the Victorian lunatics right under that grass, that's why it's so green.'

Alexander thought of Hooker, nearly mentioned him, then decided not to.

'Mary told me about your war game,' his father started up again, 'and the way you organize everybody. I admire that, the ability to organize. I was never a capable commander. I expect you've inherited that from your maternal great grandfather. Inheritance often hops a generation or two you know. You probably haven't inherited anything from me at all, or your mother, but everything from your great grandfather. You're probably a Midley through and through, and he must have murdered quite a few people to have made all that money. There's a crime in every millionaire they say, and certainly in every politician. Had he lived longer, old Midley would have become Prime Minister I expect. Think how many people they murder from behind the safety of a fountain pen. Such power! But to kill with one's own hands, subtly, to rid the world of unhappiness; that should be considered as an achievement. There ought to be a Nobel prize for euthanasia.'

The visitor's bell sounded from up inside the large grey building.

'You'll have to go now,' his father said. 'Were you waiting for it anxiously?'

'Not at all,' Alexander protested. And he hadn't, and he didn't want his father to think he had.

'I ramble on, I know. But your visits do me good. The doctors have said so. They know who you are. I tell them everything, my analysts.'

They walked across the permitted lawn, joining the other patients and visitors on the terrace steps and following them through the French windows into the main recreation room.

'I have two analysts you know. A man and a woman. The man is very keen on euthanasia, but the woman isn't. I find that interesting. It has something to do with the male killer instinct perhaps; the ability to contemplate the disposal of someone else's life clearly and without emotion.'

In the entrance hall his father unexpectedly bent down and gave him a kiss on the forehead and squeezed both his hands. There were tears in his eyes and he tried a brave smile.

'I'm very proud of you Alexander,' he said, then turned and ran up the stairs to take up his position at the window on the first landing. Getting there before other patients seemed to be very important to him.

Alexander headed for the door. He felt empty, sad, not sure. Was it the mention of the two analysts. Somehow he hadn't imagined his father being examined regularly. It brought home the reality of the medical treatment he must be undergoing.

A bearded man with ginger hair and glasses, wearing a white coat, stopped him.

'You're Alexander, aren't you? Richard Northey's son?' he asked in a broad Scottish accent.

'Yes?'

An arm across the shoulders, an affectionate pat on the back.

'I'm his doctor. Just thought you should know how well your father has been lately and how cheerful he's become since you've been visiting him. I hope you can keep doing so, there is such a marked improvement.'

His father had been talking about him, then.

'I'm not sure how often I can come,' Alexander said. 'It's not always easy for me to find the time.'

'To find the time or to get away from your grandparents? I know all about you Alexander, every detail. I probably know more about you than you know yourself. But a secret's a secret with me. I'm only concerned about the well-being of my patient, and right now it wouldn't suit him to have them know you were coming here. He knows they'd stop you.'

They were right in the centre of the hall, people were passing to left and right.

'He has some pretty wild ideas sometimes, your father, but much of what he says makes sense. He has a great mind if we can only get it to function properly again. So the more you are able to do for him the better. He needs to feel that someone outside is doing his bidding, that he is not completely lost and locked up.'

Another white-coated doctor across the hall beckoned.

'I have to go now,' he said. 'Good luck with all your projects anyway, and don't let him down.'

Alexander left the hospital and waited at the bus stop, aware that it was now a beautiful afternoon, yet not able to enjoy it. He turned and saw the inmates up at the first floor window, his father there in the middle, waving, rather stupidly.

The bus came, he got on, looked out, waved, not knowing whether he could still be seen.

He felt very unsettled.

He wanted to believe that his father was stable, but he was mad. He was in hospital, he was taking drugs, his mind was not functioning properly, and mentioning murder was part of the insanity.

Yet the doctor had said three things very clearly: he needs to feel that someone is doing his bidding; much of what he says makes sense; good luck with all your projects and don't let him down.

Did killing little Timmy make sense if Mary was going to be saddled with a half-wit for the rest of her life?

For the first time during these holidays he wanted to see Hooker. He needed someone else's opinion. 'Great idea,' Hooker would say, 'I know where I can get you a miniature coffin half price.'

Hooker wouldn't be any help at all.

He got off at the Three Horse Shoes and walked round the back to the car park where he had left his bicycle. He then cycled home, the long way, round Hermit's Wood to come down Gifford's hill passing the Northey cottages.

No sign of life, the door closed.

He stopped, got off his bike, leaned it against the wall and went in through the open gate.

He needed to see her, needed to talk to someone who knew his father.

Mary answered his knock on the door, holding the baby. It

was so pale and white it was nearly translucent and its awful domed forehead was repulsive. She was feeding it, holding a gurgling bottle to its wet, dribbling lips.

'I just went to see your Dad,' Alexander said.

'Thought you had.'

'He said . . .'

'That we ought to get rid of this.' She nodded at the baby. 'I've worked it all out. We'll do it so's it looks like a drowning accident in the river.'

'What sort of accident?'

'I'll say I was sitting in a boat with him and the boat tipped over. Everyone thinks I'm stupid so they'll believe me.'

'But just dropping a baby into the river doesn't mean it'll drown. It might float.'

'Oh, I'll hold him under before you find him. I'll drown him, then you'll find him, all wet. You'll be the hero, see, and I'll just be silly and scared as they'd expect me to be.'

She had worked it all out. She was always much brighter than he thought.

'When?' he asked.

'Best at night. You can say you heard some screams, my screams. I'll wander around all wet in the fields till they find me, but you find the baby first; it'll be easy.'

She pulled the bottle out of the baby's mouth and it started screaming straight away.

'Oh belt up you little sod!' she said through clenched teeth, and shoved the teat back in its mouth.

'I'll signal you from here, you can see the light from your room. I'll flash three times.'

'Twice,' he corrected.' Three times is too obvious.'

'Right. The signal will mean I'm taking Timmy down to the boat house. We can wedge him under the old punt or somewhere till he's dead, then I'll drop in the water too and run off. You find him and take him up to the house saying you heard me scream.'

'But what will you say?'

'I'll say the baby couldn't sleep so I took him down to rock him in the boat and fell over in the dark.'

'Why don't you come up to the house then? Wet, saying you've had the accident?'

'Cause I wouldn't. I'd be scared wouldn't I . . .? And I'd try and rescue the baby and scream. And you'd come and help, then I run away. That's what would happen. That's the story. Dad said you'd help and I can't do it alone.'

A look of panic came into her eyes.

'What about your mother?'

'She's out at Bingo tomorrow night. She always goes Wednesdays and doesn't get back till late. We'll do it then.'

'So soon?'

He wasn't ready.

But she was. Clearly. If it was going to be done, then the sooner the better.

He left her in the doorway, got back on his bicycle and pedalled off down the lane, through the Hernmead gates, up the drive, the derelict barn to the left used by Simcock to park his tractors, Five Acre field on the right with the Simcock cows, the line of willows and, in the distance, on the other side of the river, the railway line along which a yellow and blue express would sometimes speed through on its way to London or Bristol.

He stood on the pedals to get up the last slope to the cobbled courtyard, then freewheeled straight down into the garage where he leaned the bike against the wall. The old Morris was out, so Grandma was probably shopping in the village; but the Rover was there so Grandpa would be in the study doing something boring like getting in a muddle with his stamp collection, which was just as well because Alexander needed to be alone.

He ran up the steps and in through the kitchen. Empty. Hilda in her room, no doubt; the place spotless, quiet, a smell of summer fruit in the air; pleasant.

He went up the back stairs to the first, then the second landing, keeping his footfalls quiet. He tiptoed along the corridor past Hilda's room and opened the end window which gave out on to the flat roof over Grandpa's dressing room. From there it was dangerous swinging himself up and over the gable, but he had done it, unseen, enough times, and now he sat quite still astride the narrow roof, his back against the chimney stack looking down on the whole estate and the surrounding countryside.

Up here he felt as though he were one with the universe, with God, and he badly needed that sort of company right now to think over his future which, at this moment in time, was clearly not in his own hands.

He felt he was involved in a chess game he did not fully understand because no one knew they were playing it; but he could see them taking part, as principal movers, as advisers, as pieces: Grandpa, Grandma, Mother, The Buzz, his father and now Mary.

He could ignore Mary; he need not help her in the proposed murder. He could delay her until he had seen his father again. His father would then either have forgotten what he had said, in which case it would be a confirmation of his madness, or he would still be locked into the idea, in which case it might well have to be reported to the doctor.

Was his role in life to help his own father through the more disastrous periods of his madness and was that why fate had demanded that they should meet? His own character, as his father had said, was probably inherited from his great grandfather, a man of power, of business acumen, of intelligence; a man who could make faultless decisions.

Successful men were masters of their own destiny and he had to be a master of his. The following twenty-four hours would be hideous, like waiting for an exam, like waiting for a beating at Clairmount if he allowed himself to be ruled by Mary. If, on the other hand, he made the decisions, told her what to do and when to do it, the elimination of the child Timothy might prove rather exciting, something to achieve which would be clever in its total secrecy. He would be pitting his wits against more than parents or prefects or masters, he would be deceiving everyone in authority, the police, the Government itself.

And he couldn't see a flaw in Mary's plan. It all made sense. If anything did go wrong it would be of her doing. He would be safe, if there was failure. But he didn't want failure, he want to go back to his father and say the deed had been done, that there had been an accident.

It was unnerving the way Mary had thought it all out so well. He liked the directness of her idea, its simplicity. He might well have complicated things too much enjoying the idea of duping his adults. But she had it just right.

A chilly wind blew up and woke him from his daydreams. He slipped himself off the gable roof on to the parapet and stepped in through the window as silently as he had gone out.

With his secret he would now join the rest of the world, the planned crime giving him a feeling of confidence he had never before experienced. From now on he would be someone to be reckoned with. He would discard his grandparents, his mother, Hilda, the Simcock brothers. They were going through life like zombies and, unlike himself, achieving nothing.

It was seven o'clock, Grandpa would be in front of the television watching some news programme and Alexander badly needed company. The old fool could at least provide that.

He slid down the stairs, leaning heavily on the polished bannisters and leaping four steps at a time, then went into the drawing room where his grandfather was seated in the wing-back chair trying to figure out, after years of owning the damn thing, how the remote control worked.

It was grunting time, acknowledgement that Alexander was a member of the family and therefore allowed to join in the viewing.

'Where've you been?'

'On the Simcock farm.'

'You've got to be careful there you know .. farms aren't what they used to be.'

The man was unbelievable.

'Interested in this programme then?'

'Any cricket?' Alexander asked.

No reaction. It was a News programme about West Germany and South Africa and Washington and all the other boring things they always went on about. But he quite liked some of the pictures and there had been another terrorist attack at an airport and the cameras were dwelling on the smears of blood and shattered glass that covered vast expanses of marbled floor – fascinating.

Every day, somewhere, people were killing other people for a belief. So why not him? Grandpa, who had decided to light a cigarette and was searching for his lighter in all his pockets and down the side of the chair, missed it all, so no comment was made, then the Home Secretary came in to justify the sending back to Pakistan of an impoverished family and Grandpa started fuming at the interviewer for even questioning the obvious need to get rid of all foreigners from these sacred British shores.

It was tiring.

It had been a long day and he was quite suddenly very pleased to be here in the comfort of his own family home, away from thoughts of Mary and her mother and her wretched baby. If he did get involved in the killing he would fear an uncontrollable guilt. And what if there was a God and a Judgment Day? Thou shalt not kill.

He got up and made noises about going to the bathroom, but actually went to his grandfather's study to look up 'Euthanasia' in the dictionary.

> The action of inducing a gentle and easy death, especially with reference to a proposal that the law should sanction the putting painlessly to death of those suffering from incurable and extremely painful diseases.

It helped.

It would be a defence.

He slipped back into the drawing room and sat in the depths of the sofa. Sport now, golf, a Spaniard hitting the white ball half a mile straight into a tiny hole, or nearly. Grandpa didn't like it. Golf was a British game and, like cricket, to be won only by British champions.

Something moving to his left made Alexander turn round and look out of the window. To his horror he saw Mary standing on the terrace waving at him, making faces, signalling him to come out and join her urgently.

Had she gone completely off her rocker?

He got up calmly and started for the door.

'Where are you going?' demanded his grandfather.

He checked that Mary had gone.

'Upstairs to my room.'

'Thought you wanted to watch the cricket?'

'I want to put on my slippers.'

Grunt.

He opened and closed the door quietly and slipped out of the house by the side entrance into the garden. Mary was right there waiting for him.

There was a smile dancing on her face, the sort of smile that demanded a pat on the back. She had done something clever, he could tell, at least something she thought was clever and that could mean disaster.

'Mother's gone out, so I got on with it.'

'Got on with what?'

'The babe's in a basket waiting for you in the boat house. I've put him under that canvas thing in the corner.

'He's there now?'

She nodded, biting her lower lip.

'But there are people on the river, they'll hear it screaming for God's sake!'

'Oh, he won't be screaming,' she said. 'He's already dead.'

He stared at her, having heard her perfectly clearly, knowing that she meant what she had said, but not wanting to understand.

'What did you say?'

'Timmy's dead. He suffocated, somehow, didn't he? Now all you have to do is push him under the water and let him go. I'll say someone stole him from his pram. Let others find him, but I've got to make myself scarce just in case Ma comes back.'

And she was gone, spinning round on her feet and running lightly down the path, disappearing behind the greenhouses.

He was numbed.

A dead baby was under the tarpaulin in the boat house.

He turned to look up at the windows. Nobody was likely to have seen them talking to each other but it was best to get back to the television.

He sneaked into the drawing room and quietly sat down.

The sports report was still on, a cricket match in which he pretended to take a fiendish interest, but the images did not register. He was trying to control the panic going on inside his head and his stomach. He would have to go casually down to the boat house and find the dead baby and put him under the water for at least half an hour. Wedge him under the punt, as Mary had said.

Christ!

A cricket captain was being interviewed which might last another God knows what. He had to get out. He stood up.

'Aren't you interested in this Alexander. I thought you wanted to see it?'

'I want to go out in the canoe before it gets dark.'

'Strange chap. You can never stay put in one place for more than two minutes. Just like your mother.'

Which wasn't true. He was always accusing his daughter of never moving, of always sitting around, always lying in bed, of being the laziest cow in Christendom. It didn't matter what he said to the old man anyway, it would be forgotten in seconds.

He left the house and checked a desire to run.

Twenty past seven, not too much time before supper.

What frightened him about Mary was that she had been so impulsive. He had noticed that in the war game. Impossible for her to explain what she was going to do, or wanted to do, then suddenly she'd be off with some strange idea which had sometimes floored him because it was quite intelligent. Like the time she had got one of the farm labourers to push her in a wheelbarrow, covered with hay, so that she could surprise Damian and capture him.

Of course, now it could be explained. She had inherited her brains from her father. Like father like daughter like son . . . like brother!

But what about her getting all wet?

He'd have to try and see her again before dark . . . Jesus . . . she had acted too quickly! Was she supposed to have dropped him in the river by accident, or had he been stolen?

He slowed his pace down as he neared the boat house in

case someone was around, lovers in the long grass, for instance. He had read that they could often be the deadliest of witnesses as they were always hiding like criminals themselves.

He opened the boat house door and stepped in.

There was nothing different that he could spot. The tarpaulin in the corner did not seem to have been moved. The old punt was there, the canoe bobbing up and down to the movement of the lapping water, and the evening sun, bright yellow, reflecting off the water on to the underside of the beamed roof.

He closed the door and stood there in the stillness, breathing in the familiar Thames dampness.

Under the heavy canvas which had at one time covered the family launch that Grandpa had sold, he would find a dead baby.

It could be unpleasant if he allowed it to be, but he had to be practical, so he crossed over the boardwalk, took hold of a corner of the stiff faded green tarpaulin and looked down on something quite astonishing.

Baby Timmy, dark blue round the lips and white cheeked was tied down in a shallow wicker basket by a network of strings to which had been taped a garland of wild flowers, and round his neck hung a crude wooden crucifix.

chapter fourteen

Mary had gone stark raving mad.

What was it supposed to be?

Had she done this to prove it was a mercy killing. Christ! It looked more like a religious sacrifice.

Alexander crouched down to look at the baby and the intricate way it had been secured in the basket, the type that was sold in kitchen shops but seemed to serve no real purpose.

The little body was wrapped tightly in its white cellular blanket, its jelly head sticking out of the top. Sown to the basket was the crude cross which he now saw was made of platted reeds, like those Hilda stuck behind the Jesus above her bed on Palm Sundays. The baby was strapped down by thick, green garden string which encircled everything, and a net work of different coloured wools had been latticed around the whole bundle to which larkspur, bindweed, and michaelmas daisies had been taped.

What did Mary expect him to do? Put it in the water and hope it would float away?

He reached out to lift it and found it quite heavy. If he had a knife he might cut the strings and release the body, but then what would he do with the basket, which was evidence. He could hardly burn it. And the moment the baby was found missing it was certain there would be a search.

He stared at the dead face, which was changing colour and getting darker. It looked more like a plasticine model than the real thing. He reached out to touch a cheek with the back of his fingers and it felt very soft, still warm, and quite horrible.

He stood up, pushed the basket to the edge of the boards with his foot, and toppled it over so that it fell face down in the water with a splash.

There were bubbles, it rocked, but it stayed afloat, half an inch or so below the surface. To the innocent eye it looked like a large piece of cardboard or the top of a log, perhaps, certainly nothing extraordinary, though the green string was intriguing.

He took a boat hook from the punt and pushed the basket towards the open river, pushed it down, trying to submerge it, to release more bubbles, rocking it in the water.

When it reached the mainstream, he gave it an extra shove, but it hardly moved. It was just a piece of lifeless jetsam struck there for all to see. He realized there just wasn't enough current.

He got into his canoe, backed it out of the boat house and went off at great speed into the middle of the river.

There was no one around to speak of. A couple with a dog far down on the opposite bank, some people on the bridge, a cabin cruiser coming up river. He waited for it to pass, keeping the canoe between it and the overturned basket which started to bob up and down in the wake.

He backed and manoeuvred so that the canoe's bows slid over the basket, and started paddling. He made remarkable progress downstream, an innocent boy in an innocent canoe, and when he drew level with Hearn Creek he gently pushed the basket into the reeds and moved on.

Time and the river would have to do the rest.

Unhurried, he paddled on towards Mapledurham Lock for several hundred yards, crossed over to the south bank and paddled up using his well-practised flick, enjoying the gentle speed.

A steamer was coming up river now, holiday-makers crowding the top deck. If they passed the reeds and saw nothing he would consider his work well done.

He waited for the big boat to go by, watched the pale faced city dwellers breathing in the fresh country evening air, sunning their faces, pointing out ducks and trees and the Simcock cows as though they were famous landmarks.

Some school kids waved at him; he waved back aware of their envy. He was their age, he was in a canoe, carefree on the river every day, little did they know that right now he was hiding the evidence of a cold-blooded murder.

The steamer went on up towards Whitchurch Bridge, no one on deck screamed out that they had seen anything unusual. He crossed over to the north bank and sped past the reeds. The basket had gone, it had disappeared.

By the time he had got back to the boat house and had docked the Xanadu and had tidied up the tarpaulin, the awful deed seemed insignificant and ready to be forgotten. He ambled slowly across Five Acre field and along Gifford's Lane then round to the drive and into the house by the front door. It was a quarter to eight, time to sit down with his grandparents for supper. He let them know he was home and went into the lobby lavatory to wash his hands.

No blood, no damned spots.

It was all up to Mary now.

'What have you been doing today?' Grandma asked when he joined them at the table.

He made it as boring as possible.

'I went on my bicycle to Whitchurch and then Mapledurham. I saw a kestrel diving for a field mouse by Hermit's Wood. I went in my canoe to Pangbourne Lock and came back, and here I am.'

She wasn't listening. She was busy serving Grandpa with the Tuesday baked beans.

Mother had gone back to London and there was nothing to talk about, so nobody talked, and Grandpa chewed away noisily at his food.

After the meal they moved to the drawing room to watch television, and at the end of the news he got up like a good boy, pecked his grandmother on the powdered cheek, nodded the goodnight to his grandfather because no great show of affection was allowed, and went off to bed.

Tonight he wouldn't read, but would sit at his bedroom window and keep watch across Hernmead meadow for any signs of activity at the Northey cottage. By now Mary would have reported Timmy missing.

Though it was not yet night, Hilda had drawn the curtains and turned down the bed. He switched on the light, undressed quickly, put on his pyjamas and brushed his teeth at the wash-basin in the corner. He then turned the lights off, pulled back the curtain a little, knelt on the window seat and was surprised to see a great deal of activity out there. The flashing of a blue police light and people around the cottage.

He opened his cupboard and found his telescope. It was quite a good telescope, a birthday present two years back from Tante Louise, who always gave him the best presents. White plastic with brass mountings, he always kept it in its box. 'An expensive instrument, not a toy,' his grandfather had said. He had borrowed it from Alexander to study the stars and had bought several books on astronomy. The old fool had then spent nights searching the distant skies for planets and had cried victory on discovering Mars, until Alexander had pointed out that he was actually looking at a beacon on a high point of the Chilterns, after which he had lost interest.

Now Alexander focused on the cottage and saw a white police Rover with red and yellow trim, parked in front of the gate and a police officer talking on the car phone. Another was in the doorway. There was no sign of Mary, or her mother.

He watched intently for a good twenty minutes, then the police left and he followed the car's progress along Giffords Lane leading to the entrance of the Hernmead drive.

Were they coming to the house?

They might. They might easily come here to ask questions.

He folded the telescope, put it back in its box and in the cupboard, drew the curtains, got quickly into bed and switched on the bedside lamp. He reached for his book, the Spectrum instruction manual, opened it up and waited.

Unable to bear the tension, he got out of bed, opened his door carefully and tiptoed out into the corridor, down the stairs to the landing and the window which overlooked the driveway.

As he reached it he saw the police car turning slowly on the gravel. He ducked. It was just possible that the keen-eyed police might see him at the window.

He waited.

The front doorbell rang.

It took ages for Hilda to go and answer, and then he couldn't hear anything that was said because she closed the lobby door. She came back in, crossed the hallway to the drawing room, and he decided to make it back to his room.

Would they ask for him? Would they want to interview him? They should. He was the one active member of the household.

So what would he say?

He would have to be very careful, very vague, and be sure not to ask for Mary. He didn't, after all, know anything.

He got into bed and opened the manual, reading the first sentence on sound bleeps, not taking in a word. He listened hard to what was going on, then thought he heard Hilda's distinctive footfall in the corridor, a footfall he had listened for in the past whenever he was sick in bed being starved by the doctor and his grandmother because he had some gastric complaint and she had brought him the odd biscuit.

The door opened and Hilda poked her head in.

'Put your dressing gown on Alexander, and your slippers, and come downstairs. Your grandfather wants a word with you.'

'What about?'

'Yours is not to reason why but just to do,' she said smugly, not for the first time.

It was like being summoned to the House Captain's room.

On the way down the stairs he saw a police officer in the hall politely holding his cap under one arm and writing notes in his pocket-book. Grandmother and Grandfather were standing by the entrance door looking like Agatha Christie suspects.

'Ah, this is Alexander,' said Grandpa. 'Alexander this police officer wants to ask you a few questions.'

Alexander was a Public School boy and therefore only spoke when spoken to. He smiled, glad that he had complete control of himself, feeling so removed from the reality of what was happening and of his involvement in the crime that had been committed, that he could dwell on what might be called an admirable sang-froid.

Had he not seen the police at Mary's door he might have been frightened and jumped to the conclusion that someone had seen him with the dead baby, but this was clearly a routine enquiry following a filed missing person's report.

'You know Mary Northey, her mother and little brother Timothy?' the officer asked him.

'Yes sir.'

'Well, little Timothy Northey has gone missing and we're

asking everyone in the area if they saw him, or saw someone with him betwen the hours of five and eight this evening.'

He thought about it, looked intelligent, answered that he hadn't seen Timothy or anyone with him during that time.

'Do you know where you were between five and eight?'

'Yes, a bit everywhere, on the river, on my bicycle. I spent quite some time in my canoe round Whitchurch Lock.'

The policeman smiled. 'Still got the old canoe then, have you?'

The officer must have been one of those present at his Weir House dramatics. Somehow it annoyed him that the man thought him funny, thought him a little screwy perhaps; but he hoped his irritation didn't show.

'Thanks for your help. If you hear of anything, or remember anything about the baby, please get in contact with us.'

Hilda showed the officer to the door and when he was gone and they were alone, as a family, Grandpa said, 'Of course, if they will let that half-wit girl look after a baby such things are bound to happen.'

'Go up to bed now,' Grandma said, giving him another goodnight kiss.

And the incident was over.

Three days passed before anything more happened.

Because the weather turned cold and grey, windy and wet, Alexander did not venture near the river, did not see Mary Northey and did not hear whether the baby had been found or not, till the Simcock brothers came panting across the lawn, having climbed over the forbidden fence, waving, beckoning him to join them.

'They've found Timmy Northey. He's been drowned. He's in the river and the police are there now!'

He was painting in the morning room at the time, without much success. Irritated by the way the water just poured down the length of the paper and how the trees failed to look like trees, he was pleased to be relieved of the self-imposed artistic chore.

Of course, to refuse to go would be suggesting that he was

frightened. He had to behave naturally, and behaving naturally for a boy of his age, in his bored holiday circumstances, was to rush down and join in any excitement available.

He followed Michael and Keith Simcock down the path across the meadow and along the river bank straight to Hearn Creek where Mr Simcock, his wife, old Tom Northey, Connie Northey, two farm labourers and several other children, including Mary herself, were standing.

From under Whitchurch Bridge came the putt-putting of the Thames Conservancy launch, but from the opposite bank, where a police Rover was parked in the field, two officers were paddling across in a rubber dinghy.

Among the reeds Alexander saw the familiar basket right side up, but containing something brown and quite unrecognizable.

No one touched it, a local fisherman who had obviously found it seemed to be in charge, stopping anyone from going near it.

Alexander looked at Mary who, up till now, had not noticed his presence. She was staring at the basket, vacantly, nothing in her expression giving away any feelings of either fear, or sadness, anticipation or excitement.

The officers in the dinghy manoeuvred in among the reeds and one of them leaned over to grab the floating object. It was heavy, covered with slime, slippery, and he had difficulty in pulling it out of the water. Deciding that it was his duty to get on with it, regardless of whether he got his uniform or bright orange day-glo life jacket filthy, he heaved the basket up, exposing its contents to those on the bank for a moment.

Strapped inside with black string and dead flowers was a greyish bundle with a recognizable infant's head, its lips black, its orbits green, covered with mucous, a crucifix tied to its little chest.

Mrs Simcock turned away in horror, Mr Simcock reached out for her to comfort her, mesmerized by the fearful sight. Everyone gasped, Mary looked on, her eyes opening a trifle wider, her mouth dropping open for a moment, her mother instinctively throwing both hands up to cover her face.

Once the basket was on board the dinghy, the officers rowed off across the river just as the Thames Conservancy launch arrived a fraction too late, both officials looking somewhat peeved at having been beaten to it.

The small crowd remained quite still, numbed by the sickening discovery, and Mary drew away from them and came towards Alexander.

Standing right in front of him, her back to the others, she looked him straight in the eyes.

'Poor little mite,' she whispered, with no expression at all on her face. 'Do you think I should tell them who murdered him?'

Alexander looked at her, unsettled, sensing that she was accusing him.

'I didn't kill him,' he protested, 'You did.'

'No I didn't Alexander. He was only asleep when I put him in the basket. I drugged him, but he was only asleep. It was you who did the drowning.'

chapter fifteen

When Alexander woke up the next morning he realized he was as frightened as he had been on the first day at Clairmount, and Amhurst; the terror of authority threatening to impose itself on his life without him being able to do anything about it.

He would have to go and see Mary Northey, somehow.

He got out of bed and went to look out of the window. There were a number of cars parked outside the cottage which he hadn't expected this early, then, through his telescope, he saw that quite a number of the people milling around had cameras. It was the press.

Downstairs his grandparents had already started breakfast and were looking through the papers.

'We're in the news, Alexander! Headlines in the *Express*!' The headline was quite astonishing.'

REED BABY MURDER

And under it a quotation from the Bible.

And when she could no longer hide him she
took for him an ark of bulrushes and daubed
it with slime and with pitch, and put the
child therein, and she laid it in the flags
by the river's brink.

Alexander read on. Timmy Northey, five months, had been the victim of a ritual murder, the work of a religious fanatic or a satanic witches coven, which the police were investigating.

'It's going to be a witch hunt I'll tell you,' Grandpa said with certain relish. 'They'll round up all the Catholics and burn them at the stake Alexander. And quite right too.'

'I don't think you should make a joke of it dear,' Grandma said. 'It's quite a horrible story and it's happened only a few yards from our own river frontage.'

Hilda came in with more coffee.

Grandpa grunted a thank you and the moment she had left the room he leaned forward to whisper to Grandma, 'You don't think *she* did it, do you?'

'Whatever for?'

'The cross. The papers said there was a cross. A Catholic! She's loony enough to think up something like that. All she'd need is the conviction that poor Connie Northey was going to bring up her child as an infidel, and she'd do it!' Alexander thought of mentioning that Hilda had a cross in her room like the one found on the baby, but he decided not to draw attention to himself. They had noted that he wasn't eating, and he had said that seeing the black face of the baby had made him sick. What no one knew was that it had been Mary's remark which had really cut his appetite.

He could no longer trust her.

Mary was dangerous.

All she had to do was point the finger at him and the police would start investigating, taking finger prints in the boat house, and with forensic science probably prove he had done the killing.

'It's Hilda, I'm sure of it.' Grandpa went on deliberately. 'Mad as a hatter that woman. All they have to do is find a motive and she'll be for the chop!' He started chortling, and winked at Alexander, 'Then perhaps we'll be able to have some decent food, what?'

His grandmother got up. 'If you're going to be silly about this Ralph, I'm leaving. I think it's a very serious matter, and it is just possible that the police will make enquiries here because of Hilda's reputation.'

'Reputation? What reputation?'

'Of being very religious.'

'Ah . . .!' He laughed some more, 'For a moment I thought you were going to accuse her of doing something sacrilegious with that Irish priest of hers.'

Alexander managed to eat his cornflakes and to drink his orange juice, but he couldn't face anything else, and when Grandpa went on to open his letters, he pulled the newspaper away from him to read what it had to say in detail about the murder.

It was a short account on an inside page, not very dramatic, but to the point, explaining how the fisherman had found the basket in the reeds, had called the police who had, understandably, compared it to the finding of Moses in the bulrushes.

As soon as he could, Alexander went out to join Michael and Keith Simcock to watch the crews from the BBC and ITN filming the river bank.

He went into the village on his bicycle and saw groups of people standing around gossiping about the event. There were loads of cars outside the Swan and the Cross Keys, the Three Horseshoes and the Black Horse, and during all this time he moved freely around and about, enjoying, suddenly, the fact that the one person at the very centre of all this was being totally ignored, and that deception thrilled him.

Home again for lunch, Hilda told him that Grandpa was delaying the meal to see the BBC and ITN news at one o'clock. In the drawing room he sat down to watch the pictures that had been taken that morning: Hermead Court came into close up, the Simcock farm, Mary's cottage, then Connie Northey and old Tom Northey. The Bible was quoted again, and then there was a shot of Mary herself watching the reeds at the river's edge as a voice misquoted some lines not mentioned in the papers:

And his sister stood afar off, to wit what
had been done to him.

'Poor girl,' his grandmother said. 'We'll have to attend the funeral, Ralph.'

'What? Never! There won't be a funeral for a long time anyway. They'll have to cut the little bugger up for an autopsy.'

'Language, dear.'

Alexander realized that if they found the drugs, they would probably trace them back to Mary, which would let him off the hook, though if they got to her, questioned her, grilled her and she broke down, she'd tell the whole story as it had happened and he would be implicated.

His whole family history would then come out.

Even the General would suffer.

After lunch he went to see Mary. He didn't pretend he was going to do anything else, but went straight to the cottage and saw her from a distance in the front garden with the empty pram posing for two photographers.

She came to talk to him as soon as they were finished.

'Glad you came,' she said. There was excitement in her eyes and a new brightness of expression on her face which irritated him. She was acting coy because of the cameramen and obviously thought herself very important.

'Can you go and see my Dad? I can't 'cause the Press follow me everywhere and Ma doesn't want them to know where he is. Can you tell what we've done and how successful it's been. You can tell him too that Ma's been paid for a story about Timmy. There's a woman in there now with her from one of the papers.'

'Could we have one more shot please, Mary?'

Mary turned on her heels and went back to pose with the pram.

She was sick.

How could she behave like that?

Had she already forgotten what happened yesterday, the swollen eyes, the brown pulpy skin, the little open mouth dribbling yellow vomit?

He'd never forget.

Sarah woke up with a fearful feeling of guilt and realized she had been dreaming of Richard.

Wasn't that extraordinary?

She felt a guilt about having considered a life with James Hobson, which would mean being unfaithful to Richard who hadn't existed in her life for thirteen years.

Lying on her stomach, her head tucked under the pillow, her legs outstretched diagonally across the double bed, she went back over her dream which was fast eluding her. They had been walking together holding hands in a large empty art gallery and Richard had said to her, and this was so clear to her that she felt it must be significant, 'The trouble with the video society is that it doesn't approve.' It made no sense, no sense at all, but the holding of the hands was still with her.

Was she still in love with him, then?

She turned over to lie on her back and looked up at the familiar ceiling.

In two or three days, the curse again, as sure as night follows day.

A cold shower for you, Sarah.

Maybe, like a bitch on heat, she'd be giving off irresistible vibrations all through lunch.

At least she had that to look forward to.

Where would dear Mr Hobson take her this time?

And what would he talk about? The new shop?

'"Time Immemorial" is an ideal name,' he'd said. 'There's a demand for antique paranormal artefacts. Crystal balls, Ouija boards, Cabbalistic charts, Tarot cards, those sort of things.'

Perhaps she should pretend to be psychic and tell his fortune, read his palm; that would give him an excuse to hold hands again.

She stretched, got out of bed, and started her day.

She drove to the shop and spent an hour there tidying up, hoovering the second-hand yellow carpet upstairs and the thick cord beige carpet downstairs. Maybe Saint James would refurbish the place, have brand new wall-to-wall Axminster fitted, along with spotlights and cupboards and a desk which would be better than the half-hearted plywood counter that had come as a fitting.

She went to the hairdresser and had a trim, a rinse, a blow dry, and when she got back to the shop he was standing at the door in an ample white raincoat, blue leather Italian shoes and bright red scarf, a cardboard box on the pavement sandwiched between his feet.

'Have you been waiting long?'

'Just this moment arrived. This is for the shop. The first display. Not for sale,' he said.

As she unlocked the door he stooped to pick up the box and, once inside, he placed it in the middle of the carpet and watched her open it up.

'It's like Christmas,' she said.

It was a marble phrenologist's head with areas of the skull marked out and engraved: THE EGOISTIC OR SELFISH SENTIMENTS. THE MORAL AND ETHICAL REGION. THE DOMESTIC AND SOCIAL FEELING. PHILOPROGENITIVENESS. APPROBATIVENESS. It was lifesize and quite beautiful.

'Nineteenth century, early Victorian. Thought it might look good in the window.'

'We haven't discussed terms yet, let alone agreed on a business contract,' she said lightly.

'Oh, I've worked all that out. Got the details in my pocket and a letter of intent all ready for you to sign. I've booked a table at the Pasquale in Beauchamp Place and once I've plied you with wines and liqueurs I am sure you will be unable to resist my proposition.'

They left the shop, he hailed a taxi, they were sitting down at a cosy little table drinking a fresh, light white wine before she had had time to fully appreciate the efficiency of it all, when he asked, 'Didn't you say your parents had a place near Pangbourne?'

'Yes.'

'Did you see the breakfast news?'

'No. . .?'

'Oh, there's been a most extraordinary murder on the river, quite macabre, a baby found in the reeds but all done up with garlands and things. It's probably in the London *Standard*,' and he asked the waiter to see if any of the staff had a copy.

The paper was handed him and he found the story on one of the inside pages. There was a photograph of Mary Northey standing by the river, looking at a bank of reeds. BABY MOSES – NO CLUE YET headlined the piece and under the photograph was a quote from the Bible.

'How extraordinary,' Sarah said. 'I know that girl quite well.'

Alexander was in the drawing room playing with the computer when his mother rang. She didn't ask to speak to him, but to Grandma who answered in the sort of tone reserved for family crises.

Though she barely said more than a 'yes' and a 'no', it was obvious what the conversation was about – a fear that because Tom Northey was their gardener the Midleys of Hernmead Court would become involved in the whole sorry business.

It was a good time to disappear out of the house, an ideal time to go to Mileswood and see his father. He told Hilda he was off on a cycle ride and left before anyone could make any objections.

He got on his bicycle and pedalled off along the drive. A fair summer's day, cumulus nimbus. All the information up there in the sky which he hadn't yet mastered. Some people could lift a finger and sense the wind's direction, look up at the cotton-wool clouds and tell immediately what the day would be like. But he couldn't. 'Geography: He has worked very well.' Not true. He hadn't worked at all well because Mr Edding was a crashing old bore and forced his possibly interested pupils to doodle, or clean their nails, or stare out of the window at nothing because of his dreary monotone voice and total lack of interest in the subject.

When he reached the Three Horseshoes he realized he'd missed the 2.10 bus so he decided to cycle all the way. Four miles. He could easily make it in an hour, and he could short-cut to Mileswood village via Lower Checkendon. He'd have to walk and push the bike up a hill or two, but after that it would be a doddle.

He liked cycling, liked being close to the nature exhibited along the side of the road. The foxgloves, forget-me-nots, the honeysuckle and clover, a cardinal beetle he saw on a daisy, two hoverflies near some red campion, an orange-tip butterfly hovering near a cuckoo flower. Tom Northey had taught him more in one afternoon's ramble last year than Mr Edding had managed to convey in two terms. Maybe he was thinking of nature study more than geography, but the subject was hardly important; it was the ability to interest.

Tom Northey, his other grandfather.

Did he know they were related?

He's ask his Dad. 'I'll ask me Dad,' he said out loud imitating Mary, and he started zigzagging up the hill, standing on the pedals, tacking up the steep climb.

Top of the hill, the common. Wind. The going was good. There was a feeling of freedom up here, and distance. The road sloped down now and he could freewheel.

'I am a jolly mur-der-rer and also a madman's son . . .' he started singing to a familiar tune.

'Happiness is deceiving the world.'

He could do anything really. If he got caught he'd be put in the hands of someone like Red Beard at the hospital who'd forgive him on principle and probably write a book on him.

Hooker knew a psychiatrist. 'They're looney themselves,' he'd said. 'Every psychiatrist has his own psychiatrist, did you know that? They analyse each other all the time because their patients come up with such hair-raising stories that it drives them bonkers. And it's all to do with sex.'

He pedalled more slowly, less eager, suddenly, to get to the hospital.

Was his father's madness to do with sex?

Mary had tried.

Goodall, Pitts.

Hooker was the only one who didn't do anything but talk about it. But then Hooker was painfully ugly.

And had dreadful spots.

There was a Panda police car ahead, parked outside a row of terraced houses.

'Nothing to do with you Saranson. They're a million miles from connecting you with the great Moses murder.'

Holy Moses!

The press were really great at dreaming up stories, though little Mary had certainly worked hard at her basket weaving.

He could see the hospital now, in the distance, a couple of hills, up and down, up and down, then the flat.

He decided to count the telegraph poles but had to give up after fifteen because they were off across a field.

Mileswood. Four red-brick cottages, a sub-post office cum general store tempting him to stop and buy a lolly with its Walls Ice Cream advertisement. But he went on. The garage, the Craven Arms, Mileswood Garden Centre with its cement pond and three gnomes, the yellow-brick police station, the big sign with its red arrow for Kate King's Kennels. He'd had a dog once. Morris, a mongrel that had got drowned down by the boat house during the flood, winters ago. Funny he hadn't thought of that before. Old Northey had found him eight days after he was missing and he was all bloated and slimy like Timmy.

Last lap.

Past the baker, the DIY, Shafter's Chemist. He knew them all from the bus ride, and now the bend and the beginning of the hospital's green iron railings.

He leaned his bicycle against the wall just inside the gate

and walked up the entrance steps and through the glass doors.

'I've come to see Mr Richard Northey,' he said to the receptionist.

He realized he shouldn't have come the moment he mentioned the name.

It was the way the woman at the desk said, 'Oh yes.' It implied too much interest, and instead of telling him to go on through to the workshop she held up her hand by way of asking him to wait a moment while she picked up the internal telephone.

'The boy, for Richard Northey, doctor.'

Pause. Smile. Receiver back in its cradle.

'Take a seat over there, he'll be with you in a moment.'

He wanted to ask who. His father or the doctor?

'The boy for Richard Northey . . .'

The boy.

As though he were expected.

It augurs badly, Saranson.

Red Beard came out of a blue door, all smiles, but hands deep in white coat pockets.

'Your father's in bed. Nothing serious. You can see him for a few minutes but not much more. I'll take you up.'

Coincidence?

For the whole ride he hadn't once thought of what he was really doing, what he might come up against.

Of course the authorities would be interested in his visit.

Timmy Northey, son of Connie and Richard Northey.

One daughter – Mary.

'We're making preliminary enquiries doctor, looking into the instability of the family.'

'There is a son of course. Illegitimate. Related to the Midleys of Hernmead Court.'

'Really? Keep an eye on that one.'

'How's Mary?' the doctor asked him. They were going up the cement stairs, past the first floor landing window, the crow's nest of the demented.

'I haven't seen her much.'

'A bit of an upset in the family.'

'Yes.'

Down a long passage to a door marked 'WARD F'. Not a large room, four beds, all empty but one. His father lying back on top of pillows wearing a beige and red tartan dressing gown, reading.

'Alexander, how lovely to see you.'

'A few minutes,' the doctor said, and he left the room.

'You shouldn't have come,' his father whispered, swinging his legs off the bed to sit upright, patting the space next to him. 'I'm being permitted solitude because of Timmy's death. I'm not supposed to know the details, but of course I do. I'm surprised they allowed you to come and see me, or perhaps I'm not surprised at all. They're probably on to Mary. We had better be careful what we say, though I've probably said too much already.'

'A bug?' Alexander suggested.

'Oh, I doubt whether a state hospital could run to that exciting sort of expense. No, they'd be more subtle anyway. It'll be in the questions afterwards. To you. To me. Specially me. Just don't talk about Timmy, that's all, to anyone. But well done.'

He put his arm round Alexander's shoulders and gave him a hug and a pat with the large hand.

'So you had the courage to do it? I didn't think you would.'

He said nothing.

'The garlands, very clever that, suggesting fanaticism.'

'That was Mary's idea.'

'Well it wasn't, Alexander. It was my idea. I told her to do that to make it look like a religious killing, which worked. But what did you do?'

'I pushed the basket out and under the water. I thought Timmy was already dead, but he wasn't. He was only drugged. So I did the killing.'

'How clever of her!' his father said, standing up. He started to pace the aisle between the beds.

'How clever of my little Mary. Her mother is cunning you

know. Mary gets that from her. She could be a danger to you.'

'Telling the police you mean?'

'Yes. Telling the police, but only if cornered. You're her failsafe if things get too difficult I expect. I've put you in a very awkward spot. I'm sorry.'

Unexpectedly he tiptoed quickly to the bed, sat down and picked up his book.

'The doctor's coming, we must talk of something else. This book is by a man called Gurdjieff. Have you ever heard of him? A genius. He elaborated on the theory about the three possible selves that make one tick, centres he called them . . .'

Red Beard was in through the door looking at his watch.

'You'll have to leave now Alexander, I'm afraid. Your father must rest.'

The goodbye embrace and kisses came very naturally; it was not in fact, till he had disengaged from his father's warm hug that it dawned on him it was the first time they had displayed so much affection. The feeling that it was so mutual, that there was such a desire to demonstrate their love, brought tears to Alexander's eyes, and he turned too abruptly to leave, and so turned again to wave.

His father waved back, smiling, but equally sad.

Once in the corridor the doctor also put his arm across his shoulders. Maybe he just happened to be the right height.

'Did he mention Mary to you?' the doctor asked.

'He asked how she was,' Alexander said with well-controlled casualness.

'And how is she?'

He'd asked that before.

'I haven't seen her, I told you.'

It annoyed Red Beard a little, but he was a professional.

'You haven't seen her since the murder?'

'That's right.'

'Have you any idea who might want to murder a little baby?'

'The papers said something about a religious fanatic.'

'But your own theory. You must have one?'

'My grandfather thinks it's our cook because she's an RC. But I doubt if that's true.'

Well fielded, Saranson.

Red Beard smiled the smile of a thwarted batsman. No go. No joy. Abandon Operation Alexander.

He left the doctor's company on the front steps of the hospital, got on his bicycle and pedalled off out between the gates not turning round this time to see if anyone was watching from the window.

A mile or so along the road, down in a dip between hills, the Panda car passed him, a uniformed officer driving a civilian passenger next to him.

When he crossed the common of Lower Checkendon, it passed him again with the same occupants.

At the bottom of Whitchurch Hill he saw it parked outside the Three Horseshoes, empty, and along Gifford's Lane he passed a walking man who looked remarkably like the police officer's passenger.

They were keeping tabs on him.

The murder hunt was on.

When he got home, Alexander realized he was completely exhausted. He had cycled the best part of ten miles, had had nothing to eat and, though he did not feel hungry, he forced himself to down a glass of milk in the kitchen, watched by Hilda.

'Where is it that you've been, then?'

'Over the hills and far away. I heard they were hang-gliding this side of Streatly, but I couldn't find out where.' A likely story which wouldn't interest her. Boy's stuff.

'Your grandparents were worried.'

'It's only just seven-thirty.'

He dutifully went to apologize in the drawing room and told Grandma and Grandpa the same story. As expected it didn't interest them, now that he was back.

'Anything on the news about the murder?' he asked directly.

'No, nothing more. Nothing at all.' Grandpa sounded disappointed.

'There's been a nasty train crash in Italy. That took up most of the news,' Grandma explained.

'Few wops less,' Grandpa mumbled. 'Are we going to eat now?'

Hilda came in on cue, announcing supper.

Veal and ham pie, tomato, lettuce, salad cream, strawberry yoghurt. Cheese and biscuits if you needed more filling.

He managed to get it down, feeling really tired, the back of his legs aching, his face burning.

'You've taken the sun today.' Grandpa noticed.

'Have the police been around again?'

'No.'

It was a natural question for an eager boy to ask. The police were exciting.

He felt better after eating, quite looked forward to watching television from the deep comfort of the sofa, which is what he did, till after the nine o'clock news and it was time to go to bed.

The pecked goodnight to one, the wave to the other. Up in his room alone, the teeth ritual, the pyjama ritual. He'd sleep well, the sleep of the burnt out cyclist.

But something caught his eye when he looked out of the window. The blue flashing light of a police car again over at the cottage. He got out the telescope and focused.

Too much activity for it to be healthy and it wasn't a police car but an ambulance, and several blue uniforms about.

He didn't waste time but took off his pyjamas and slipped on his jeans and T-shirt again, tied up his sneakers, tight. Down the stairs, two at a time, round to the kitchen and out of the door.

'Where are you going you evil boy, it's time for bed!'

'There's an ambulance over at the Northey's. I'm going to see what's happening.'

Logical behaviour. The more curious he was the more natural it would seem.

Despite his aching calves, he ran. Out by the kitchen-garden door, down the path, over the fence into Hernmead meadow and across through a thousand buttercups to the hedgerow separating the field from the lane.

The ambulance was wide open, a police Panda was there, two other cars, five officers, several men in hacking jackets, two or three local onlookers.

He squeezed himself through a gap in the hedge and crouched behind a sycamore tree. It was a good vantage point, looking down on the small garden, the cottage door clearly in view.

It opened, a man came out carrying one end of a stretcher. The stretcher appeared, someone lying unconscious under a blanket. The second stretcher-bearer was in command giving directions on how to negotiate the narrow gate.

Mrs Northey appeared in the doorway, pale and distraught, then he saw the patient's face. His father, Richard Northey, hair dishevelled, mouth open, eyes tightly closed.

Was he dead?

And what was he doing here? How had he got here?

No sign of Mary.

'She could be a danger to you, maybe we should do something about that . . .'

Had his own father committed murder for him? Run away from the hospital and come here to kill his own daughter to silence her?

Stunned, fearing that he might be watching the end of a terrible tragedy in which he had taken a major part, he jumped out of his skin when someone put a hand on his shoulder.

He turned and found himself staring at Mary.

She was smiling, very nearly grinning.

'Poor Dad,' she said. 'He came round to the house to check I was all right 'cause he thought I might tell on you, and they caught him. They knew he'd come here sooner or later. They think he killed the baby you see, because he went missing the other night when you did it. That's why it had to be done that day. All arranged between Dad and me. He hid somewhere in the hospital, covering for me. Covering for us.'

'But how did he get here?'

'Taxi, I expect. They're not prisoners in that place.'

Then she crouched down next to him and put her finger to her lips. They were closing the ambulance doors and everyone was getting back into their respective cars.

'They believe he did it 'cause he had a reason,' she whispered. 'He had the motive, as they say. Little Timmy wasn't his, see, and he didn't want a little bastard hanging around us for the rest of our lives, using his name.'

Sarah was entertaining 'Saint James' at home when the telephone rang. She and her guest were sitting next to each other on the sofa, drawing plans.

She had decided he was a saint because he had come up with the sort of proposal over lunch which she had never allowed herself to hope for in her wildest dreams. He was going to back her, financially, inject all the money necessary into the shop to gut it, redesign it, refurbish it and stock it as an antique shop dealing exclusively with art nouveau and art deco. The premises would be given a Maxwell Fry look and she would manage it in partnership. He did not seem to be primarily after her body, though he was continually flattering her; it was a straight business deal which would be legalized through lawyers. His interest was in the shop site, its established name and her own, apparently obvious, capabilities as a salesperson.

He had been married, twice divorced, had never had children, adored female company and she still couldn't tell whether he was bi or just camp. He'd squeezed her knee several times in way of fun, and helping her in and out of taxis he had held her arm tightly when it was quite unnecessary.

He was older than she, an older man rather than an elderly one, and this she found pleasing because it made her feel much younger. The only possible black mark against him were his teeth, which were so perfect that she feared them false rather than capped. Did aged lovers put their dentures in a glass before they kissed you? Such a question had crossed her mind as he had refused a cocktail olive and seemed to have difficulty with the peanuts.

Then the telephone had rung.

'Sarah, it's mother. Something quite dreadful has just happened over the Northey baby affair.'

She had spent the whole afternoon at the shop with Saint James and she had rung her mother to find out everything about the killing. She had not allowed it to upset her; she had managed to push any thoughts of Alexander or Richard right to the back of her mind, and now that things were beginning to develop favourably for her, mother would of course put a damper on it all with some new panic.

'What now?' she asked, a little too pointedly.

'The police have arrested Richard Northey for the murder. Alexander doesn't know anything, of course. Thank God we've managed to keep the truth from him despite all the problems; but both Daddy and I do feel it would be wise for him to go back to London and stay with you as soon as possible. There's too much going on around here and we just can't keep an eye on him all the time.'

She closed her eyes and took a deep breath. She had to remain calm, she had to contain her deep resentment and growing anger at this ill-timed intrusion. Whenever there was the slightest hope of bettering her chances in life, Mummy, Daddy or beastly little Alexander were always sure to put a kybosh on it.

'Fuck!' she mouthed across the room at Saint James who was watching her discomfiture with some amusement.

'All right mother, I'll come and get him tomorrow after lunch.'

'Can't you come before?'

'I'm stock-taking and have someone coming to help me in the morning.' She made a face at Saint James who raised his eyebrows at the lie.

'Can't that wait? We really don't want Alexander to get

mixed up with police enquiries and gossip dear. And we can't keep him in without a good reason.'

'Eleven o'clock. I'll come as soon as I can, Mother. I have someone here right now.'

'Oh, all right dear. See you tomorrow then.'

Her own sharpness and her mother's ability to sound crestfallen to the lowest degree of despression combined to make her feel unbelievably shitty; but a line had to be drawn somewhere or she would never have a private life. The message, if she started to think about it, was, of course, shattering.

Richard . . .

She did not give herself the chance to dwell on it but returned to the sofa to sit next to her benefactor.

'Is the "him" you have to collect tomorrow a dog?' Saint James asked.

'No,' Sarah replied, nearly amused. 'He's a bit more trouble than a dog.'

'A parent then, a father perhaps? Fathers are always a great deal of trouble.'

'That's true. Mine is a nuisance sometimes, a pain always, but it's not him. I have a son.'

'Do you? Now that is a surprise. And how old is this son?'

'Thirteen.'

'What a terrible responsibility.'

The evening was ruined of course, and the rest of the week which they had planned would be ruined too. She had intended inviting Saint James to stay instead of spending nights in hotels, but now she wasn't sure she could. A relationship might have blossomed, she wouldn't have minded; on the other hand this setback might stop her making a fool of herself.

'He lives here with you, I presume?'

'Most holidays he stays with my parents. They're worried at the moment because of this murder committed so close to the house. They don't want him to be nosing around.'

When the papers released Richard's name as the accused,

would Alexander put two and two together? The letters she had shown him were all signed Richard.

'Does he go to a boarding school?'

'Amhurst.'

'And when do the holidays end?'

'Another three, long weeks.'

It gave him the opportunity of patting her on the knee and leaving his hand there. 'Three weeks isn't too long.'

He might as well have added 'I can wait'. It was implied. He understood the situation.

'As soon as he's gone back,' he said, 'I think you should come and spend a weekend with me in Wiltshire or, better still, if you think the boy would enjoy it, come this weekend. There's plenty of room, and if he's at all artistic there are hundreds of things to look at. I've got a horse he can ride, and the countryside around there is very exciting.'

'That would be wonderful,' she said and, without hesitation, without even thinking about it, she gave him a thank-you kiss on the cheek and he took hold of her chin and turned her face to give her a peck on the mouth.

He looked straight into her eyes and she managed to look back, smiling. He had blue eyes, deep blue, slight veins showing along the length of his nose. He had a good mouth, sensuous, a sort of small wart on his chin. How old could he be, sixty? Late fifties for sure.

'Are you going to invite me to stay tonight?' he asked.

'The spare room is being re-painted,' she lied, 'and the only place you could sleep would be with me. I don't suppose you'd want to do that?'

'Oh, we do like fishing for compliments! Why don't I take you out to dinner so you can forget that your son is unexpectedly being dumped on you?'

She kissed him again, a kiss that developed into a tender embrace, which she wasn't at all sure she enjoyed.

Tante Louise would think her an idiot if she didn't grab hold of this opportunity, whatever shape it came in. 'You are no longer young, Sahara; how many women of your age get such a chance?' Besides, it would mean she would be able to pay back what she owed her; the very flexible loan without which 'Time Immemorial' would never have existed. 'Can we buy your partner out?' Saint James had asked. 'Two's company and all that?'

He had been after her body then. But she'd be getting a good price for it.

'I must go and powder my nose,' she said, breaking away, and went upstairs.

She had made the bed carefully that morning in case she invited him home and now that she had, why was she balking at what she had actually planned? 'A woman, Sahara, can prostitute herself; but a man cannot. Well, a young man can, but it is not quite the same thing. So you should never be too prim about allowing yourself to be ravished. I have done it quite a few times and it has always been an adventure well rewarded!' Tante Louise had then shown her a sapphire ring of some value and a diamond brooch. 'I always insisted on jewellery, or property. I was never apparently worth a property, but I did quite well with the jewels.'

She sat down in front of her mirror and switched on the searchlight which would reveal all the cracks and crannies.

Surprisingly she didn't look too bad; the hairdresser had done a good job, her hair was nice, she was probably worth what he would have to pay for her. Millions!

More confident, she changed her shoes for something less comfortable but more chic, sprayed herself liberally with scent, dropped her gold cigarette case and matching lighter into an evening handbag and was ready for anything.

'Don't close your eyes and think of England, Sarah dear,' she said to herself switching off the lights and going down the stairs. 'Keep your eyes wide open and think of what it would be like if he wasn't interested.'

chapter sixteen

'So, Alexander, you are off back to school today?'

'Yes.'

'And you have come to say goodbye?'

'Yes.'

'That is nice.'

Tante Louise not only had pins in her mouth but a cigarette as well, and the smoke was blinding her left eye which was watering. She was pinning up a lace dress on an old wooden mannequin in the basement of his mother's shop and standing back to gauge the result.

'What do you think? I found it, believe it or not, in a trunk in the attic of my parents' old farm in Normandy. It was my grandmother's ball gown. Look at the dentelle here, isn't it beautiful?'

'It is very delicate,' Alexander said.

'What can I offer you?' she asked, crossing over to a table to stub out her cigarette in the ashtray. 'A Coca-Cola, a fizzy lemonade, a glass of milk? We have a refrigerator here now. She got down on her haunches with difficulty to tuck up the hem of the old dress.

'Nothing, thanks.'

'What time is your train?'

'After lunch. 2.25.'

The whole place was a bit of a mess due to the re-decoration going on. Upstairs, the builders had started on shelves and alcoves for the display of antiques, so everything else had been piled up in corners or packed in cardboard boxes and stored down here. His mother seemed to have worked pretty hard. Everything was clearly marked – hats, gloves, coats, blouses, shirts. Tante Louise was in the middle of it all, circling the mannequin on her knees.

'Are you looking forward to going back?'

'Not particularly, but I don't mind.'

'You had an eventful holiday, anyway. Plenty to tell your friends.'

He shrugged his shoulders.

'I went to Wiltshire, if that's what you call eventful.'

'And you had all that terrible excitement because of le petit Northey. How *was* Wiltshayer and Monsieur Hobson and all his antiques?'

'He was quite pleasant.

'Pleasant? Is that all? I thought he had been extremely generous to you?'

'He was, yes.' Alexander agreed.

'Did he not give you a very handsome chess set worth a great deal of money?'

'He did, yes.'

'Why do you think he did that? To win you over, to make you like him?'

'I expect so.'

'A bribe then?'

'Sort of.'

He loved the way she saw right through people and blurted out what she thought.

'Is your mother fond of him, do you think?'

'Difficult to say.'

'Is it? Is it Alexander. Why is it difficult to say?'

She was always like that, Tante Louise, as soon as she got on to relationships between men and women she seldom let go. He liked it because it made him think.

'I can never tell with mother whether she likes people or not. The more she says bad things about them the more she wants to like them, usually.'

'And does she say bad things about Monsieur Hobson?'

'Enough. It's more to sound me out though, I expect. More to draw me out.'

'Do they sleep together?'

It wasn't really any of her business, but she was so natural about such things that it made him feel adult talking about it.

'I expect so.'

'You expect so? Don't you know? When you were all at his house, which is a palace I understand, where did Sahara sleep?'

'We each had our own rooms, but I heard him go into hers, and she into his some nights.'

'You cannot hide anything from the young,' she said getting up and again stepping back to admire her handiwork.

'Is his home such a palace?'

'It's pretty big, twenty-seven rooms, but most of it is stocked with old furniture for sale. Its his place of business. The Abbey goes back to the fourteenth century but the modern part was built by a Sir Henry Martinmore in 1785. George III.'

'That sounds very learned. And what do you think of Monsieur Hobson taking over this shop?'

'Why not, if you don't mind.'

'I don't mind at all. I am being payed off handsomely. Besides I think your mother and he maybe very happy together, as partners.'

He said nothing to that.

He noticed that the stairs had been altered. Though he'd come down them he hadn't realized what the builders had done. It was quite clever, knocking down a wall so as to expose the steps, giving the whole basement a feeling of space. He went up half way to sit on them and look down.

Tante Louise was appraising her work again.

'I am giving the dress and the mannequin to your mother as a re-opening present. I think it should be put in the window, don't you?'

'It does look very theatrical,' Alexander said.

'That means you approve?'

'Absolutely.'

'But it's still wrong you know. The skirt should be lower, the ankles should be hinted at but not seen . . .'

'Shaken but not stirred?' he suggested.

'What is that?'

'I was quoting. James Bond.'

'Ah! The great detective.'

He didn't correct her. There were areas in Tante Louise's

education that lacked a knowledge of British culture.

He watched as she crouched down to alter the line of the hem again.

'Do you think the police will find her out?'

The question did not register immediately, Tante Louise asked it so casually.

'I'm sorry?'

'Mary. Do you think the police will find out that she did it?'

'Did what?'

'Oh, Alexandre, you know and I know that Mary killed her little brother and put him in that basket. I know because I taught her how to weave and how to sow, and the work on that basket was her work. I would recognize it anywhere, and I know you know, because you know everything.'

'The work on the basket?' he questioned.

'The police came round with the basket they found little Timmy tied up in. They showed it to anyone who knew the Northey family. The way Mary plaited that cross and the way the wool and the string were tied was clearly her work.'

He was so taken aback that he was unable to cover his surprise. It was all to do with timing. He had hesitated too long before sounding astonished and the more he waited now without saying anything the more he was confirming her suspicions.

'You don't have to say anything Alexandre, but I will have to do something.'

He wasn't sure what she meant.'

'I'm sorry?' he said again.

'I will have to tell the police what I know. Mary is a minor; all that will happen to her is that she will be put into care for a while and the death of her brother put down to diminished responsibility. But poor Richard, her father, he was recovering. Imagine what will happen to him, taking the blame.'

He remained silent but felt the tips of his fingers go quite cold and his stomach tighten.

'I thought I would hear the story from you first Alexandre, what you know about it.'

'I don't really know what you're talking about,' he faltered.

'You are very loyal,' she said, 'but murder is murder. If she were allowed to get away with it she might become a dangerous criminal when she is older.'

She was going to report Mary, and Mary would tell the truth. He would be implicated, he would be put into care for diminished responsibility.

'Truly,' he repeated, 'I don't know what you're talking about.'

Tante Louise straightened up and turned slowly to look at him.

'Alexandre, mon petit, do you think that Mary could have managed to survive all the questioning she went through during those few days after Timmy's death without talking to someone? She came to me. I know everything. I know about you visiting Richard, who is your real father, I know about him asking you to help Mary, and I know about you drowning the baby.'

From where he was, sitting above her, he could easily hit her with something heavy if there was something heavy around.

If he could trick her into staying right there, he might be able to do it.

But he had to think fast. Very fast.

'It's down a bit on the right,' he said.

'What is, the hem?'

She studied it, bent double on her knees to measure.

'Is that someone upstairs in the shop?' Alexander asked.

'I didn't hear anything; but check, please.'

He went up the stairs quickly, his mind racing, desperately searching the empty room for a weapon, anything heavy. On the floor, against one wall next to the telephone was the marble phrenology head. He tiptoed across and lifted it up with both hands. It was very heavy and he had to clutch it against his stomach, but there was a chance it would work; if she stayed where she was it might work. He started down the steps.

She was still kneeling at the foot of the mannequin. He could throw it at her head and stun her and after that have the time to think. But he had to take advantage of this perfect position.

He lifted the head ready to throw, and she turned round.

'What are you doing with that?'

'Thought you wanted it down here.'

'No . . . your mother wants it in the window so that passers-by will know the shop has changed . . .'

She turned to face the dress. He pushed the head up into the air with both hands as though he were putting an exceptionally heavy shot, but it did not rise. It's sheer weight stopped any possible elliptic progress short, and it dropped like a cast iron ball to crunch down into the base of Tante Louise's spine.

The sound she emitted was an agonized yelp. She reeled, tried to reach back with her hands, then fell forward, her face hitting the mannequin's thighs so brutally that she brought it down with a crash.

She moaned, tried to utter something, then gave up the struggle, it seemed, for life.

Terrified at the horrendous scene, Alexander stood on the stairs unable to move. To his horror her whole body started to twitch violently. It reminded him of a horse he had seen being shot at a point-to-point when it had fallen at a fence. It had jerked as she was jerking now, her legs kicking out senselessly, her arms shooting out from underneath her like a badly manipulated puppet.

He couldn't stand the sight and ran up the stairs to stop in the middle of the empty shop not knowing what to do.

Was she dying? Should he go for help or wait till it was over? But how long would it take?

And what about an explanation?

He could leave. Just leave and hope that the police would believe she had been attacked by an intruder.

What of finger prints? They'd find his all over the place, but that wouldn't matter because they'd accept that he visited the shop regularly.

He listened. There was no sound from downstairs. He tiptoed to the top step and looked over.

Her legs were tucked underneath her, her head slumped lifelessly across the broken mannequin.

He went down.

Very cautiously he approached her, circled her, leaned down to listen for any sound of breathing.

There was no movement. Nothing.

It seemed she was dead.

How to check? Take her pulse.

He reached out for her wrist, felt around. Her hand was limp and he could feel nothing.

Her heart?

He didn't want to do that. He didn't want to thread his hand into her dress and feel those huge soft breasts.

He stood back and moved her head with his foot.

The expression on her face was hideous. The eyes, wide open, were bulging out in shock, the mouth leered in a paralysis that exposed the top gums and all the teeth clenched by a petrified jaw.

She was dead.

An impulse murder.

He looked at the phrenology head that had rolled off her on to the floor.

No blood.

A clean killing.

He could probably get away with it if he made it look like a petty robbery gone wrong.

He now acted with remarkable speed and clarity of mind.

Going to one of the boxes he fished out a pair of black velvet evening gloves and put these on. He picked up the head, carried it up the stairs and put it on the floor in its place, wiping it all over carefully. It was quite undamaged. He went back down the stairs, found Tante Louise's handbag, opened it, emptied the contents, picked out her wallet, took out the five ten-pound notes he found in there with the Visa and Access cards, hurled the bag across the room, emptied her purse of small change and thrust all the money and cash in his pockets. He looked around at anything else he might have touched that could be incriminating. Deciding there was nothing, he took off the gloves, replaced them in the box and switched off the basement lights. Up the stairs he switched off the ground floor lights, left everything exactly as it was, opened the shop door and walked out into the street.

There was a woman on the other side of the road concentrating on how she was pushing her shopping basket, a Mother's Pride delivery man re-arranging the bread in the back of his van, a Chelsea Pensioner shuffling along the pavement holding his walking stick like a divining rod; none of them noticed him or were interested in him.

He sauntered off, hands in pockets, forcing himself to believe that he was just out shopping, deliberately stopping to look into a newsagent's uninteresting window, aware that a block of flats opposite had enough windows to justify the fear that someone might be observing his behaviour.

He had killed in cold blood.

Twice.

He was thirteen, the son of an innocent lunatic, a lunatic probably himself.

He had killed Tante Louise.

The moment he got on to the train at Victoria, waved his mother goodbye and sat down next to Hooker as they moved off, he knew he had got away with it.

Safety in numbers, safety in being part of a group. No one would think he could have done it. He had left no clues.

He had walked home calmly, let himself into the house, had gone upstairs to wash his hands, (just in case), had changed into his school clothes, had put his jeans and T-shirt and sweater in the washing machine downstairs in the kitchen, and had waited, watching television, all neat and tidy for his mother to come back from wherever she had gone.

His mother had returned with a little farewell present from Habitat, a clear plastic executive game with chrome balls that had to be dropped through certain holes to get a score. It was nice, it would be fun, and they had gone to an American hamburger bar for lunch and a giant strawberry milkshake that had made him feel quite sick.

But he had eaten, and he had managed to appear cheerful and totally unconcerned about anything except, perhaps, going back to school.

'Did you go and say goodbye to Tante Louise?'

'Yes.'

'How was she?'

'Busy. She was pinning a dress on a dummy. She didn't have much time for me so I didn't stay long.'

Hooker looked out of the window, neither sad nor happy, then turned to him.

'You heard about Pitts, I suppose?'

'No. What?'

'Gone to Eton. Can you beat that?'

'How?'

'How do you think, dummy. Frigged off some well connected old queen, I expect.'

Marriott came down the carriage counting heads and looking for trouble.

'Good holiday, Saranson?'

'Yes thank you, Marriott.'

'He's been made Head of House,' Hooker said, 'so he'll probably behave himself. Most tyrants become quite pleasant once they've reached their zenith. We'll just have to watch out for Parminger now. He's a mean sod, anything could happen with him. But at least we're past fagging. I pity the new boys though; seen any of them?'

'Nope.'

'Two in the next carriage. Very weedy, but in Head's House there's apparently the son of a cabinet minister. Something important in drainage I expect.'

'You are full of shit, Hooker,' Alexander said.

'Not me, him!'

And both collapsed with laughter.

Christ, he felt grateful for Hooker's stupid company, and for everyone else's. It was getting safer and safer as the train took them away from London.

At the small Sussex station, school transport was waiting for them. The first glimpse of the college up on the hill drew moans and groans from all the others, but not from him.

Amhurst would be a refuge.

Once he'd settled his stuff in the dorm, he found his tuck box in the House Stores where he had left it, pulled the key on the end of its silver chain from his pocket and opened it up. The smell of stale apples and mouldy biscuits was surprisingly pleasant, and so was the sight of the Superman box in which he kept his pens. *His Observer Book of Freshwater Fish* sent an immediate shiver down his spine, reminding him of the reeds and Timmy. He would give it to Hooker, if Hooker wanted it.

Someone came in behind him and hit him hard on the back.

'Hallo Saranson, had a good summer?'

'Abysmal thanks. How was yours Pollgate?'

'Great, went to France, Germany, Austria and Italy – and I'm in the Junior First Eleven.'

Pollgate slammed a brand new pair of football boots on his tuck box and left. He seemed taller and too damned self-assured.

Well he hadn't been to France, Germany, Austria or Italy, and he wasn't in the Junior First Eleven, but he had drowned a baby and killed an old lady of seventy.

The realization that neither of his victims were exactly strong opponents who could have put up a struggle, jarred, and butted him closer to the craven reality of what he had done. But he knew that to survive he had to forget, and to that end he put in a great deal of effort and energy, searching out old friends, listening to what they had done in the holidays, talking to those who were interested in what he had done.

He slept well that night in a new bed next to new friends. If he hadn't made many the term before it was because he had still been shy and unsure of himself and hadn't even needed them. Now he was confident and felt happier surrounded by the nonsensical behaviour of schoolboys together. Before Lights Out he ragged with the best of them, hit out with pillows, risked lines; but his wildness was appreciated, laughed at. Clowns, he knew, were always popular. Reckless clowns were admired.

He got through the first day without thinking too much of Tante Louise. He expected to be summoned to The Buzz's study to be told of her death, or for someone to tell him they'd seen something about his mother's shop in the paper being the site of a gruesome murder, but no one said anything.

During French dictation the following day, however, The Buzz came into the classroom to ask for him and he had to follow him down the cloisters and round the Upper Quad to his study, in fear and trepidation as to what might be awaiting him.

'This is Detective Inspector Hull, Saranson, he's come to ask you a few questions. I'd best leave you alone, but if you want me I'll be in the library. Go back to your classroom when the Inspector has finished with you.'

The last few words instantly calmed the uncontrollable anxiety building up within him. Stepping into the musty book-lined study that smelt oppressively of stale tocacco smoke, he had panicked on seeing two plain-clothes officers, but it seemed they were not here to detain him.

'This is my Detective Sergeant, Alexander. We've just come down from London, we work for the crime squad, Scotland Yard.'

He looked as impressed as they expected him to be.

He managed a wide-eyed innocence, nervously interlocking his fingers behind his back and allowing his shoulders to drop to make himself feel smaller and look more vulnerable.

'I don't know whether your family have contacted you yet, but I have some sad news for you.'

He blinked, managed apprehension.

'Madame Louise Rimbaud, your Godmother, I understand, was killed two days ago in your mother's shop. We believe she was attacked and we need some information.'

He said absolutely nothing at all, but opened his mouth a

little, swallowed hard, then wiped his perfectly dry nose with the back of his hand very quickly.

'Your mother told us that you visited her in the shop just before you caught the train down, is that correct?'

'Yes, sir.'

'Do you remember at what time you visited her in the shop? It is important.'

Alexander looked straight at the Dectective Inspector and straight at the Detective Sergeant, then down at The Buzz's filthy blue carpet. It was not only stained with spilt tea and coffee but had burns in it where the old idiot banged out his pipe.

'It must have been about eleven-thirty, sir.'

'Why do you say that?'

'I had lunch with mother at about twelve-thirty, sir. May be it was a bit earlier because I went shopping before the lunch.'

'Where did you go shopping?'

He had to be careful, they could check. They would check, not because he was a suspect, but because they would want to be sure that what he said was reliable.

'Nowhere in particular. I went window shopping in the King's Road.'

'And then?'

'I went home and waited for Mummy.'

He nearly corrected it to Mother, but let it go. He was only a child. A minor.

'When you saw Madame Rimbaud in the shop, where was she, upstairs or downstairs?'

'Downstairs, sir.'

'And what was she doing?'

'She was putting a dress on, sir. Not on herself, on a dummy, sir. It was an old-fashioned dress.'

'Did you see anything at all in the shop that looked out of place? Anything heavy?'

He looked puzzled, and looked thoughtful.

'No, sir,' he said at last, noting their disappointment and deriving some pleasure at having produced such an anti-climax.

'Have I forgotten anything, Sergeant?'

'I don't think so sir. You didn't see anyone else in or around the shop, Alexander?' the Sergeant asked.

'No, sir. No one at all sir. Sorry, sir.'

And he was told that that was all and he returned to the French class and only told Hooker about the police cross-questioning when they got away from everyone else during the mid-morning break.

'You'd think Mother or my grandparents would let me know about Tante Louise dying,' he complained.

'I expect the police asked them not to. They probably wanted to grill you cold in case you had done it.'

'I liked Tante Louise,' Alexander said.

Which was true.

At breakfast the following Monday, he was surprised to receive a letter franked 'Pangbourne' in Mary's childish handwriting.

'Girlfriend, Saranson?' Parminger commented, handing him the heart-and-flowered envelope.

He opened it. It was in code.

She constantly surprised him. The code dated back to the first war game when he had devised a way of sending messages from one outpost to the other. He had never told her the code because he had only used her as the courier, and he had never thought she would have known how to decipher it. But she had. Not only deciphered it, but had now written a letter in it.

It was a fairly simple code, that of swapping round the first and last letters of every word so that THE CAT SAT ON THE MAT read EHT TAC TAS NO EHT TAM. With three-letter words it was easy to crack, of course, but with longer words you could get bogged down pretty quickly.

'Rothem sah neeb yerv lli eincs eht tccidena,' the first line ran. 'Mother has been very ill since the accident'.

Hooker looked over his shoulder and guffawed.

'Oh creeps! She's writing to him in code. The old first-and-last-letter job. Bit aged for that aren't you, Saranson, or is your sex life so perverse that you do it backwards?'

Others laughed, which drew attention to the table, but

Alexander managed a smile. 'It's from my six-year-old cousin, bumhole, who can write a darn sight better than you.'

It shut Hooker up, and he folded the letter, put it in its envelope and patiently waited for breakfast to be over before going to the bogs to read it in peace.

> 'Did you hear that Tante Louise is dead? She was killed in your mam's shop in London no one knows who did it. I have seen Dad once but he has gone to an other hospital in Kent. Don't write . . .'

The next day he got a letter from his grandfather which gave him little comfort.

> 'I am sure you will have been sad to learn of Louise Rimbaud's untimely death. She was attacked by a burglar one must presume, while tidying up your mother's boutique. The police are still making enquiries and I will let you know of any interesting developments.'

His closest relatives, it seemed, had no idea how upset he might have been on learning about Tante Louise's death from the police. They were, on reflection, a remarkably unsentimental and insensitive lot, and he really felt that his mother should at least have rung him up and told him if she couldn't be bothered to write him a letter.

Days passed, a week, two weeks. He heard nothing more.

He forgot Tante Louise, like he forgot his mother, Blake's Garden Mews, his grandparents, Hernmead Court. Time was a great eraser of unpleasant memories. He concentrated on cultivating a happy lunatic image, not conforming to the expected keenness to get his House colours or the idolization of those who played games brilliantly, but rather making fun of the establishment's sacred cows.

Late one afternoon before Evensong, he went to the school Chapel for choir practice and somehow felt very protected there. Though he had imagined he might feel oppressed or feel a guilt welling up inside him when surrounded by all the religious artefacts, he only sensed a peaceful contentment in there, even a forgiveness which bolstered his ego to the point of rashness.

'Saranson, are you singing off key deliberately?'

'No, sir. I think my voice is breaking, sir,' he said, then he burped, which got a laugh. 'And my wind is breaking, sir,' he added, which got a roar.

The music master, never one too competent with discipline, brought his conductor's stick down on a pew with a crash.

'Silence all of you! I will not be made fun of by anyone, however foolish you may think I am. Apart from it being insubordinate, it is also extremely bad manners in such a place as this. Among other things you boys are here to learn good manners, so good manners, Saranson, you will be taught.'

'Yes, sir, sorry sir.'

'It's no use saying sorry to me now. It's too late. You had better keep your apologies for the Headmaster, for that is to whom I am going to report you.'

A profound silence fell on the young singers.

'Go, Saranson, to the back of the chapel. We of Amhurst School Choir are no longer interested in your voice, let alone you. It is high time that you all learned that however lenient a master is with his classes no one can abuse that leniency. You seem of late to think, Saranson, that you can get away with murder. Well I assure you that you cannot.'

Alexander felt like making a rude sign as he made his way out of the choir stalls. Instead he simply said quietly under his breath, 'Oh you're wrong, sir. So very wrong!'

chapter seventeen

Since receiving Geoffrey's letter regarding Alexander's visit to his house in June, Sarah hadn't been too happy to see white envelopes on the hallway floor. White envelopes and buff envelopes could contain bad news and this particularly thin one from Wiltshire didn't make her jump with joy. It should have been thick, very thick, containing a contract of several pages for her to sign; but as she hadn't seen Saint James for well over a week and he hadn't rung her as promised, she feared the worst.

And the worst it was.

'My dear Sarah,
Following a meeting with my lawyers and accountants yesterday, I have reluctantly decided not to involve myself further in any form of expansion programme for a few months. It is a tax problem, which will be resolved, but I am afraid that my investment in your.shop must, for the time being, be delayed . . .'

It was not unexpected.

The police had covered the whole shop with their fingerprinting powder, had questioned him for hours about his movements on the dreadful day, he had become quite incensed by their suggestion that he was a suspect, and he had fled to the country the moment his innocence had been proved and accepted.

'Some people bring you good luck, others bring you bad,' he had said on their first meeting. 'I'm terribly superstitious and I know you'll bring me good luck.'

Well she hadn't.

Either to him or to herself.

She was, as she had quite often told friends, 'a disaster area', and she sensed that this present run of catastrophes was not yet over. Last night, for example, while she was watching something mindless on the television in an attempt to forget what had happened, she had been paid a visit by another Scotland Yard detective, in the company of a uniformed officer. This man's sheer iciness had turned her to jelly. It had been unsettling, because she could usually be quite masterful with people of his ilk. Insurance salesmen, surveyors, the underlings of the top guys – the clerk for instance, who had worked for her solicitor at the time of the divorce and had been so superior to begin with. She had tamed him. But this man had been different. She had been unable to gauge what power he had, or how he could use it against her, and his tone had suggested continually that whatever she said was probably untrue.

He'd asked her about her relationship with Louise before they had become business associates, and how the shop had come about, and it had suddenly occurred to her that, of course, she was a prime suspect, much more than poor James, because she probably stood to benefit from the death. She did not know this for sure, but it was probable that Tante Louise had made a will in her favour, not having any close relations of her own.

'I understand that on the morning of Mrs Rimbaud's death you went shopping. Is that correct?'

'Yes. Alexander, my son, was going back to school that day, taking the 2.25 from Victoria, and I wanted to buy him something, because I always do. I also needed to get groceries because Louise and I were to meet later that afternoon to go through the stock.'

'After you had finished your shopping,' he said, taking out his notes, 'you came back here and waited for Alexander?'

'I didn't wait. He was already here.'

'Where had he been?'

'To see Madame Rimbaud to say goodbye, and also to go shopping. He always goes shopping on his last day, a final look at the world outside he calls it.'

'You have no idea which shops he visited?'

'No, but I believe that some other police officers went down to his school to question him, so I presume he told them.'

'I have studied his file, Madame, thank you. We tend to be methodical in these instances and get as many versions of the same event as possible. Now, I wonder if you could let me have a pair of his shoes, the ones he was wearing that day. Also his clothes, a white cotton T-shirt and jeans. We need them for laboratory tests.'

She had only just closed the door when the telephone had rung and, inevitably, her mother was at the other end of the line.

'Sarah dear, I think you'll have to come over tomorrow, things are getting very complicated. We've had the police here for two hours asking us about Alexander, though how he could be connected with Timmy's death or Louise's I don't know, but they seem to think so. And now a doctor from Mileswood Hospital has just rung insisting he must talk to us. Something to do with Richard Northey.'

She said nothing about the visit she'd just had from the police but had felt so weary, so utterly exhausted by the incessant pummelling she seemed to be getting from every direction, that she'd promised her mother she would be over first thing and then had gone straight to bed with a potent dose of valium to sleep, sleep, sleep.

Now Saint James's letter.

The one person she needed most was no longer alive, Tante Louise, it was really quite unbearable.

She had gone to the shop after saying goodbye to Alexander at Victoria station, and she had found a crowd of people blocking the entrance to the premises watching the comings and goings of the police, who had been called by the builders. They had found the body when bringing in materials from their yard. She didn't want to think about that day, but she would have to think about what her mother had said concerning a link between the Northey baby's death and Tante Louise's.

During their lunch before he had taken the train to Amhurst, Alexander hadn't talked about Tante Louise, or even mentioned the baby. She had walked on to the platform with him looking at all the other little boys, similarly dressed, aware that one or two of the older ones, the seventeen and eighteen year olds, were virtually men and looked her over as though she was up for grabs. She'd spotted one quite good-looking youth who had blatantly given her the eye.

'Who's that?'

'No idea. He's at another school. We're not the only ones going back today you know.'

It had been a reprimand. 'You should know that Mummy.' She had checked her watch to see how much longer she would have to put up with him. One mother was walking away searching for a handkerchief in her handbag, and one quite extraordinary sight had been a middle-aged father, unashamedly letting tears run down his cheeks. Did some parents really love their children so much? She had been a very great distance from feeling tearful about Alexander's departure.

'I'll get in here mother. Hooker's waiting for me.'

It was his incredible confidence. He hadn't needed her there at all. She had wondered, in fact, why she had bothered to come to the station. 'Goodbye Alexander, have a good term,' she'd said.

She'd given him a smile and a little wave and had walked back up the platform. As she'd passed the carriage of the older boys she'd made the mistake of turning around. A tall fair-haired boy had winked at her.

How could they be so aware, so awake, so astute at their age? She hadn't been.

She had a cup of coffee, got dressed, dabbed her nose with a little make-up, not really caring what she looked like. She'd get through the day because the valium was probably still having some effect and the deep sleep had helped enormously.

She locked up the house, got into her car and drove off, thankful that it was a dry, reasonably sunny day.

She became suspicious when she turned out of the mews into Fulham Road and a badly parked car pulled off the kerb. Could it be the police, and were they following her?

Instead of turning right again to meet up with the Cromwell Road and so on to the M4, she turned down left after St. Stephen's Hospital, left again in the King's Road, and yet another left in order to pass the shop.

There wasn't anyone there. No police officer standing outside today. They had done their job and taken all the finger prints they needed. She had been told she could go back and clean up whenever she wanted to, thank you. Well she wouldn't go in there for quite a while, not until every-ting had been sorted out.

Madame Rimbaud, she had been told, had actually died of a heart attack following a blow delivered to the base of her spine with a heavy blunt object. A dent in the basement cord carpet corresponded to the convex shape of the marble head found on the ground floor. There was a possibility that this had been used to assault her.

Having taken all these odd turnings she fully expected to see the car follow her, but it didn't. All that was happening was that she was going off her head, imagining things that were not really happening and probably not being aware of what reality was truly about any more.

When she eventually got to Hernmead Court she saw a white Ford Fiesta parked in the driveway which she presumed belonged to the doctor from Mileswood.

She had managed not to think about his visit during the drive, about him, or Richard, or Alexander or even Saint James. She had listened to Radio 3 until the music had become too dramatic when she had switched to Capital and had allowed herself to be browbeaten by the disco pop and commercials. Nothing like it, she had decided, to stop you thinking about and mulling over anxieties.

She didn't want to live in London anymore, she certainly didn't want to live at Hernmead and the greater distance she could put between herself and Weir House, with all its sad memories, the better.

A niece had arrived to sort things out, she'd heard. Tante Louise's sister's daughter, and she really didn't want to get involved with her, specially as she didn't apparently speak a word of English.

She let herself in through the front door, heard the murmur of conversation in the drawing room, found Mother and Father in there listening intently to a ginger-bearded young man wearing glasses who was sitting on the sofa.

Next to him, biting her nails, knees together, bare feet in

leather shoes, was Mary Northey who grinned inanely on seeing her come in.

What on earth was she doing there?

'Oh, Sarah, come in, come in,' said her father, nervous as hell, standing up, re-arranging chairs, desperately wanting to get everyone to sit in a circle but not managing it.

Mother was on the prie-dieu, rather lower than everyone else, hands in her lap holding her spectacles, numbed it seemed by yet another terrible revelation.

Sarah sat down on the edge of an armchair and fished out a cigarette from her handbag as introductions were made.

'This is Dr Stuart from Mileswood Hospital; my daughter Sarah Saranson. Doctor Stuart has some rather unsettling news I'm afraid, which I think he had better tell you himself.'

The nervous, apologetic cough, a series of restless movements, hands into pockets, hands out of pockets, sitting down in the other armchair, getting up again to move an ashtray, sitting down again; her father was a mess.

She noted that Dr Stuart was watching all this with keen interest.

'I've brought Mary along,' the young man started to explain in his pleasingly soft Scottish brogue, 'because she wants you to know what she intends telling the police concerning the death of her baby brother Timmy.'

He reached out and took Mary's hand in way of confirming that he was carrying out her wishes, not the other way round.

'As she is not over eloquent and it took her some time to explain to me exactly what happened, she has asked me to be her spokesman.'

Mary smiled up at him.

'I am her father's, Richard Northey's, doctor at the hospital, and therefore I know everything.'

He looked straight at Sarah who glanced at both her parents quickly. Father was clenching his teeth, clasping his hands and staring at the carpet. Mother hadn't moved at all.

'I know, for example, Mrs Saranson, that Alexander is Richard's son and that Mary is therefore his half-sister. Mary knows this too.'

Sarah lit her cigarette expecting to have difficulty in holding her lighter without shaking, but she was surprised to find that her hand was remarkably steady.

'I also know, which you do not,' Dr Stuart continued, 'that Madame Louise Rimbaud was Richard's mother.'

She inhaled and blew out a cloud of smoke very slowly.

She could not work out what it would mean, nor its importance immediately. What registered, however, was the fact that Tante Louise, over all these years, had not helped her out for her sake, but for Richard's. The generosity to Alexander and herself had not been because she was fond of her as a person, but because she was her son's grandmother.

It was a terrible betrayal.

Her mind raced.

Tante Louise and Tom Northey?

It was possible.

Richard at Weir House, often enough, knowing?

'Did Richard know she was his mother?' she asked.

'Oh, yes.'

'Did Mary?'

'Yes, Mary knew, but only quite recently.'

Father was confused, Mother looked at Sarah for a moment, tears in her eyes, and looked away.

'What Mary has come to tell you,' Dr Stuart went on, 'or rather what she has asked me to tell you on her behalf, is that she believes Alexander was responsible for Louise Rimbaud's death, not knowing that she was his grandmother, because Madame Rimbaud knew he had killed the baby Timothy.'

She stubbed out her cigarette and stood up, walked over to the window and stared out at the lawns and the river.

All she was aware of was of what she was doing.

It was an act.

She had just heard some appalling news but right now, right this very moment, it was not affecting her because she hadn't had time to understand what it would mean.

Her instant reaction had delayed the moment of truth, standing by the window looking out was delaying the moment of truth, but any second now something awful would link her conscience to what she had just been told and she would go to pieces.

'The police have already worked all this out Mrs Saranson, and will shortly be arresting your son. They are only waiting for Mary's signed statement. But, as I explained, Mary wished to tell you what she was going to do.'

The link registered as Sarah turned round to smile gratefully at Mary.

It was the black cardboard box under the television set in which the computer keyboard she had bought Alexander had been packed. Like dominoes knocking each other down, minute details of her life with Alexander collapsed. The computer, his delight, the executive game, his delight, the Thousand Island sauce when he had eaten his last hamburger, his delight, the one brief moment of sadness in his eyes when he had looked out of the train window to wave goodbye, but which both of them had fought, oh, so successfully, not to acknowledge.

What would they do to him?

And a mother's anger suddenly welled up.

'Exactly what does Mary intend reporting to the police?'

And Dr Stuart brought out a piece of paper from his wallet pocket and read out a draft of the statement he had prepared with the girl.

It recounted how Richard Northey had convinced his daughter Mary that her life and her mother's life would be made easier if the newly born baby died, and how she might go about killing it with Alexander's help. It further recounted how she had drugged the child with adult aspirin and whisky mixed in its bottle, how she had tied the baby in the basket with garlands and the cross to make it look like a religious sacrifice, and how she had passed the seemingly lifeless baby to Alexander who had somehow drowned it, not realizing that it was still alive. Later, Mary had confessed to Madame Rimbaud what she had done, and Madame Rimbaud had immediately visited her son at Mileswood. She had found him ready to cover for his daughter, having already taken steps to do so by going missing the evening before. It was she who had driven him to Connie Northey's cottage where he had taken it upon himself to confess to the mercy killing, thus clearing both his children.

'So Alexander is hardly guilty of murder!' Sarah protested. 'He didn't know what he was doing.'

'That would be for a jury to decide, Mrs Saranson, but I doubt whether Timmy's death will be the crime your son will be tried for. The police are concerned about Madame Rimbaud's death.'

'And what proof have you, or they got that he had anything to do with it?'

'I personally have no proof at all, but I understand that they have enough evidence to satisfy a court that he could have done it, if it was found that he had a motive. This,' Dr Stuart continued, holding up the draft statement, 'would seem motive enough.'

Sarah looked at her mother who still hadn't moved and seemed to be completely paralysed by the news. Her father was looking at his outstretched, highly polished brown shoes, a vacant expression in his eyes.

What was going on in his mind?

The awful things the neighbours would say?

The dreadful slur on the family name?

He looked up, smiled at her through a sigh and got to his feet.

'I think we should thank Dr Stuart, and especially Mary for telling us all this. I think, Mary,' he said moving towards her to pat her on the head, 'that you have been a remarkably honest and brave girl, and we are very grateful. I will contact the family solicitor immediately for advice, and I think, Sarah, that you should ring up Amhurst now and tell the Headmaster that we are coming down this afternoon. I'll do it if you would rather not.'

'Compassion and leadership when our backs are to the wall.' He had said it years ago to her when a business partner of his had gone bankrupt and had tried to drag him down too.

Would he help Alexander now, rather than wash his hands of the whole business?

'Are we all going to Amhurst?' she asked.

'I think we should. The boy will need to know he is not being abandoned.'

'I'll ring straight away.'

'What could happen to a boy of Alexander's age if he were found guilty of murder, Dr Stuart?' her father asked as she started towards the door.

'I think he would be put under psychiatric care. But, if I may venture one small piece of advice, having studied the sensitivity of children at such an age, I would suggest that he is not told that Madame Rimbaud was his grandmother until he has been prepared to receive such news.'

'You think that we should perhaps keep that a secret within the family?'

'If it is at all possible, yes,' Dr Stuart replied.

'If it is possible,' Sarah's mother repeated, getting to her feet. 'So far we don't seem to have been very successful in keeping any secrets from him. That's why all this has happened.'

And Sarah, saddened by the incredible distress her parents were suffering, left the room to go and ring Alexander's school.

Lunch. Over-stewed beef served as roast, under-baked potatoes, watery cabbage, thick salty gravy over everything, followed by bread and butter pudding containing three sultanas if lucky. They got better food in prison.

Alexander was hungry because he hadn't eaten any breakfast and he hadn't eaten any breakfast because of two things. He had actually gone into a blind funk during a sleepless night at the thought of the choirmaster reporting him to the Head, and he had received a letter from his father, the opening lines of which had cut what little appetite he had had until he was able to read it later in secret.

My dear Alexander,

Burn this letter the moment you have read it for it will

incriminate you. I would not write it, let alone send it, if there was any other way of reaching you, but I have virtually been put behind bars since Timmy's death and need to know that you are aware of my love and admiration for you. You will be going through the roughest seas of your life very shortly. You have committed, because of me, *the* cardinal sin and, as Albert Camus once said, "The only serious moral problem is murder." I do not speak of Timmy's, but of Tante Louise's. I understand why, but you need not have feared her, for she was on your side, on my side, on *our* side and would have defended us to the last.

She was – unbeknownst to you – my mother, your grandmother.

Alas!

Will anyone tell you I wonder? Or will they hide it from you believing that we all need to be protected from ourselves?

You will be put under similar care to myself Alexander; the trick cyclists will enter your brain with irrelevent questions from now on.

Answer them all whichever way you like and realize, indeed *enjoy* the fact that from now on you will be considered insane.

Have fun. Madness allows total freedom of thought, if not movement. I have dreamt so many dreams and lived them through. I have been Machiavelli and have motivated revolutions; I have been the Pope and sanctified the truly deserving. No one knows this but myself.

Am I mad, I ask myself every day?

None of us are normal, we are told, but some of us are a trifle less normal than others.

When you emerge, and I emerge, we will meet and we will have a marvellous time together. We will be so rich compared to others, having experienced everything our dreams allowed.

Perhaps they will put us together one day and we will build a model of the theatre at Epidaurus, or Delphi and serve up Greek tragedy knowing from personal experience what true tragedy does to the soul.

Do not allow yourself to descend into your own purgatory.

There is no one else's.

And that door need never be opened.

My mother understood this and tried to take the key from me, but I kept it and used it. Throw it away my son, it is the only evidence that evil exists. Mary, our benefactor of saintly and heavenly name, will post this, somehow, and she will be our courier and keep us in touch.

She is, if truth be known, madder than me.

So understands.

Never be discouraged and remember, at all times, that you have seen the light, and not they, and that the sheer brightness of awareness drives one so wild with joy that they become jealous and have to certify you as unstable.

Do not, mon beloved fils, care a fig!

I love you.

Your demented, crazed, psychopathic Father.

PS. There are no laws for the insane. It is the perfect state.

He had read it in the dormitory bathrooms. He had been unable to find matches, so had torn the letter up in tiny pieces and flushed them down the six lavatories, then had been surprised by one of the cleaners who had said she would report him.

'There are no laws for the insane,' he had said to her, and had put out his tongue.

Now the bread and butter pudding was going down a treat, and he realized he had no fear of the world because he was no longer alone and had the best identity in the world.

But, waiting for him outside Hall, was Parminger.

'You're to report to the Head's study in ten minutes, Saranson,' he said with clear relish. 'And it's so serious that I'm not to let you out of my sight till I deliver you there. So we'll take a walk round the Chapel.'

Alexander fell into step next to him.

'Any idea what you've done wrong to deserve such attention Saranson?'

'There are no laws for the insane,' Alexander said. 'So I wouldn't know.'

'You're off your rocker!'

On the chapel quadrangle, reserved for visitors' cars, Alexander saw his grandfather's Rover.

Next to it was parked a dark green Ford Granada, a uniformed police officer waiting behind the wheel.

'Shit!' said Alexander lightly.

'That's a beating offence, Saranson,' Parminger said, concerned.

'Oh, I don't think anyone can beat me now,' Alexander replied. 'Not at anything.'